François de Salignac de La Mothe- Fénelon

The Adventures of Telemachus, the Son of Ulysses

In XXIV Books. Written by the Archbishop of Cambray: Vol. I

François de Salignac de La Mothe- Fénelon

The Adventures of Telemachus, the Son of Ulysses
In XXIV Books. Written by the Archbishop of Cambray: Vol. I

ISBN/EAN: 9783337100742

Printed in Europe, USA, Canada, Australia, Japan

Cover: Foto ©Andreas Hilbeck / pixelio.de

More available books at **www.hansebooks.com**

THE
ADVENTURES
OF
TELEMACHUS,
THE
SON of ULYSSES.

In XXIV BOOKS.

WRITTEN by the
ARCHBISHOP of CAMBRAY.

To which is added,
The ADVENTURES of
ARISTONOUS.

Done into Englifh
By Mr. LITTLEBURY *and* Mr. BOYER.

Adorned with Twenty-four PLATES,
And a Map of TELEMACHUS's Travels,
All curioufly Engraved by very good Hands.

The SEVENTEENTH EDITION,
Carefully Revifed and Corrected.

VOL. I.

LONDON:
Printed for J. BROTHERTON, J. BUCKLAND, W. STRAHAN, W.
HINTON, J. RIVINGTON, R. BALDWIN, W. JOHNSTON, G.
KEITH, HAWES, CLARKF, and COLLINS; B. LAW, T. BECKET,
R. and Q. WARE, M. RICHARDSON, and B. COLLINS.

M.DCC.LXVI.

A
DISCOURSE
UPON
EPIC POETRY,
AND THE
EXCELLENCE
OF THE
POEM of *Telemachus.*

I F we could relish *Truth* in her naked Simplicity, she would not need to borrow any Ornaments from Imagination to attract our Love: But her pure and delicate Light does not sufficiently affect the grofs Senfes of Men; and the nice Attention she requires is too great a Reftraint on their natural Levity.

The Origin and End of Poetry.

B   In

In order to inſtruct Men, we muſt not only enlighten their Underſtanding with pure Ideas, but likewiſe preſent them with ſenſible Images, to keep them ſteady in a fixed View of Truth. This is the Source of Eloquence, Poeſy, and of all the Sciences that depend upon Fancy; and which Man's Weakneſs renders neceſſary. The ſimple and immutable Beauty of Virtue does not always affect him; nor is it ſufficient to point out Truth to him, unleſs at the ſame time we repreſent her amiable to his Eyes (*a*).

We ſhall conſider the Poem of *Telemachus* according to theſe two Views, *viz.* to *inſtruct* and to *pleaſe*; and endeavour to ſhew, That the Author has inſtructed better than the Ancients, by the Sublimity of his Moral; and has pleaſed no leſs than they, by the Imitation of all their *Beauties.*

Two Sorts of Heroic Poetry. There are two Ways of inſtructing Men, in order to make them good: The firſt, by ſhewing them the Deformity of Vice, and its fatal Conſequences; which is the chief End of *Tragedy:* The ſecond, By unveiling to them the Beauty of Virtue, and its happy Iſſue; which is the proper Character of the *Epopœa,* or *Epic Poem.* The Paſſions that belong to the former, are *Terror* and Pity; as *Admiration* and *Love* are proper to the latter. In the one, the Actors ſpeak; in the other, the Poet makes the Narrative.

Definition and Diviſion of Epic Poetry. An *Epic Poem* may be defin'd, *A Fable related by a Poet, in order to raiſe the Admiration, and inſpire the Love of Virtue, by repreſenting to us the Action of a Hero*
favoured

(*a*) Omne tulit punctum, qui miſcuit utile dulci;
Lectorem delectando, pariterque monendo.
                                        Hor. *Art. Poet.*

favoured by Heaven, who brings about a great Enter-prize, notwithstanding all the Obstacles he meets in his way. Therefore there are three Things in the *Epic Poem, viz.* The *Action*, the *Moral*, and the *Poefy*.

I. *Of the* EPIC ACTION.

The Action ought to be *Great, One, Entire, Marvellous*, and of a *certain Length. Telemachus* has all thefe Qualities. In order to be convinced of it, let us compare him with the two Models of *Epic* Poetry, *Homer* and *Virgil*.

Qualities of the Epic Action.

We fhall confine ourfelves to fpeak of the *Odyffey*, whofe Plan and Defign is more agreeable to that of *Telemachus*, In that Poem, *Homer* introduces a wife King returning home from a foreign War, in which he had given fignal Proofs of his Prudence and Valour : In his Way, he meets with violent Storms, which force him into divers Countries, whofe Manners, Laws, and Politics he had thereby an Opportunity to learn. From hence naturally arife Abundance of Incidents and perillous Adventures. But the Hero of the Poem, knowing what Diftractions his Abfence muft occafion in his Kingdom, furmounts all Obftacles ; defpifes all the Pleafures of Life ; difregards even Immortality itfelf ; and renounces all, that he may eafe his People, and fee again his dear Family.

Defign of the Odyffey.

In the *Æneid*, a pious and courageous Hero, who is efcap'd from the Deftruction of a powerful Kingdom, is deftin'd by the Gods to preferve its Religion, and to fettle another Empire, more great and glorious

Subject of Virgil's Æneid.

glorious than the former. This Prince, who is chosen King by the unfortunate Remainder of his Country-men, wanders a long while from Shore to Shore, and, in the several Countries he visits, learns all that is necessary for a King, a Legislator, and a High-Priest. At last, finding an *Asylum* in a remote Country, from whence his Ancestors drew their Descent, he defeats several powerful Enemies who opposed his Settlement; and lays the Foundation of an Empire, which was one day to conquer all the Universe.

The Action of *Telemachus* compre-
Plan of
Telemachus. hends all that's great in both those Poems. There we see a young Prince, animated by the Love of his Country, going in quest of his Father, whose Absence occasioned the Misfortunes of his Family and Kingdom. This Prince exposes himself to all manner of Dangers; signalizes his Magnanimity by heroical Virtues; refuses Crowns more considerable than his own; and travelling through several unknown Countries, learns all that should qualify him hereafter to rule his People, with the Prudence of *Ulysses*, the Piety of *Æneas*, and the Valour of both; like a wise Politician, a religious Prince, and an accomplished Hero.

The *Epic* Action ought to be one.
The Action
ought to be
one. For an *Epic* Poem is not either a History, like *Lucan's Pharsalia*, and *Silius Italicus's Punic* War; nor the whole Life of a Hero, like the *Achilleid* of *Statius*. The *Unity* of the *Hero* does not make the *Unity* of the *Action*: For a Man's Life is full of Inequalities. He continually changes his Designs, either through the Inconstancy of his Passions, or by the unforeseen

Accidents

Accidents of Life. Whoever fhould defcribe the *whole Man*, would draw a fantaftic Picture, made up of a *Contraft* of oppofite Paffions, without either Coherence or Order. And therefore an *Epic* Poem is not the Panegyric of a Hero fet up for a Pattern, but the Recital of fome One great and noble Action propofed for Imitation.

It is with Poetry, as with Painting; the Unity of the principal Action hin-ders not the bringing in feveral particular Incidents. The Defign is formed from the Beginning of the Poem; and the Hero brings it about by furmount-ing all Obftacles. 'Tis the Recital of all the Op-pofitions he meets with, that makes up the *Epifodes:* But all thefe *Epifodes* depend upon the principal Action, and are fo interwoven with it, and fo con-nected together, that the whole prefents to our View but one fingle Picture, confifting of feveral Figures, ranged in excellent Order, and in a juft Proportion and Symmetry.

Of Epifodes.

I fhall not in this Place enquire, whether *Homer* fometimes drowns his main Action in the Length and Multiplicity of his *Epifodes*; whether his Action be double; and whether fometimes he lofes fight of his principal Hero? 'Tis fufficient to obferve here, that the Au-thor of *Telemachus* has, in all the Parts of his Work, imitated the Regularity of *Virgil*, by avoiding all the Defects that are charged on the *Greek* Poet. All our Au-thor's *Epifodes* are coherent, and fo artfully inter-woven one with another, that the firft naturally brings on the next. His principal Perfons never difappear; and his *Tranfitions* from the *Epifode* to the main *Action*, ftill preferve and make us fenfible

The Unity of Action of Telemachus, and the Co-herence of the Epifodes.

of

of the Unity of the Defign. In the fix firſt Books, wherein *Telemachus* fpeaks, and relates his Adventures to *Calypſo*, this *Epiſode*, in imitation of that of *Dido*, is contrived with ſo much Art, that the *Unity* of the principal Action remains perfect and entire; the Reader being in ſuſpence, and ſenſible from the Beginning, that both the Stay of that Hero in the Iſland, and what paſſes there, is but an Obſtacle to be ſurmounted. In the XIIIth and XIVth Books, wherein *Mentor* inſtructs *Idomeneus*, *Telemachus* is not preſent, being then in the Army; but then 'tis *Mentor*, one of the principal Perſons in the Poem, who does every thing with regard to *Telemachus*, and for his Inſtruction: So that this *Epiſode* is perfectly well connected with the principal Deſign. 'Tis likewiſe a great Piece of Art in our Author, the bringing into his Poem *Epiſodes* that do not reſult from his principal Fable, without breaking either the *Unity* or *Continuity* of the Action. Theſe *Epiſodes* find a place here, not only as important Inſtructions for a young Prince, which is the Poet's main Deſign, but becauſe they are related to his Hero at a time of Inaction, to fill up the Vacancy. Thus *Adoam* acquaints *Telemachus* with the Manners and Laws of *Bœtica*, during a Calm that happens in a Sea Voyage; and *Philoctetes* recounts to him his Misfortunes, whilſt that young Prince is in the confederate Camp, expecting the Day of Battle.

The Action ought to be entire. The *Epic Action* ought to be *entire*; which *Entireneſs* ſuppoſes three things: The *Cauſe*, the *Diſtreſs*, and the *Unravelling*. The *Cauſe* of the Action ought to be worthy of the Hero, and agreeable to his

his Character. Such is the Defign of *Telemachus*, as was fhewn before.

The *Diftrefs* ought to be *Natural*, and arifing from the Action itfelf. In the *Odyffey*, it is *Neptune* that makes it ; in the *Æneid*, the Wrath of *Juno* ; in *Telemachus*, it is *Venus*'s Hate. The *Diftrefs* of the *Odyffey* is natural, becaufe, in the Courfe of Nature, no Ob-ftacle is more to be dreaded by Sea-faring Men, than the Sea itfelf. In the *Æneid*, the Oppofition of *Juno*, a conftant Enemy of the *Trojans*, is a noble Fiction. But the Hate of *Venus* againft a young Prince, who defpifes Voluptuoufnefs thro' a Love of Virtue, and fubdues his Pafíions by the Help of Wifdom, is a Fable drawn from Nature, which, at the fame time, comprehends a fublime Moral.

Of the Di-ftrefs.

The *Unravelling* ought to be as *natural* as the *Di-ftrefs*. In the *Odyffey*, *Ulyffes* comes among the *Phæ-acians*, relates to them his Adven-tures ; and thofe Iflanders, who were great Lovers of Fables, charm'd with his Tales, furnifh him with a Ship to return home ; which *Unravelling* is *plain* and *natural*. In the *Æneid*, *Turnus* is the only Obftruction to the Set-tlement of *Æneas*, who, to fpare the Blood both of his *Trojans*, and of the *Latins*, whofe King he is foon to be, puts an end to the Quarrel by a fingle Combat. This is a noble *Unravelling*. That of *Telemachus* is, at once, both Natural and Great. That young Hero, in obedience to the Commands of Heaven, conquers his Love for *Antiope*, and his Friendfhip for *Idomeneus*, who offer'd him both his Crown and his Daughter ; and facrifices the moft violent Paffions, and the moft endearing and even innocent Pleafures, to the pure Love of Virtue. He

Of the Un-ravelling.

embarks

embarks for *Ithaca* on board the Ships that are fur-
nish'd him by *Idomeneus*, for whom he had performed many signal Services. When he comes near
his Country *Minerva* caufes him to put into a
little defart Ifland, where fhe difcovers herfelf to
him After having accompanied him, without his
Knowledge, through tempeftuous Seas, unknown
Lands, bloody Encounters, and all the Evils that
can try human Courage and Wifdom ; fhe at
length conducts him to a folitary Place, where fhe
acquaints him with the End of his Labours, and his
future Profperity : and fo leaves him. As foon as
he is going to enjoy Felicity and Repofe, the Goddefs difappears, the Marvellous ceafes, the heroic
Action is at an end. 'Tis in Affliction that a Man
fhews himfelf to be a Hero, and for that purpofe
has need of a Divine Support. 'Tis only after he
has fuffer'd, that he is capable to go alone, to fteer
his own Conduct, and to govern others. In the
Poem of *Telemachus*, the Obfervation of the minuteft Rules of Art is accompanied with a profound
Moral.

General Qualities of the *Diftrefs* and *Unravelling* of the E-pic Poem. Befides the *Diftrefs*, and general *Un-*
ravelling of the *main Action*, every *Epi-*
fode has its peculiar *Diftrefs*, and *Unra-*
velling, which ought, every one of them,
to have the fame Qualities. *Epic* Poetry does not affect the furprizing Adventures of modern Romances ; for Surprize alone produces but a very imperfect and tranfitory Paffion.
The *Sublime* lies in the Imitation of fimple Nature ;
in preparing the Incidents fo delicately, as that they
may be unforefeen; and in the conducting them fo
artfully, as that every Thing may appear *Natural.*
Thus we are neither uneafy, nor in fufpenfe, nor
taken

taken off from the *principal Object* of *Heroic Poetry,* which is *Inſtruction,* to attend an imaginary Intrigue, and fabulous Unravelling. This is allowable in a Romance where the main Deſign is to amuſe : But in an *Epic* Poem, which is a kind of *Moral Philoſo-phy,* ſuch Adventures are Conceits below its Gravity and Noblenefs.

The Author of *Telemachus* has not only avoided the Intrigues of modern Romances, but likewiſe that *Extrava-gance* with which ſome reproach the An-cients. He neither makes *Horſes* ſpeak, nor *Tri-pods* walk, nor *Statues* work. The *Epic* Action ought to be *marvellous,* but *probable* at the ſame time. We do not admire what we look upon as impoſſible : And therefore the Poet ought never to ſhock Reaſon, though he may ſometimes exceed Nature. The Ancients have introduc'd the *Ma-chinery* of the Gods into their Poems, not only in order to bring great Events about by their Interpo-ſition, and thereby unite the *Probable* and the *Wonder-ful*; but likewiſe to teach Men, that the moſt Cou-rageous and the Wiſeſt can do nothing without the Aſſiſtance of the Gods. In our Poem, *Minerva* conſtantly guides *Telemachus :* Whereby the Poet ren-ders every thing poſſible to his Hero ; and gives us to underſtand, that, without Divine Wiſdom, Man is not able to do any thing. But this is not the ut-moſt of his Art : The *Sublime* lies in his concealing the Goddeſs under an human Form. Not only the *Probable* but the *Natural* likewiſe, unites here with the *Marvellous.* All is *Divine,* and yet appears to be *Human.* Nor is this all : For, if *Telemachus* had known that he was conducted by a Goddeſs, his Me-rit would have been the leſs, as he would have had

The Action ought to be marvellous.

too powerful a Support. *Homer*'s Heroes generally know what the immortal Gods are doing for them : Whereas our Poet, by concealing from his Hero the *marvellous* Part of the Fiction, caufes his Virtue and Courage to be the more admir'd.

Of the Du-
ration of the
Epic Poem.

The *Duration* of the *Epic* Action is longer than that of *Tragedy*, in which the Paffions are predominant ; and nothing that's violent can be of long Continuance. But Virtues and Habits, which are not to be acquired all of a fudden, are proper for the *Epic* Poem, whofe Action confequently muft have a greater Length. The *Epopœa* may contain the Actions of feveral Years ; but, in the Opinion of the Critics, the Time of the principal Action, from the Place where the Poet begins his Narrative, ought not to exceed the Compafs of one Year ; as the Time of a Tragic Action ought not, at moft, to take up above one Day. However, *Ariftotle* and *Horace* are filent about it ; and *Homer* and *Virgil* feem to have obferv'd no fix'd Rule in that refpect. The Action of the whole *Iliad* takes up but fifty Days ; and that of the *Odyffey*, from the Beginning of the Poet's Narrative, about two Months ; that of the *Æneid* about a Year ; and *Telemachus* fpends but one Summer from his failing from *Calypfo*'s Ifland to his Return to *Ithaca*. Our Poet has chofen a middle way between the Impetuofity and Vehemence with which the *Grecian* runs to his Conclufion, and the majeftic and meafur'd Proceeding of the *Latin* Poet, who fometimes feems to be flow, and to lengthen out his Narration too much.

Of the E-
pic Narra-
tion.

When the Action of the *Epic* Poem is long, and not continu'd, the Poet divides his Fable into two Parts ; the one,

one, in which the Hero fpeaks, and relates his paft Adventures ; the other, wherein the Poet only gives the Narrative of what afterwards befals his Hero. Thus *Homer* does not begin his Narration till after *Ulyſſes* is fail'd from the Iſland of *Ogygia* ; nor *Virgil* his, till after *Æneas* is arriv'd at *Carthage.* The Author of *Telemachus* has perfectly imitated thofe two great Models. Like them he divides his Action into two Parts ; the principal of which contains what he himfelf relates, and begins where *Telemachus* concludes the Recital of his Adventures to *Calypfo.* He takes little Matter in hand, but treats it at large, and beftows no lefs than Eighteen Books upon it. The other Part is of far greater Extent, both for the Number of Incidents, and the Space of Time : But is much more contracted as to Circumftances ; fo that it takes up only the firft fix Books. By this Divifion of what our Poet relates, and of what he makes *Telemachus* recount, he retrenches the Time void of Action, fuch as his Captivity in *Egypt*, his Imprifonment at *Tyre*, *&c.* He fhortens the Time of his Narration. He joins together both the *Variety* and *Continuity* of the Adventures. All is in Motion, all is in Action throughout his Poem. His principal Perfons are never idle ; and his Hero never difappears.

II. *Of*

II. *Of the* MORAL.

1. Of the Manners.

Virtue may be recommended both by *Examples* and *Inſtructions*, either by the *Manners* or by the *Precepts :* And in this our Author far ſurpaſſes all other Poets.

We are certainly indebted to *Homer's* vaſt *Invention*, for having perſonalized the divine Attributes, human Paſſions, and phyſical Cauſes; and thereby open'd a rich and inexhauſtible Foundation of noble Fictions, which animate and enliven every thing in Poetry. But his *Religion* is little elſe than a Heap of Fables, which have nothing in them that conduces to make the

Characters of *Homer's* Gods.

Deity either reverenced or beloved. The *Characters* of his Gods are even below thoſe of his Heroes : Nor have *Pythagoras, Plato, Philoſtratus,* tho' Heathens like himſelf, juſtified his having thus debaſed the *Divine Nature*, under pretence that what he ſays of it is an *Allegory*, ſometimes *Phyſical,* ſometimes *Moral.* For, beſides that 'tis againſt the Nature of the Fable, to make uſe of Moral Actions to expreſs Phyſical Effects, they thought it of dangerous Conſequence to repreſent the Conflicts of the Elements, and the common *Phænomena* of Nature, by vicious Actions aſcribed to the heavenly Powers, and to teach *Morality* by *Allegories,* which litterally point out nothing but Vice.

Homer's Fault may in ſome meaſure be extenuated, by conſidering the Darkneſs, Ignorance and Manners of the Age he liv'd in, and the ſmall Progreſs Philoſophy had made in his Time. But, without entering into ſuch an Enquiry, let it ſuffice to obſerve,

obferve, that the Author of *Telemachus*, in imitating
what is beautiful in the Fables of the *Greek* Poet,
has avoided two great Faults for which he is blamed.
Like *Homer*, he perfonalizes the divine Attributes,
and makes them inferior Deities ; but he never brings
them in, but upon fuch Occafions as merit their
Prefence ; nor does he ever make them fpeak or act
but in a manner worthy of themfelves. He *artfully
joins together* Homer's *Poetry with the Philofophy of*
Pythagoras. He fays nothing but what the Heathens
might have faid ; and yet he has made them fay
what is moft fublime in *Chriftian Morality*, and
thereby has fhewn, that this Morality is written in
indelible Characters in the Heart of Man, and that
he would infallibly difcover them there, if he follow'd the Dictates of pure and fimple Reafon, in order to deliver himfelf entirely up to that Sovereign
and Univerfal Truth, which enlightens all Spirits,
juft as the Sun enlightens all Bodies, and without
which any Man's Reafon is nothing but Darknefs and
Error.

The Ideas our Poet gives of the Deity,   His Notions
are not only worthy of him, but like-   of the Deity.
wife infinitely endearing and amiable to
Men. Every thing infpires Confidence and Love ;
a gentle Piety ; a noble and free Adoration due to
the abfolute Perfection of the Infinite Being ; and
not a fuperftitious, gloomy, and fervile Worfhip,
which feizes upon, and depreffes the Heart of Man,
when he looks upon G o d only as a powerful Legiflator, who punifhes with Rigour and Severity the
Breach of his Laws.

He reprefents G o d to us a Lover of Mankind ;
whofe Love and Beneficence are not given up to the
blind Decrees of a fatal Deftiny, nor merited by the

pompous

pompous Appearance of an outward Worſhip, nor
ſubjeċt to the fantaſtic Caprice of the Heathen Deities; but ever regulated by the immutable Law of
Wiſdom, which cannot but love Virtue, and deals
with Men, not according to the Number of the *Animals* but of the *Paſſions* they ſacrifice.

Of the Man-
ners of *Ho-
mer's* Heroes.
The *Characters Homer* gives to his
Heroes are more eaſily juſtify'd than
thoſe he aſcribes to his *Gods*. It is certain, he paints Men with Simplicity,
Strength, Variety, and Paſſion. Our Ignorance of
the Cuſtoms of a Country, of the Ceremonies of its
Religion, of the Genius of its Language; the general Fault of Men in judging of all according to the
Taſte of the Age they live in, and of their own Nation; the Love of Pomp and falſe Magnificence,
which has adulterated pure, primitive Nature: all
theſe may lead us into Error, and make us look upon
That as inſipid, which was highly eſteem'd in ancient
Greece.

Of the two
ſorts of *Epic*
Poetry, the
Pathetic and
the *Moral.*
Although it ſeems more Natural and
Philoſophical to diſtinguiſh *Tragedy* from
the *Epic* Poem, by the Difference of their
reſpeċtive Moral Views, as we did at
firſt; yet we dare not determine, whether, as *Ariſtotle* ſuggeſts, there may not be two
ſorts of *Epic* Poems, the one *Pathetic*, the other
Moral; one, where the great *Paſſions* reign; the
other, where the great *Virtues* triumph. The *Iliad*
and *Odyſſey* may ſerve for Inſtances of thoſe two
kinds: For in the one, *Achilles* is naturally repreſented with all his faults; ſometimes ſo ſavage and
intraċtable, as to preſerve no manner of dignity in
his Anger; and ſometimes ſo furious, as even to
ſacrifice his Country to his Reſentment. Although
the

the Hero of the *Odyſſey* be more regular than the youthful, hot, impetuous *Achilles* ; yet neverthefs the wiſe *Ulyſſes* is often falſe and deceitful ; becauſe the Poet draws Men with Simplicity, and as they generally are. Valour is often allay'd with a fierce and brutiſh Revenge ; and Policy is generally join'd with Lying and Diſſimulation. To paint after the Life, is painting like *Homer*.

Without criticizing upon the different Views of the *Iliad* and *Odyſſey*, a curſory Obſervation of their various Beauties may ſuffice to raiſe an Admiration of the Art with which our Author joins together, in *These two ſorts of Epic Poems are join'd in Telemachus.* his Poem, thoſe two ſorts of *Epic* Poetry, the *Pathetic* and the *Moral.* We behold in that wonderful Picture an admirable *Mixture* and *Contraſt* of *Virtues* and *Paſſions :* It offers to the Sight nothing too great; but equally repreſents both the *Excellence* and *Meanneſs* of Man. It is dangerous to ſhew us one without the other : but nothing is more profitable than to lay them both together before our Eyes ; for perfect Juſtice and Virtue require, that a Man ſhould, at once, value and deſpiſe, love and abhor himſelf. Our Poet does not raiſe *Telemachus* above Humanity, but makes him only fall into ſuch Weakneſſes as are compatible with a ſincere Love of Virtue ; and his very Weakneſſes ſerve to reform him, by inſpiring him with a Diſtruſt of himſelf, and of his own Strength. He does not render the Imitation of him impoſſible, by beſtowing an unblemiſh'd Perfection upon him ; but excites our Emulation, by ſetting before our Eyes the Example of a young Man, who with the ſame Imperfections every Man finds about him, performs the moſt noble and virtuous Actions. He has united together, in the Character

racter of his Hero, the Courage of *Achilles*, the Wisdom of *Ulysses*, and the Piety of *Æneas :* For *Telemachus* is passionate like the first, without being savage ; politic, like the second, without being deceitful ; and tender, like the third, without being voluptuous.

2. Of Moral Precepts and Instructions.

Another way of instructing 'is by Precepts. The Author of *Telemachus* joins together noble Instructions, with heroic Examples ; *Homer's* Morality, with *Virgil's* Manners. His Morality, however, has three Excellencies, which were wanting in that of the Ancients, whether Poets or Philosophers. It is *sublime* in its Principles, *noble* in its Motives, and *universal* in its practical Uses.

Qualities of the Morality of Telemachus.

1. Sublime in its Principles.

First, Sublime in its Principles. It results from a profound Knowledge of human Nature. It leads a Man into his own Heart ; unfolds to him the secret Springs of his Passions ; the latent Windings of his Self-love ; the Difference between false and solid Virtues. From the Knowledge of Man, it soars to the Knowledge of G o d himself. It makes us everywhere sensible, that the infinite Being incessantly works within us, in order to render us both Good and Happy ; that he is the immediate Source of all our Knowledge, and of all our Virtues ; that we are no less indebted to him for our Reason, than for Life itself ; that his sovereign Truth ought to be our sole Light and Guide, and his supreme Will the Rule of all our Affections ; that, for want of consulting that universal and immutable Wisdom, Man sees nothing but deluding Phantoms ; and, for want of hearkening to it, hears nothing but the confused Noise of his Passions ;

fions; that folid Virtues are like fomething foreign
planted in us; and are not the Refult of our own Endeavours, but the Work of a Power fuperior to Man,
which acts in us when we do not obftruct it, and of
whofe Operation we are fometimes infenfible, by reafon of its Delicacy. We are taught, at laft, that
without this firft and fovereign Power, which raifes
Man above himfelf, the moft fhining Virtues are but
Refinements of Self-love, that makes itfelf the Center of all, becomes its own Deity, and is, at once,
both the *Idolator* and the *Idol.* Nothing is more to be
admired, than the Picture of the Philofopher whom
Telemachus faw in Hell, and whofe only Crime was
the having idoliz'd his own Virtue.

Thus our Author's Morality is calculated to make
us forget our own Being, in order to refer it wholly
to the Supreme Being, and to render us his devout
Adorers; as the Defign of his Politics is to make us
prefer the public before the private Good, and to
infpire us with the Love of Mankind. The Syftems
of *Machiavel* and *Hobbes*, and of *Puffendorff* and
Grotius, two more fober Authors, are well known.
The two firft, uuder the vain and falfe Pretence, that
the Good of Society has nothing in common with the
effential Good of Man, which is Virtue, lay down
no other Maxims of Government, but Craft, Artifice, Stratagems, Tyranny, Injuftice and Irreligion.
The two laft Authors ground their Politics wholly
on Pagan Principles, which even fall fhort either
of *Plato*'s Commonwealth, or *Tully*'s Offices. 'Tis
true, thefe two Modern Philofophers have labour'd
to be profitable to human Society, and have refer'd
almoft every thing to the Happinefs of Man in a
Civil Capacity. But the Author of *Telemachus* is an
Original, in having united the moft perfect Politics,
with

with the Notions of the moſt conſummate Virtue. The great Principle on which his whole Syſtem turns, is, That the whole World is but an univerſal Commonwealth, and every Nation like a large Family. From this beautiful and glorious Idea reſult what the Politicians call the *Laws of Nature, and of Nations,* equitable, generous, and full of Humanity. Every ſingle Country is no more conſider'd as independent from the reſt; but all Mankind as an indiviſible Whole. We are no longer confined to the Love of our own Country alone; but our Affection is immeaſurably enlarged, and we embrace, with univerſal Friendſhip, all the Sons of Men. From hence ariſes a Love for Strangers; the mutual Confidence between neighbouring Nations; Good Faith, Juſtice and Peace among the Princes of the Univerſe, as well as between the private Men of each State. Our Author teaches us likewiſe, that the Glory of a Supreme Governor lies in making Men both Good and Happy; that the Prince's Authority is never more firmly ſettled, than when it ſtands on the Affections of the People; and that the true Riches of a Kingdom conſiſt in retrenching all the falſe Appetites of Life, in being contented with Neceſſaries, and with thoſe Pleaſures which are ſimple and innocent. By this he ſhews, That Virtue not only contributes to qualify Man for future Felicity; but alſo actually renders Society as happy as it can be in this Life.

2. The *Morality of Telemachus is Noble in its Motives.*   *Secondly,* The Morality of *Telemachus* is Noble in its *Motives.* His great Principle is, That the Love of *Decency* is to be preferred before the Love of *Pleaſure,* as *Socrates* and *Plato* uſed to ſpeak; or the *Honeſt* before the *Agreeable,* according to *Tully's* Expreſſion. Behold the Source of noble Sentiments, Greatneſs

Greatnefs of Soul, and all Heroic Virtues! 'Tis by thefe pure and elevated Ideas that he overthrows, in a more affecting manner than by Difputation, the vain Philofophy of thofe, who *make Pleafure the only Spring which moves the human Soul.* Our Poet fhews, by the excellent Morality he makes his Heroes fpeak, and the generous Actions he caufes them to perform, how far the Love of *Decency* and of *Perfection,* may prevail with a noble Spirit, and make him facrifice his Pleafure to the toilfome Duties of Virtue. I am not ignorant, that this heroic Virtue paffes for a *Chimera* among vulgar Souls, and that the Men of Fancy and Imagination have endeavoured to explode this fublime and folid Truth by many frivolous and defpicable Witticifms; becaufe finding nothing in themfelves equal to thofe great Sentiments, they therefore conclude, that human Nature is not capable of them. Thefe are *Dwarfs,* who judge of the Strength of Giants by their own. Minds that are continually grovelling within the narrow bounds of *Self-Love,* will never be able to comprehend the Power and Extent of a Virtue that raifes Man above himfelf. Some Philofophers, who otherwife have made ufeful Difcoveries, have yet been fo far hurried away by Prejudice, as not fufficiently to diftinguifh between the *Love of Order,* and the *Love of Pleafure;* and to deny, that the Will may be as ftrongly moved *by the clear View of Truth,* as *by the blind Senfation of Pleafure.* One cannot ferioufly read *Telemachus,* without being convinced of that great Principle. There we fee the generous Sentiments of a noble Soul, which conceives nothing but what is great; of a difinterefted Heart, which continually forgets itfelf; of a Philofopher, who is not confined either to himfelf, or his own Nation,

or

or indeed to any thing particular ; but who refers all to the common Good of Mankind, and all Mankind to the fupreme Being.

In the *Third* Place, the *Morality* of *Telemachus* is, in its Practical Ufes, Uni-verfal, extenfive, fruitful, and adapted to all Times, Nations, and Conditions. Here are taught the Duties of a Prince, who is at once a King, a Warrior, a Philofopher, and a Legiflator. Here is difplayed the Art of governing different Nations ; the Way of maintaining Peace abroad with our Neighbours ; and yet of having ftill at home a warlike Race of Youth, always ready to defend the Kingdom ; of enriching the Nation without falling into Luxury ; and of finding a Medium between the Exceffes of a *Defpotic Power*, and the Diforders of Anarchy. Here are difpenfed Precepts for Agriculture, Com-merce, liberal Arts, civil Government, and the Education of Children. Our Author brings into his Poem, not only heroic and royal Virtues, but even fuch as are proper for all Conditions. While he is forming the Mind of his Prince, he inftructs no lefs every private Man in his Duty.

margin: 3. The Mo-rality of Te-lemachus is Univerfal in its practical Ufes.

The End of the *Iliad* is to reprefent the fatal Con-fequences of Divifions among the Generals of an Army. The *Odyffey* lets us know, what Prudence, joined with Valour, may enable a King to do : And the *Æneid* defcribes the Actions of a pious and cou-rageous Hero. But all thefe particular Virtues do not render Mankind happy. *Telemachus* excels all thefe Plans, in the Greatnefs, Number, and Extenfive-nefs of his Moral Views ; fo that we may fay, with the Philofopher who has criticized upon

Ho-

Homer, * *The moſt profitable Gift the
Muſes ever beſtowed upon Men, is* Te-   * The Abbot
lemachus: *For, if the Happineſs of Man-*   *Terraſſon.*
*kind could reſult from a Poem, it would ariſe from
this.*

Of the P O E T R Y.

It is an excellent Obſervation of Sir *William
Temple,* That the Powers of *Muſic,* the Beauty of
Painting, and the Force of *Eloquence,* ought to be
united in *Poetry :* But, as *Poetry* differs only from
Eloquence in that it paints with *Enthuſiaſm,* we rather
chuſe to ſay, That *Poetry* borrows its *Harmony* from
Muſic, its *Paſſions* from *Painting,* its *Force* and
Juſtneſs from *Philoſophy.*

The Style of *Telemachus* is polite,
clean, flowing, magnificent, and hath   Harmony
all the Copiouſneſs of *Homer,* without   of the Style of
his Luxuriancy of Words. He never   *Telemachus.*
falls into *Tautology* ; and, when he ſpeaks twice of
the ſame things, he does not call back the ſame
Images, much leſs does he uſe the ſame Expreſſions
over again. All his Periods fill the Ear with their
Numbers and *Cadency*; nor is it ever ſhock'd with
harſh Words, abſtruſe Terms, or affected Turns.
He never ſpeaks merely for the ſake of ſpeaking, or
only of pleaſing: All his Words carry a Thought,
and every Thought tends to the making of us good.

Our Poet's *Images* are no leſs *perfect,*
than his *Style harmonious.* To paint,   Excellence
is not only to deſcribe Things, but to   of the Paint-
repreſent their Circumſtances in ſo lively   ings of *Tele-*
and ſo affecting a manner, that we may   *machus.*

fanſy

fanfy we fee them. As the Author of *Telemachus*
had ftudy'd the Heart of Man, and was acquainted
with all its Springs, fo he paints the Paffions with admirable Art. When we read his Poem, we can fee
nothing but what he fets before our Eyes; we have
no Ears but for his Perfon fpeaking: He warms, he
rouzes, he tranfports us; and we feel all the Paffions
he defcribes.

The Poets generally make ufe of two
Ways of Painting, *viz*. *Similies* and *De-*

Of the Si-
milies and De-
fcriptions of
Telemachus.

fcriptions. The *Similies* of *Telemachus*
are *Juft* and *Noble*. The Author does
not raife the Mind too far above his
Subject by extravagant Metaphors; neither does he
perplex it by too great a Variety of Images. He
has imitated all that is great and beautiful in the Defcriptions of the Ancients, their Combats, Games,
Shipwrecks, Sacrifices, and the like; without dwelling on trifling Things that make the Narrative flag;
and without debafing the Majefty of the *Epic* Poem
by the Defcription of low and difagreeable Things.
Sometimes he defcends to Particulars: But he never
fays any thing but what deferves Attention, and
contributes to the Idea with which he'would imprefs
us. He follows Nature in all its various Forms. He
knew perfectly well, That all manner of Difcourfes
ought to have *Inequalities*, and be fometimes *fublime*
without Bombaft, and fometimes *plain* without being
low. It is a falfe Tafte to affect Embellifhments
every-where. His Defcriptions are magnificent, but
natural; fimple, and yet agreeable. He not only
paints to the life, but his Pictures themfelves are
amiable. He joins Truth of Defign, to Beauty of
Colouring; the Fire of *Homer*, to the Majefty of
Virgil.

Virgil. Nor is this all; the Defcriptions in this Poem are not only calculated to pleafe, but to inftruct at the fame time. If the Author fpeaks of a rural Life; it is to recommend its lovely Simplicity of Manners. If he defcribes Games and Combats; it is not only to celebrate the Funeral of a Friend or of a Father, as in the *Iliad* and *Æneid*; but in order to chufe a King who may furpafs all other Men in Strength of Mind as well as Body, and who may be equally capable of bearing the Fatigue of both. If he reprefents to us the Horrors of a Shipwreck; 'tis to infpire his Hero with Conftancy of Mind, and with an entire Refignation to the Gods, in the utmoft Dangers. I might run over all thefe Defcriptions, and find in them the like Beauties: But I fhall content myfelf with obferving, that in this *new Edition*, the Sculpture on the dreadful *Ægis* (or *Shield*) which *Minerva* fends to *Telemachus*, is full of Art, and contains this fublime Moral, *That Sciences and Agriculture are the Buckler of a Prince, and the Support of a Kingdom: That a King armed with Wifdom always feeks Peace, and ever finds plentiful Supplies againft all the Calamities of War in a well difciplined and laborious People, whofe Minds and Bodies are equally inured to Toil.*

Poetry draws its Force and Juftnefs from Philofophy. We fee every-where in *Telemachus,* a rich, lively, and agreeable Imagination, and, at the fame time, a juft and profound Judgment. Thefe two Qualities feldom meet in the fame Perfon: For the Mind muft be in an almoft continual Motion to invent, to raife the Paffions, and to imitate; and at the fame time, in a perfect Tranquillity, to judge as faft as it invents, and, among a thoufand Thoughts that offer

Philofophy of *Telemachus.*

offer themfelves, to felect the moft proper. The Imagination muft fuffer a fort of Rapture and Enthufiafm, whilft the Mind, calm in her Dominion, curbs and directs it as fhe pleafes. Without this Tranfport, which animates all, the Narration appears cold, languid, abftracted, hiftorical; and, without this exquifite and over-ruling Judgment, it is falfe and deceitful.

Comparifon of the Poetry of *Telemachus* with *Homer* and *Virgil.*

The *Fire* § of *Homer*, efpecially in the *Iliad*, is impetuous and fierce, like a flaming Whirlpool that fets all in Combuftion. The Fire of *Virgil* has more Light than Warmth, but is ever equally bright. That of *Telemachus* warms and enlightens at once, according as there is occafion either to perfuade or ftrike the Paffions. When this Flame fhines out, it gives, at the fame time, a gentle and inoffenfive Heat; fuch as we find in the Difcourfes of *Mentor* upon Politics, and in thofe of *Telemachus* expounding the Laws of *Minos*, &c. Thefe pure Ideas fill the Mind with their gentle Light; whereas

§ Mr. *Pope*, in his Preface to the Tranflation of *Homer*'s *Iliad*, has this Obfervation, "Where this *Poetical Fire* "appears, though attended with Abfurdities, it brightens "all the Rubbifh about it till we fee nothing but its "own Splendor. This Fire is difcern'd in *Virgil*; but "difcern'd as through a Glafs, reflected and more fhining "than warm, but every-where equal and conftant. In "*Lucan* and *Statius*, it burfts out in fudden, fhort, and "interrupted Flafhes: In *Milton*, it glows like a Furnace "kept up to an uncommon Fiercenefs by the force of Art: "In *Shakefpeare*, it ftrikes before we are aware, like an "Accidental Fire from Heaven: But in *Homer*, and in "him only, it burns every-where clearly, and every-where "irrefiftibly."

as *Enthufiafm* and *Poetic Fire* would offend, like the
too fierce Rays of the Sun, which dazzle the Sight.
When there is no more occafion for Reafoning, but
only for Acting; when the Truth is clearly difcover'd; and when the Mind hefitates merely from
Irrefolution; then the Poet excites a Fire and a
Paffion that determines; and bears away the debi-
litated Soul, which wanted Courage to refign herfelf to Truth. The *Epifode* of the Amours of *Telemachus* in the Ifland of *Calypfo*, is full of this fort of
Fire.

This excellent and judicious Mixture of *Brightnefs*
and *Warmth*, diftinguifhes our Poet from *Homer* and
Virgil. The *Enthufiafm* of the firft makes him
fometimes forget the Rules of Art, neglect Order,
and trefpafs upon the Bounds of Nature. The
Strength and rapid Flight of his great Genius hurry'd him away in fpite of himfelf. The pompous
Magnificence, the found Judgment, and Conduct of
Virgil, fometimes degenerate into a too formal Regularity, wherein the Poet feems to dwindle into an
Hiftorian. The latter, however, is far better liked
by our *Philofophical Modern Poets*, than the former;
undoubtedly, becaufe they are fenfible, that 'tis far
eafier to imitate *by Art* the great Judgment of the
Latin Poet, than the noble Fire of the *Grecian*, which
Nature alone can beftow.

Our Author cannot but pleafe all forts of Poets,
whether they be *Philofophers*, or only Admirers of
Enthufiafm. He has united the Clearnefs and Soli-
dity of the *Underftanding*, with the Charms of the
Imagination; he proves Truth as a Philofopher; he
renders the Truth he has proved amiable by the
Sentiments he excites. With him all is folid, true,
perfuafive, and engaging; without any Witticifms

C

or glittering Thoughts, which are only defign'd to make the Author admir'd. He has followed the great Precept of *Plato*, who fays, *That whoever writes, ought to conceal himfelf, difappear, and be forgotten; and only fet forth the Truths he intends to perfwade, and the Paffions he means to purify and refine.*

In *Telemachus* all is *Reafon*, all is *Thought*. This makes it a Poem for all Nations, and for all Ages. All Foreigners are equally affected with it. Nor do the *Tranflations* that have been made of it into Languages lefs nice and polite than the *French*, efface its original Beauties. The learned Defendrefs * of *Homer* affures us, *That the* Greek *Poet lofes infinitely by a Tranflation, it being impoffible to convey into it the Force, Noblenefs, and Spirit of his Poetry:* But we make bold to fay, That *Telemachus* will ever preferve in all Languages, its Strength, Noblenefs, Spirit, and effential Beauties. The Reafon of it is, becaufe the Excellency of this Poem does not lie in the happy and harmonious ranging of the Words, nor even in the Beauties borrow'd from the Imagination ; but in a fublime Tafte of Truth, in noble and elevated Sentiments, and in the natural, delicate, and judicious manner of treating them. Such Beauties are of all Languages, Times, and Countries, and equally affect found Judgments, and great Souls, throughout the Univerfe.

* Madam Dacier.

Firft Objection againft *Telemachus.*

Several Objections have been rais'd againft *Telemachus* ; *and, firft of all,* That it is not in Verfe or Rhime.

Anfwer.

Verfification, according to *Ariftotle, Dionyfius* of *Halicarnaffus,* and *Strabo,*

is

is not eſſential * in an *Epic* Poem, which may be written in Proſe, as well as ſome Tragedies are written without Rhimes. A Man may make Verſes without *Poetry*; and write very poetically without verſifying. *Verſification* may be learn'd or imitated by Art, but a Man muſt be born a Poet. Poetry doth not conſiſt in the fixed Number, and regular Cadence of Syllables; but in a lively Fiction, bold Figures, and the Beauty and Variety of Images. It is That Enthuſiaſm, That Fire, That Impetuoſity, That Energy, That Something in the Expreſſions and Thoughts, which Nature alone can beſtow. All theſe Qualities are found in *Telemachus*, whoſe Author therefore has perform'd what *Strabo* ſays of *Cadmus*, *Pherecides* and *Hecateus*; *He has perfectly imitated Poetry, except only his not obſerving the Meaſure of it, but he has preſerv'd all the other Poetical Beauties.* This M. *de la Motte* has happily expreſs'd in one of his Odes †, to this Effect:

In this our Age another Homer *lives,*
And all that's great in ancient Greece *revives:*
By VIRTUE's *ſelf this Poem was deſign'd;*
T' inſtruct the World, and to reform Mankind;
That TRUTH's *ſtupendous Heights the Bard might*
                                                    [climb,
Th' indulgent Muſe unfetter'd him from Rhime.

Moreover, I doubt, whether the Conſtraint of Rhimes, and the ſcrupulous Regularity of our *Eu-*
ropean,

---

* This is beſt exemplified by our great *Engliſh* Poets, who have written in *Blank Verſe.*
† Firſt Ode of M. *de la Motte* to the *French* Academy.

ropean Conftruction, together with the fixed and
meafured Number of Feet, would not very much
flacken the Flight and Vehemence of Heroic Poetry. Effectually to ftrike and raife the Paffions,
Order and Connection muft often be difregarded;
and therefore the ancient *Greek* and *Roman* Poets,
who painted and defcribed every thing with Vivacity and Tafte, made ufe of *inverted Phrafes*, and
their Words having no fix'd Place, they marfhal'd
them as they thought convenient. The *European*
Languages are a Compound of the *Latin*, and of
the *Jargons* of all the barbarous Nations, that fubdued the *Roman* Empire. Thefe *Northern* People,
like the bleak Climate from whence they came,
froze up every thing by a frigid Formality of *Syn-
tax*; being unacquainted with that beautiful Variety of long and fhort Syllables, which fo well ex-
prefles the delicate Motions of the Soul. They pro-
nounced every thing with the fame Coldnefs, and
knew no other Harmony in Words, than the vain
Jingle of final Syllables of the fame Sound. Some
Italians, and a few *Spaniards*, have endeavour'd to
free their *Verfification* from the Torture
of Rhime; in which Attempt an *Eng-*
lifh Poet * has had wonderful Succefs,
and has likewife very happily begun to
introduce *Inverfions* of Phrafes into his
Language. Who knows but the *French* may one
Day refume that noble Liberty of the *Greeks* and
Romans ?

* I fuppofe
the Author
means *Mil-*
ton.

There are thofe, who, thro' a grofs
Ignorance of the noble Freedom of the
Epic Poem, have found fault with *Tele-*
machus, for being full of *Anachronifms.*

2d Objec-
tion againft
Telemachus.

The

The Author of this Poem has herein imitated the Prince of the *Latin* Poets, Anfwer. who could not be ignorant, that *Dido* was not co-temporary with *Æneas*. *Pygmalion*, in *Telemachus*, Brother to the fame *Dido*; *Sefoftris*, who is fuppos'd to have liv'd about the fame time, *&c.* are not Faults any more than the *Anachronifm* of *Virgil*. Why fhould we blame a Poet for breaking through the Order of Time, when it is fometimes a Beauty to break through the Order of Nature ? I own, it would not be allow'd to contradict a Hiftory in a Matter of Fact not far off from the prefent Time; but as to remote Antiquity, whofe Annals are fo un-certain, and wrapt up in fo great Obfcurity, a Poet, in the Opinion of *Ariftotle* and *Horace*, ought fome-times to follow Probability rather than Truth. Some Hiftorians have written, that *Dido* was chafte; *Pene-lope* loofe; that *Helen* was never in *Troy*, or *Æneas* in *Italy*; and yet *Homer* and *Virgil* have not fcrupled to deviate from Hiftory, in order to render their Fables more inftructive. Why fhould the Author of *Tele-machus*, whofe Defign was to inftruct a young Prince, be deny'd the Liberty of bringing together the Heroes of Antiquity, *Telemachus*, *Sefoftris*, *Neftor*, *Idome-neus*, *Pygmalion*, and *Adraftus*, in order to exprefs in the fame Picture, the Characters of good and bad Princes, whofe Virtues were to be imitated, and whofe Vices to be avoided ?

Some few find fault with the Author of *Telemachus*, for having related in his 3d Objec-tion againft *Telemachus*. Poem the Story of the Amours of *Ca-lypfo* and *Eucharis*, and feveral other Defcriptions of that Nature, which feem too paffio-nate.

The

An⌠wer.   The beſt Anſwer to this Objeƈtion is,
the Effeƈt which this Poem wrought on
the Mind of the Prince for whoſe Inſtruƈtion it was
written : Perſons of an inferior Condition ſtand not ſo
much in need of being caution'd againſt the Dangers
to which Elevation and Power expoſe thoſe who are
deſtin'd to wear a Crown. If our Poet had written
for a Man who was to paſs away his Life in Obſcu-
rity, ſuch Deſcriptions would, indeed, have been of
no great Uſe to him ; but for a young Prince, in the
midſt of a Court where Gallantry paſſes for Politeneſs, where every Objeƈt muſt unavoidably awaken
his Reliſh for Pleaſure, and where all that ſurround
him, are buſy to ſeduce him; nothing, certainly,
was more neceſſary, than to repreſent to him, with
that amiable Modeſty, Innocence, and Wiſdom, that
are conſpicuous in *Telemachus*, all the alluring Arts
of criminal Love ; than to paint to him that Vice in
its imaginary Beauty, in order to make him ſenſible
afterwards of its real Deformity ; than to ſhew him
the whole Depth of the Abyſs, to prevent his falling
into it, and even to keep him from coming near the
Brink of ſo horrid a Precipice. 'Twas therefore a
Piece of Wiſdom worthy our Author, to caution his
Diſciple againſt the extravagant Paſſions of Youth,
by *Calypſo's* Fable ; and to give him, in the Story
of *Antiope*, the Example of a chaſte and lawful
Love. By repreſenting to us, in this manner, that
Paſſion, ſometimes as a Weakneſs unworthy of a
great Soul, ſometimes as a Virtue worthy of a Hero,
he ſhews us, that Love is not below the Majeſty of
Epic Poetry, and thereby he unites, in his Poem, the
tender Paſſions of modern Romances, with the heroic
Virtues of ancient Poetry.

Some

Some are of opinion, that the Author of *Telemachus* exhaufts his Subject too much through the Luxuriancy and Rich- nefs of his Genius ; that he fays all, and leaves nothing for others to think ; that, like *Homer*, he fets whole Nature before our Eyes ; whereas we are generally better pleafed with an Author, who, like *Horace*, comprehends a great deal of Matter in a few Words, and gives his Readers the Satisfaction of unfolding his Hints.

4th Objec- tion againft *Telemachus.*

'Tis certain, that it is not poffible for the Imagination to add any thing to our Poet's Pictures : But, as the Mind attends his No- tions, it both opens and extends itfelf. When he only intends to defcribe, his Paintings are finifhed and perfect ; and when he inftructs, his Knowledge is fruitful, and we difcover a vaft Extent of noble Thoughts, which did not at firft appear, and which even all his fertile Eloquence did not exprefs. He leaves nothing for Fancy to imagine, and yet affords the Mind a great deal of Matter for Reflection. This is properly adapted to the Character of the Prince for whom alone this Work was defigned. There fhone in him, through his Infancy, a fruitful and happy Ima gination, an elevated and extenfive Genius, which made him relifh the Beauties of *Homer* and *Virgil.* Thefe great natural Parts fuggefted to our Author the Defign of a Poem proper to cultivate them, and which fhould comprehend the Excellencies of thofe two Poets. This Affluence of fine Images was effen- tial in fuch a Work, to employ the Imagination, and form the Tafte of the Prince ; and to give him an Opportunity of acquiring, as it were, of his own ac- cord, the Truths prepared for his Mind, and to turn them into Nourifhment. 'Tis plain enough, that

Anfwer.

C 4　　　　　　　thofe

thofe Beauties might as eafily have been fuppreffed, as brought forth, and that they refult from Defign as well as Fecundity, in order to ferve both the Occafions of the Prince, and the Views of the Author.

It has alfo been objected, That neither the Hero, nor the Fable of this Poem have any Relation to the *French* Nation; whereas *Homer* and *Virgil*, by choofing *Actions* and *Actors* out of the Hiftorians of their refpective Countries, have interefted the *Greeks* and *Romans*.

5th Objection againft Telemachus.

Anfwer. If our Author has not interefted the *French* Nation in particular, he has done more, for he has interefted all Mankind. His Plan is much more extenfive than either of the two ancient Poets. It is far greater to inftruct all Men at once, than to confine one's Precepts within a particular Country. Self-love makes every thing center in itfelf, and fubfifts even in the Love of one's Country: But a generous Mind ought to have more enlarged Views.

Yet, after all, *France* had a particular Concern and Satisfaction in a Work, calculated to form a King, who might one Day govern her, according to her *Exigencies* and *Defires*, like a Father of his People, and a Chriftian Hero. The Dawning of that Prince's Life, gave at once, both the Hopes and the Firft-Fruits of that future Happinefs. The Neighbours of *France* began already to fhare in it, as an univerfal Felicity: And fo the Fable of the *Greek* became the Hiftory of the *French* Prince.

The Author had ftill a more excellent Defign than that of pleafing his own Nation; for he meant to ferve her, without her Knowledge, by contributing towards the forming of a Prince, who, even in his infant Sports, feem'd to be born to compleat her Felicity

and

and Glory. That auguſt young Prince reliſhed Fables and Mythology; and therefore it was proper to take advantage of his Taſte, and to ſhew him the Solid and the Beautiful, the Simple and the Great, in what he admired; and to imprint in his Mind, by affecting Examples, the general Principles, which might arm him againſt the Dangers incident to royal Birth, and imperial Power.

With this View, a *Greek* Hero, an Imitation of *Homer*'s and *Virgil*'s Poetry, and the Hiſtories of other Countries, Times and Events, ſuited perfectly well; and were, perhaps, the only Means to ſet the Author at full Liberty to draw and paint, with Truth and Force, all the Dangers that threaten Sovereigns in all ſucceeding Ages.

By a natural and neceſſary Conſequence, theſe univerſal Truths often have ſome Analogy to the Hiſtories and Circumſtances of the preſent Age. For theſe *Fictions*, abſtracted from all Application, and intended to inform the Infancy of a young Prince, contain Precepts for all the Moments and Periods of his Life.

This Applicability of general Leſſons of Morality, to all manner of Circumſtances, raiſes our Admiration of the Author's fruitful Fancy, Penetration and Wiſdom; but does not excuſe the Injuſtice of his Enemies, who have maliciouſly endeavour'd to find in his *Telemachus* certain *odious Allegories*; and who, to turn his wiſeſt and moſt moderate Counſels into injurious Satires againſt thoſe for whom he had the higheſt Veneration, have inverted the Characters, fixed imaginary Reſemblances to them, and poiſon'd his pureſt Intentions. Could the Author, with any Honeſty, ſuppreſs thoſe fundamental Maxims of wholeſome Morality and Politics, becauſe the moſt cautious Manner of delivering them that could be thought of, was not able to ſkreen them from the Malice of Critics.

C 5

Upon

Upon the whole matter, our illuftrious Author has united in his Poem the greateft Beauties of the Ancients : For he has all the Enthufiafm and Profufion of *Homer*, and all the Magnificence and Regularity of *Virgil.* Like the *Greek* Poet, he paints every thing with Force, Simplicity and Life : There is Variety in his Fable, and Diverfity in his Characters ; his Reflections are moral ; his Defcriptions lively ; his Imagination fruitful ; and every-where one meets that Spirit and Fire which Nature alone can beftow. Like the *Latin* Poet, he perfectly obferves the Unity of the Action, the Uniformity of the Characters, the Order and Rules of Art: His Judgment is profound, and his Thoughts lofty and elevated ; whilft he unites the Natural with the Noble, and the Simple with the Sublime. Every-where *Art* becomes *Nature.* But our Poet's Hero is more perfect than either the *Greek*'s or the *Latin*'s ; for his Morality is more pure, and his Sentiments more noble. From all this we may conclude, that the Author of *Telemachus* has fhewn by his Poem, That the *French* are capable of all the Delicacies of the *Greeks*, and of all the great Sentiments of the *Romans* ; and that the Elogy of the Author, is the Elogy of his own Nation.

The END *of the Difcourfe on the* Epic Poem.

THE

Book.I.

THE
ADVENTURES
OF
TELEMACHUS,
THE
SON of ULYSSES.

BOOK I.

The ARGUMENT.

Telemachus, *led by* Minerva *under the Shape of* Mentor, *having suffered Shipwreck, lands in the Island of the Goddess* Calypso, *who was still lamenting the Departure of* Ulysses. *She gives him a kind Reception, is smitten with Love of him, offers to make him immortal, and desires to know his Adventures. He relates his Voyage to* Pylos

and

and Sparta; *his being shipwrecked on the Coast of* Sicily; *the Danger he was in of being sacrificed.on the Tomb of* Anchises; *how* Mentor *and he assisted* Acestes *in repelling an Incursion of* Barbarians; *and how that King acknowledged that Service, by giving them a* Phenician *Ship to return home.*

A L Y P S O continu'd disconsolate for the Departure of *Ulysses:* Her Grief was so violent, that she thought herself unhappy in being immortal: Her *Grotto* no more echo'd to her tuneful Voice: The Nymphs that served her durst not speak to her: She often walk'd alone on the flowery Turf, with which an everlasting Spring had edged her Island round. But these beautiful Walks were so far from asswaging her Grief, that they served only to revive the sad Remembrance of *Ulysses.* whose Company she had so often enjoyed in those Places. Sometimes she stood still and wept, watering the Shore with her Tears; and always turning her Eyes to that Side where *Ulysses*'s Ship, ploughing the Waves, finally vanished from her Sight: When, on a sudden, she perceiv'd the broken Pieces of a Vessel just wreck'd; the Oars and broken Seats of the Rowers scatter'd here and there upon the Sands; the Mast, Rudder and Cordage floating near the Shore.

Immediately after this, she descry'd two Men at a distance, one of them appearing to be aged, and the other, though young, resembling *Ulysses*; the same Sweetness and Dignity in his Looks, the same Stature and majestic Port. The Goddess presently knew him to be *Telemachus,* the Son of that

that Hero. But though the Deities of this Order far furpafs all Men in Knowledge, yet fhe could not difcover who was the venerable Perfon that accompany'd *Telemachus:* For the fuperior Gods conceal from the inferior whatever they pleafe; and *Minerva,* who, in the Shape of *Mentor,* accompany'd *Telemachus,* would not be known to *Calypfo.*

In the mean time, *Calypfo,* inwardly rejoiced at this Shipwreck that had brought the Son of *Ulyffes,* fo like his Father, into her Ifland, advanced towards him; and, without feeming-to know who he was, How had you, faid fhe, the Confidence to enter my Ifland? Know, young Stranger, that none unpunifhed come within my Dominions. Under fuch menacing Language fhe endeavoured to cover the Joy of her Heart, which in fpite of herfelf appeared in her Face.

Telemachus anfwered, Oh! whoever you are, whether a Mortal or a Goddefs (though fure your Afpect fpeaks you a Deity) can you be unmoved at the Misfortunes of a Son, who, feeking his Father through the Dangers of Winds and Seas, has feen his Ship dafhed in Pieces againft your Rocks? Who, I pray, reply'd the Goddefs, is that Father you feek? He is called *Ulyffes,* faid *Telemachus,* and is one of thofe Kings, who, after a Siege of ten Years, deftroy'd the famous City of *Troy.* His Name is celebrated in all Parts of *Greece* and *Afia,* for his Valour in Fight, and much more for his Wifdom in Council: But now he wanders over all the Extent of the Seas, and runs through the moft terrible Dangers. His Country feems to fly from him. His Wife *Penelope,* and I, who am his Son, have loft all Hopes of feeing him again. I run the fame Hazards he has done, to learn where he is. But, what do I fay!

It

It may be he is now bury'd in the profound Abyfs of the Sea. Oh Goddefs! pity our Misfortunes; and if you know what the Fates have done, either to fave or deftroy *Ulyffes*, vouchfafe to inform his Son *Telemachus*.

Calypfo, fill'd with Amazement and Compaffion to find fo much Wifdom and Eloquence in fo much Youth, could not fatiate her Eyes with looking on him, and ftood for fome time filent. At laft fhe faid to him, We will inform you, O *Telemachus!* what has happened to your Father; but the Story is long to tell, and tis high time to repofe yourfelf after all the Fatigues you have endured. Come into my Habitation, and I will receive you as my Son : Come, you fhall be my Comfort in this Solitude, and I will give you Felicity, if you know how to enjoy it.

Telemachus follow'd the Goddefs, who was furrounded by a Crowd of young Nymphs, and furpafs'd them all in Stature, as a well grown Oak of the Foreft raifes his lofty Head above the reft of the Trees. He admir'd the Luftre of her Beauty, the rich Purple of her long and floating Robes ; her Hair carelefly, but gracefully, ty'd behind her Neck ; the Fire that darted from her Eyes, and the Sweetnefs that tempered this Vivacity. *Mentor* with down-caft Eyes, and modeft Silence, follow'd *Telemachus*.

Arriving at the Entrance of *Calypfo's* Grotto, *Telemachus* was furprized to fee whatever could charm the Eye, cover'd under the Appearance of rural Simplicity. There was neither Gold nor Silver to be feen, no Marble nor Columns, no Paintings nor Statues : But the Grotto was cut into divers Vaults within the Rock, which were

in-

incrufted with Shells and Rock - work. The
Tapeftry was a young Vine, extending its tender
Branches equally on every Side. The gentle *Zephyrs* preferv d a refrefhing Coolnefs in this Place,
fecure from the fcorching Heat of the Sun..
Springs of pure Water ran fweetly murmuring
through the Meadows, that were painted with Violets
and Amaranths, and formed divers natural Baths,
as clear and as bright as Cryftal. A thoufand fpringing Flowers enamell'd the green Carpet that furrounded the Grotto. There was an entire Wood of
thofe tufted Trees that bear golden Apples, and put
forth Bloffoms in all Seafons, yielding the fweeteft
of all Perfumes. This Wood feem'd to crown the
beautiful Meads, and make an artificial Night, which
.the Beams of the Sun could not penetrate. Here
nothing was ever heard, but the Singing of Birds,
or the Noife of a Rivulet, which rufhing from the
Top of a Rock, falls down in foaming Streams, and
runs away through the Meadow.

The Grotto of the Goddefs was on the Defcent
of a Hill, from whence might be defcry'd the Sea,
one while clear and fmooth as Glafs, at another
time vainly angry with' the Rocks, againft which
it broke, roaring, and fwelling its Waves like
Mountains. From another Side, was feen a
River, in which were many little Iflands, boider'd
with flowering Lime-trees, and lofty Poplars that
rear'd their ftately Heads to the Clouds. The feveral Channels that formed thefe Iflands, feem'd to
play and fport between the Banks; fome rolling
their Waters with Rapidity; others more gently
and quietly; and others, after many Windings,
returning, as it were, to the Spring from whence
they

they came, feem'd unwilling to leave the charming
Place. One might fee, afar off, many Hills and
Mountains hiding their Heads in the Clouds, and
forming fuch odd and unufual Figures, as yielded a
moft agreeable Profpect. The neighbouring Hills,
were covered with green Vine-branches that hung
in *Feftoons*, the Grapes of which furpafs'd the richeft
Purple in Colour, and could not conceal themfelves
under the Leaves; the Vine bent beneath the
Weight of its own Fruit. The Fig-tree, the Olive,
and the Pomegranate, with all kinds of other Trees,
cover'd the reft of the Country, and made it one
great Garden.

Calypfo, having fhew'd *Telemachus* all thefe Beauties of Nature, faid to him, It is time for you to
repofe yourfelf, and fhift your wet Garments; after
which, we will fee one another again, and I will tell
you fome things that fhall affect your Heart. Having faid this, fhe caus'd them both to enter into the
moft private and retir'd Part of a Grotto, adjoining
to that in which fhe dwelt. Her Nymphs had taken
care to light in it a large Fire of Cedar-wood,
which fill'd the Apartment with an agreeable
Scent, and had left all neceffary Apparel for the
two Strangers. *Telemachus*, finding that the Goddefs had defign'd him a Tunick of the fineft
Wool, whiter than Snow, with a Gown of Purple, richly embroidered with Gold, was, like a
young Man, infinitely pleafed with this Magnificence. Hereupon *Mentor* faid to him, in a grave
Tone, Are thefe, O *Telemachus!* the Thoughts
that ought to poffefs the Heart of the Son of *Ulyffes?*
Think rather to maintain the Reputation your Father
has acquir'd, and to overcome the Perfecutions of
Fortune. A young Man, who loves the Vanity of
Drefs,

Drefs, like a Woman, is unworthy of Wifdom and Renown. The Heart, that knows not how to fuffer Pain, and defpife Pleafure, has no juft Claim to Glory.

Telemachus, with a deep Sigh, anfwered, May the Gods deftroy me, rather than fuffer Effeminacy and Senfuality to feize my Heart. No, the Son of *Ulyffes* fhall never be fubdued by the Charms of an indolent and unmanly Life. But what Favour of Heaven has brought us, after our Shipwreck, to this Goddefs, or Mortal, who receives us with fo much Goodnefs ?

Tremble, reply'd *Mentor,* left in the End fhe overwhelm you with Evil ; be more afraid of her deceitful Sweetnefs, than of the Rocks that fplit your Ship. Death and Shipwreck are lefs dreadful than the Pleafures that attack Virtue. Take heed, how you believe what fhe fhall fay to you. Youth is full of Prefumption ; it hopes every thing from its ownfelf ; though nothing in the World be fo frail, it fears nothing, and vainly relies upon its own Strength ; lightly confiding, and without any Precaution. Beware of hearkening to the foft and flattering Words of *Calypfo,* which glides along like a Serpent beneath the Flowers. Fear the conceal'd Poifon, diftruft yourfelf, and determine nothing without my Counfel.

/After this, they return'd to *Calypfo,* who waited for them : And prefently her Nymphs, dreffed in white, with their plaited Hair, brought in a plain Repaft, but exquifite for Tafte and Neatnefs, confifting of Birds that they had taken with Nets, and of Venifon that they had killed with their Bows. Wine, fweeter than Nectar, flow'd from the Jars of Silver into golden Bowls that were

crown'd

crown'd with Flowers. All forts of Fruit that the
Spring promifes, and Autumn ripens, were in profufion brought in Bafkets, and four young Nymphs
began to fing. Firft, They fung the War of the
Gods againft the Giants; then the Amours of *Jupiter* and *Semele*; the Birth of *Bacchus*, and his
Education under the Care of old *Silenus*; the Race
of *Atalanta* and *Hippomenes*, who conquer'd by the
means of the golden Apples gathered in the Garden
of the *Hefperides*. Laft of all, they fung the War
of *Troy*, and extolled the Valour and Wifdom of
Ulyſſes to the Heavens. The chief of the Nymphs,
whofe Name was *Leucethoe*, accompany'd their fweet
Voices with her tuneful Lute. When *Telemachus*
heard the Name of his Father, the Tears that flow'd
down his Cheeks gave a new Luftre to his Beauty.
But *Calypfo* perceiving that he could not eat, and
that he was feized with Grief, made a Sign to the
Nymphs, and prefently they began to fing the Fight
between the *Centaurs* and the *Lapithæ*, and the Defcent
of *Orpheus* into Hell, to bring back from thence his
dear *Eurydice*.

The Repaft being over, the Goddefs took *Telemachus* afide, and faid to him, You fee, O Son of
the great *Ulyſſes!* with what Favour I receive you :
I am immortal, and no Mortal can enter into this
Ifland without being punifhed for his rafh Attempt ;
nay, even your Shipwreck fhould not fecure you
from the Effects of my Indignation, if I did not
love you. Your Father had the fame Happinefs
you now enjoy ; but, alas! he knew not how to
ufe it. I detained him a long time in this Ifland,
and, had he been contented, he might have lived
with me in an immortal Condition : But a fond
Paffion to return to his wretched Country, made
him

him reject all thefe Advantages. You fee what he has loft for the fake of the Ifle of *Ithaca*, which he could not fee again. He refolv'd to leave me; he went away, and I was reveng'd by a Storm. After his Veffel had ferv'd for Sport to the Winds, it was buried under the Waves. Make a right Ufe of fo fad an Example; for, after his Shipwreck, you can never hope to fee him again, nor ever to reign after him in the Ifland of *Ithaca*. Forget this Lofs, fince you find a Goddefs that offers to make you happy, and to prefent you with a Kingdom. To thefe Words *Calypfo* added many more, to fhew him how happy *Ulyffes* had been with her. She related his Adventures in the Cave of the *Cyclop Polyphemus*, and in the Country of *Antiphates*, King of the *Leftrigons*; not forgetting what happen'd to him in the Ifland of *Circe*, Daughter of the Sun; nor the Dangers he pafs'd between *Scylla* and *Charybdis*. She defcribed the laft Storm that *Neptune* had rais'd againft him when he left her, intimating that he had perifh'd in it; but conceal'd his Arrival in the Ifland of the *Pheacians*.

Telemachus, who at firft had too eafily abandon'd himfelf to Joy, upon his being fo well receiv'd by *Calypfo*, now began to perceive her Artifice, and the Wifdom of thofe Counfels that *Mentor* haft juft given him. He anfwer'd in few Words; O Goddefs, pardon my Grief, which at prefent I cannot overcome; it may be, hereafter, I may have more Force to relifh the Fortune you offer me. Give me leave at this time to bewail my Father; for you know better than I, how much he deferves to be lamented.

Calypfo,

Calypso, not daring to prefs him any farther on that Subject, feign'd to fympathize with him in his Afflic- tion, and to fhew herfelf paffionately concern'd for the Lofs of *Ulyffes* ; but that fne might the better dif- cover the Means to reach his Heart, fhe afk'd him, in what manner he had fuffer'd Shipwreck, and by what Adventures he was brought to her Ifland? The Relation of my Misfortunes, faid he, would be too long. No, no, reply'd fhe, I am in pain to know them, and therefore give me that Satisfaction. After much Solicitation, fhe prevail'd with him, and he be- gan thus.

I departed from *Ithaca*, with Intention to enquire of thofe Kings which are return'd from the Siege of *Troy*, what they knew concerning my Father: The Lovers of my Mother *Penelope* were furpriz'd at my Departure, which I had taken care to conceal from them, becaufe I was well acquainted with their Per- fidioufnefs. But neither *Neftor*, whom I faw at *Pylos*, nor *Menelaus*, who received me with Affection at *Lace- dæmon*, could inform me whether my Father were ftill alive. Weary with living always in Sufpence and Uncertainty, I refolv'd to go into *Sicily*, where I had heard my Father had been driven by the Winds: But the fage *Mentor*, who is here prefent, oppos'd this rafh Defign, reprefenting to me, on the one hand, the *Cyclops*, who are monftrous Giants that devour Men ; on the other, the Fleet of *Æneas* and the *Trojans*, who were upon that Coaft. Thefe *Trojans*, faid he, are highly incens'd againft all the *Greeks*, and they would take a fingular Pleafure to fhed the Blood cf the Son of *Ulyffes*. Return there- fore, continu'd he, to *Ithaca* ; perhaps your Father, who is a Favourite of Heaven, may arrive there as

foon

foon as you. But if the Gods have refolv'd his Deftruction, and he is never more to fee his Country,
at leaft, it becomes you to revenge him againft his
Rivals, to deliver your Mother, to fhew the World
your Wifdom, and let all *Greece* behold, in you, a
King as worthy to reign, as ever *Uiyffes* was himfelf.
This Counfel was wholefome and honourable, but I
had not Prudence enough to follow it, and hearken'd
only to my own Paffion; yet the wife *Mentor* lov'd
me to fuch a Degree, that he condefcended to accompany me in that Voyage, which I rafhly undertook againft his Advice; and the Gods permitted that
I fhould commit a Fault, which was to cure me of
my Prefumption.

Whilft he fpoke, *Calypfo* look'd earneftly, and not
without Aftonifhment, upon *Mentor*. She thought
fhe perceiv'd fomething divine in him, but could
not difintangle the Confufion of her Thoughts;
which caufed her to continue apprehenfive and diffi-
dent in the Prefence of this unknown Perfon; but,
fearing to difcover the Diforder of her Mind, Proceed, faid fhe to *Telemachus*, and fatisfy my Curiofity;
which he did in this manner.

We fteer'd for fome Time with a favourable Wind
for *Sicily*; but then, a black Storm arifing, depriv'd
us of the Sight of Heaven, and involv'd us in the
Obfcurity of Night : But by fome Flafhes of Lightning, we perceiv'd other Ships expos'd to the fame
Danger, and fo a difcover'd them to be the Fleet of
Æneas; they were no lefs formidable to us than the
Rocks themfelves. In that Moment I comprehended, tho' too late, what the Heat of imprudent Youth
had hinder'd me from confidering before. *Mentor*,
in the midft of this Danger, appear'd not only refolute

lute and intrepid, but more chearful than he us'd to
be. 'Twas he that encouraged me, and I felt that
he infpir'd me with invincible Fortitude. He calmly
gave out all neceffary Orders, when the Pilot was
confounded. I faid to him, my dear *Mentor*, why
did I refufe to follow your Counfels? Am I not unhappy, to have been defirous of depending upon my-
own felf, at fuch an Age as has no Forefight of Futurity, no Experience of Things paft, nor Moderation
to govern the prefent? Oh! if ever we efcape this
Storm, I refolve to diftruft myfelf as I would my
moft dangerous Enemy, and to believe you alone for
ever.

To this *Mentor* anfwer'd fmiling, I fhall not
blame you for the Fault you have committed: 'Tis
enough that you are fenfible of it, and make it
ferve hereafter to moderate your Defires. Perhaps,
when the Danger is paft, Prefumption will return;
but however, Courage muft now fupport you;
Before we launch into Danger, we muft forefee,
and ever dread it; but when once in it, we have
nothing left but a generous Contempt of it. Shew
yourfelf therefore, the worthy Son of *Ulyffes*, and let
your Courage be greater than all the Dangers that
threaten.

I was charm'd with the Sweetnefs and Magnanimity of the wife *Mentor*; but I was much more
furpriz'd, when I faw with what Dexterity, he
brought about our Deliverance. The *Trojans*
were fo near, that they could not fail to difcover who we were, as foon as the Light fhould appear; which *Mentor* knowing, and in that Inftant
perceiving one of their Ships, which was feparated
by the Tempeft from the reft of the Fleet, to be
fomething like ours, except certain Garlands of
Flowers

Flowers that fhe carry'd at the Stern, he immediately hung up the like on the fame Part of our
Ship, and faften'd them himfelf with Ribbands of
the fame Colour with thofe of the *Trojans.* He
order'd the Rowers to bow themfelves as low as
they could upon their Benches, that they might not
be difcover'd by the Enemy. In this manner we
pafs'd thro' the midft of their Fleet, whilft they
fhouted for Joy to fee us, fuppofing we were their
Companions, whom they thought to be loft. We
were forc'd along with them, by the Violence of the
Sea, for a confiderable time ; but at laft we found
means to lag a little behind, and whilft they were
driven by the Impetuofity of the Winds towards the
Shore of *Africa,* we exerted our utmoft Efforts to
gain by the Help of our Oars the neareft Coaft of
Sicily,

We arriv'd as we defign'd ; but that which we
fought, prov'd almoft as fatal to us as the Fleet
we avoided : We found upon that Coaft of *Sicily*
more *Trojans,* and confequently Enemies to all *Greeks* ;
for old *Aceftes,* of *Trojan* Lineage, reign'd in thefe
Parts. As foon as we got afhore, the Inhabitants
taking us either to be fome other People of the
Ifland come to furprize them, or elfe Strangers that
defign'd to feize their Country, burnt our Ship in
the firft Tranfport of their Rage, and kill'd all our
Companions ; referving only *Mentor* and me to be
prefented to *Aceftes,* that we might inform him of
our Defigns, and whence we came. We were
brought into the Town with our Hands ty'd behind
our Backs, and our Death was deferr'd only to make
us a Spectacle to a cruel People, as foon as they
fhould know we were *Greeks.*

We

We were ftraightway prefented to *Aceftes*, who fat with a golden Sceptre in his Hand, diftributing Juftice, and preparing himfelf for a great Sacrifice. He afk'd us, with a fevere Voice, of what Country we were, and the Occafion of our Voyage? *Mentor* immediately anfwered, We come from the Coaft of *Great Hefperia*, and our Country is not far from thence. By this means he avoided the telling him that we were *Greeks*. But *Aceftes* would hear no more, and taking us for Foreigners that conceal'd fome bad Defign, he commanded us to be fent into a neighbouring Foreft, there to ferve as Slaves to thofe who look'd after the Cattle. This Condition feem'd more terrible to me than Death. I cry'd out, O King! order us rather to fuffer Death, than to be treated fo unworthily. Know, that I am *Telemachus*, the Son of the wife *Ulyffes*, King of the *Ithacans*. I feek my Father thro' every Sea; and if I can neither find him, nor return to my own Country, nor avoid Servitude, take that Life from me which is intolerable.

Scarce had I pronounc'd thefe Words, when all the People in a Rage cry'd out, *The Son of the cruel* Ulyffes *muft die, whofe Artifices have deftroy'd the City of* Troy. O Son of *Ulyffes!* faid *Aceftes*, I cannot refufe your Blood to the *Manes* of fo many *Trojans*, whom your Father precipitated to the Banks of black *Cocytus*. You and your Conductor fhall die. At the fame time, an old Man of the Company propos'd to the King, that we fhould be facrific'd on the Tomb of *Anchifes*. Their Blood, faid he, will be grateful to the Soul of that Hero. *Æneas* himfelf, when he hears of fuch a Sacrifice, will be overjoy'd to perceive how much you love what was dearer to him than all the World.

Every

Every one applauded his Propofition, and all their
Thoughts were bent to put it in Execution. We
were fed to the Tomb of *Anchifes*, where two Altars were erected, and the facred Fire kindled. The
Knife was brought, we were crowned with flowery
Garlands, and no Mercy could fave our Lives. Our
Fate was determined, when *Mentor* calmly defired
to fpeak with the King; and having received Per-
miffion, faid, O *Aceftes !* If the Misfortunes of
young *Telemachus*, who never carried Arms againft
the *Trojans*, may not plead for him, at leaft let your
own Intereft move you. The Knowledge I have acquir'd, to prefage and foretell the Will of the Gods,
informs me, That, before the End of three Days,
you will be attack'd by a barbarous People, who
will come down like a Torrent from the Mountains,
to overwhelm your City, and ravage your whole
Country. Haften to prevent them; arm your People, and from this Moment begin to fecure within
your Walls the rich Herds and Flocks you have in
the Fields. If my Prediction be falfe, you may facrifice us when the three Days are expir'd; but if,
on the contrary, it prove true, remember, that no
one ought to take away the Lives of thofe, by
whom his own was preferv'd.

Aceftes was aftonifh'd at thefe Words, which
Mentor fpoke with more Affurance than he had ever
found in any Man. I fee, faid he, O Stranger!
that the Gods, who have granted you fo fmall a Share
in the Favours of Fortune, have, in recompence,
given you fuch Wifdom as is more valuable than the
higheft Profperity. At the fame time, he put off
the Sacrifice, and iffued out all neceffary Orders,
with the utmoft Diligence, to prevent the Attack,
of which *Mentor* had forewarned him. On all

D   Sides

Sides were to be seen old Men and Women trembling for fear, and accompanied with great Numbers of young Children, bath'd in Tears, and retiring into the City. The lowing Oxen and bleating Sheep left the rich Pastures, and came in Droves; whose Numbers were too great to be provided with Housing for them all. The Noise and Tumult of People pressing to get in was such, that no one could understand another. In this Disorder, some took an unknown Person for their Friend, and others ran they knew not whither. But the principal Men of the City, thinking themselves wiser than the rest, suspected *Mentor* to be an Impostor, who had fram'd a false Prediction to save his Life.

Before the third Day was expir'd, whilst they were full of these Imaginations, a Cloud of Dust was seen rising upon the Descent of the neighbouring Hills; and an innumerable Multitude of *Barbarians* appear'd in Arms: These were the *Hymerians*, a savage People, together with those who inhabit the Mountains *Nebrodes*, and the Summit of *Agragas*, where a Winter reigns which the Zephyrs never could mitigate. All those who had despis'd the Prediction of *Mentor*, lost all their Slaves and their Cattle. Upon this, the King said to *Mentor*, I forget that you are *Greeks*; our Enemies are become our faithful Friends; the Gods have sent you to save us; I expect no less from your Valour, than from the Wisdom of your Counsels; hasten therefore to assist us.

Mentor shews in his Eyes a Boldness that damps the Spirits of the fiercest Warriors. He takes up a Shield, a Helmet, a Sword, and a Lance; he draws up the Soldiers of *Acestes*, puts himself at their Head, and advances in good Order towards the Enemy.

Enemy. *Acestes*, tho' full of Courage, could only follow him at a Distance, by reason of his Age. I follow'd him more close: But I could not equal his Valour. In the Fight, his Cuirass resembled the immortal *Ægis* of *Minerva*. Death flew from Rank to Rank, where-ever his Blows fell. He was like a Lion of *Numidia*, provok'd by cruel Hunger, which, falling upon a Flock of feeble Sheep, kills, tears, and swims in Blood, whilst the Shepherds, far from assisting their Flock, fly trembling away from his Fury.

These *Barbarians*, who hop'd to surprize the City, were themselves surpriz'd and defeated. The Subjects of *Acestes* were animated by the Example and Voice of *Mentor*, and felt a Vigour which they thought themselves utterly incapable of. With my Lance I kill'd the Son of the *Barbarian* King: He was of my Age, but much taller than I ; for these People are descended from Giants of the same Race with the *Cyclops*. He despis'd so weak an Enemy ; but I, not at all daunted at his prodigious Strength, or his fierce and savage Looks, push'd my Lance against his Breast, and made his Soul gush out at the Wound, in a Torrent of black and reaking Gore. As he fell, he was like to crush me in Pieces by his Fall. The Sound of his Arms echo'd in the Hills. I took the Spoil, and return'd to *Acestes* ; *Mentor* having entirely broken the *Barbarians*, cut them in Pieces, and pursued the Runaways to the Woods. So unexpected a Success made *Mentor* to be regarded as one beloved and inspir'd by the Gods ; and *Aces-tes*, from a Sense of Gratitude, shew'd his Concernment for us, if the Fleet of *Æneas* should return to *Sicily*. He gave us a Ship to carry us without Delay to our own Country ; made us many rich Pre-

sents,

fents, and prefs'd us to haften our Departure, to prevent all the Misfortunes of which he was apprehenfive. But he would not give us either a Pilot or Mariners of his own Nation, for fear they might be expos'd to too much Hazard upon the Coafts of *Greece.* He committed us to the Care of certain *Phenician* Merchants, who, trading with all the People of the World, had nothing to fear; and order'd them to bring back the Ship, when they had landed us fafe at *Ithaca.* But the Gods, who fport with the Defigns of Men, had ftill referv'd us for farther Calamities.

The E N D *of the* F I R S T B O O K.

T H E

THE
ADVENTURES
OF
TELEMACHUS.

BOOK II.

The ARGUMENT.

Telemachus *relates how he was taken in the* Tyrian·
Ship, by the Fleet of Sefoftris, *and carried Prifoner
into* Egypt: *He gives a Defcription of that fine
Country, and of their King's wife Government.   He
adds, that* Mentor *was fent into Slavery to*
Æthiopia; *That he himfelf was reduced to the Condition of a Shepherd in the Defart of* Oafis; *That*
Termofiris, *a Prieft of* Apollo, *comforted him, by
perfuading him to imitate that God, who had once
been a Cowherd to King* Admetus; *That* Sefoftris
*having, at laft, been informed of the wonderful
Things he had effected among thofe who tended his:*

Flocks

Flocks and Herds, had recall'd him ; and being con-
vinc'd of his Innocence, promifed to fend him back to
Ithaca : *But that* Sefoftris's *Death involv'd him in*
new Misfortunes; and that he was imprifon'd in a
Tower on the Sea-fhore, from whence he faw the new
King Bocchoris *perifh in a Fight againft his rebel-*
lious Subjects, who were offifted by the Tyrians.

HE *Tyrians,* by their Infolence, had
highly provok'd the King of
Egypt, whofe Name was *Sefoftris,*
and who had conquer'd many
Kingdoms. The Riches they had
acquir'd by Trade, and the impreg-
nable Strength of *Tyre,* which
ftands in the Sea, had render'd this People fo proud,
that they not only refus'd to pay the Tribute which
Sefoftris impos'd upon them in his Return from the
Conquefts he had made, but affifted his Brother,
who had confpir'd to murder him amidft the Re-
joicings of a folemn Feftival. In order therefore to
humble their Pride, *Sefoftris* refolv'd to difturb their
Commerce at Sea ; and commanded all his Ships to
feek out and affault the *Phenicians.* One of his
Fleets met with us, as foon as we loft Sight of the
Sicilian Mountains, when the Harbour and Land
feem'd to fly from behind us, and lofe themfelves in
the Clouds. At the fame time we faw the *Egyptian*
Ships advancing towards us like a floating City.
The *Phenicians* perceived, and endeavoured to avoid
them, but it was too late ; their Ships were better
Sailors, their Mariners more numerous, the Wind
favour'd them, they boarded us, took us, and carried us Prifoners to *Egypt.* I told them, but in
vain, that we were not *Phenicians;* they hardly
vouch-

Book II.

vouchfafed to hear me ; they look'd upon us as Slaves,
in which Merchandize they knew the *Phenicians*
traded, and thought only of making the beft of their
Prize. We already took notice, that the Waters of
the Sea began to have a whitifh Caft from the Mixture of thofe of the *Nile* ; and we faw the Coaft of
Egypt almoft level with the Sea. We arrived foon after in the Ifland of *Pharos*, not far from the City of
No ; and from thence were carried up the *Nile* to
Memphis. If the Grief we felt, by reafon of our
Captivity, had not render'd us infenfible of all Pleafure, our Eyes would have been charm'd with the
fruitful Country of *Egypt*, like a delicious Garden,
every-where watered with numberlefs Streams. We
could not turn our Eyes on either Side of the River,
without difcovering many wealthy Cities; Country-
feats delightfully fituated ; Lands richly covered every
Year with a Golden Harveft, without ever lying fal-
low ; Meadows full-ftock'd with Cattle ; Hufband-
men bowing under the Weight of the Fruits which
the teeming Earth had brought forth; and Shepherds that made the Echoes, on every Side, repeat
the Sweet Sound of their Pipes and Flutes.

Happy, faid *Mentor*, is the People who are govern'd by a wife King : They live in Plenty, and
love him to whom they owe their Felicity. Thus,
faid he, O *Telemachus!* you ought to reign, and be
the Delight of your People, if ever the Gods give
you the Poffeffion of your Father's Kingdom. Love
your People as your Children ; relifh the Pleafure of
being belov'd by them ; and carry yourfelf fo, that
all the Tranquillity and Happinefs they enjoy, may
lead them to remember, that they are the rich Prefents of a good King. Kings, whofe only Purpofe is
to render themfelves dreaded, and to bring their Sub-

jects

jects low, in order to make them more submissive, are the Plagues of Mankind. They are, indeed, fear'd, as they desire; but they are hated, detested, and have more reason to be afraid of their Subjects, than their Subjects have to fear them.

I answer'd, Alas! *Mentor*, 'tis not our present Business to consider by what Maxims a King ought to reign: We shall never see *Ithaca* again: We shall never see our Country, or *Penelope* more. And though *Ulysses* should return full of Glory to his Kingdom, he will never have the Satisfaction of seeing me there; nor I that of obeying him, and learning the Rules of Government from him. No, Let us die, dear *Mentor*, for we are allow'd no other Thought: Let us die, since the Gods have no Compassion for us.

As I thus spoke, my Words were interrupted with deep Sighs. But *Mentor*, tho' he could be apprehensive of approaching Evils, knew not what it was to fear them when they had happen'd. Unworthy Son of the wise *Ulysses*, cry'd he, Dost thou suffer thy self to be overcome by thy Misfortunes? Know that ye shall one Day see again both *Ithaca* and *Penelope*. You shall even see him in his former Glory, whom you never knew; the invincible *Ulysses*, whom Fortune cannot conquer, and who, in greater Misfortunes than your own, admonishes you never to despair. O! if he should hear, in distant Regions, where he is driven by the Winds and Sea, that his Son knows not how to imitate him, either in Patience or Courage, such News would overwhelm him with Shame, and prove more heavy than all the Misfortunes he has yet suffered.

After this, *Mentor* caus'd me to observe the Fertility and Happiness that was seen over all the Country
try

try of *Egypt*, wherein there were reckoned two and
twenty thousand Cities. He admir'd the regular
Government of thefe Places; the Diftribution of
Juftice which was every where exercis'd with regard
to the Poor, againft the Oppreffion of the Rich; the
good Education of Youth, who were inur'd early
to Obedience, Labor, Sobriety, and the Love of
Arts or Learning; the due Obfervations of all the
Ceremonies of Religion; a generous and difinterefted Spirit; a great Defire of Reputation; an univerfal Sincerity in their Dealings with Men; and
that Reverence of the Gods, which every Father took
care to infufe into his Children. He thought he
could never enough admire this beautiful Order. He
would often cry out, O! how happy is that People, that
is thus govern'd by a wife King! But yet more happy is that King, who, while he beftows *Happinefs*
on fo great a People, finds his own in *Virtue*. Such
a one is more than fear'd; he is beloved. Men not
only obey him, but they obey him with Pleafure.
He reigns univerfally in their Hearts; and every
Man is fo far from defiring his Death, that he fears it
above all Misfortunes, and would readily facrifice
his own Life for his.

I hearken'd with Attention to what *Mentor* faid;
and, as he fpoke, I found my Courage to revive in
the Bottom of my Heart. As foon as we were arriv'd at the rich and magnificent City of *Memphis*,
the Governor commanded us to be fent to *Thebes*,
in order to be prefented to the King *Sefoftris*, who,
being highly incens'd againft the *Tyrians*, had refolv'd to examine us himfelf. So we proceeded in
our Voyage up the River *Nile*, till we came to the
famous *Thebes*, which has an hundred Gates, and
was the Refidence of that great King. This City

appear'd

appear'd to us of a vaſt Extent, and more populous
than the moſt flouriſhing Cities of *Greece.* The Orders are excellent, in all that regards the Neatneſs
and Conveniency of the Streets, the Courſe of the
Public Waters, the Baths, the Improvement of Arts
and Sciences, and the common Safety. The Squares
are adorn'd with Fountains and Obeliſks. The
Temples are Marble, of a plain, but majeſtic Architecture. The Palace of the Prince is itſelf alone
like a great City; 'tis full of Marble Pillars, Pyra-
mids, Obeliſks, *Coloſſean* Statues, and Furniture of
ſolid Gold and Silver.

They who took us, inform'd the King, that they
found us on board a *Phenician* Ship. For he had al-
lotted certain Hours of every Day, in which he re-
gularly heard all his Subjects that had any thing to
ſay to him, either by way of Complaint or Advice.
He neither deſpis'd nor rejected any Man, and thought
he was a King for no other end than to do good
to his Subjects, whom he lov'd as his Children. As
for Strangers, he receiv'd them with Kindneſs, and
was always deſirous to ſee them, becauſe he thought
it a uſeful and advantageous Thing to be inform'd
of the Cuſtoms and Manners of remote Nations;
and this Curioſity of the King occaſioned our being
brought before him. He was ſeated on a Throne of
Ivory, with a golden Sceptre in his Hand. He was
aged, but comely, full of Sweetneſs and Majeſty.
He daily diſtributed Juſtice to the People with ſuch
Patience and Wiſdom, as made him admir'd without Flattery. After he had ſpent the whole Day in
doing Juſtice, and taking care of the public Affairs,
he refreſhed himſelf in the Evening in hearing Diſcourſes of learned Men, or converſing with the beſt
of his People, whom he knew how to chuſe and admit,

mit into his Familiarity. During his whole Life,
he could not be blam'd for any thing, except for
triumphing with too much Pomp over the Kings he
had conquer'd, and confiding too much in one of
his Subjects, whose Picture I shall draw by and
by.

When he saw me, he was mov'd with my Youth,
and my Affliction, and asked me my Country and
my Name, whilst we wonder'd at the Wisdom that
flow'd from his Lips. I answer'd, You have undoubtedly heard, O great King! of the Siege of
Troy, which lasted ten Years, and the Destruction of
that City, which cost so much *Grecian* Blood. *Ulysses*, my Father, was one of the principal Kings who
ruin'd that Place. He now wanders through all the
Seas, without being able to return to the Island of
Ithaca, which is his Kingdom. I seek my Father,
and by a Misfortune resembling his own, have been
taken Prisoner. Restore me to my Father and Country, and may the Gods preserve you to your Children, and make them sensible of the Pleasure of living under so good a Father.

Sesostris continued to look upon me with an Eye
of Compassion; but being desirous to know if I
spoke the Truth, he referr'd us to be examined by
one of his Officers, commanding him to enquire of
those that took our Ship, whether we were *Greeks* or
Phenicians? If they are *Phenicians*, said the King,
let them be doubly punish'd; first, because they are
our Enemies, and then, because they have endeavour'd to deceive us by a base Falsehood : But, if,
on the contrary, they are *Greeks*, I will have them
to be treated favourably, and sent back into their
own Country in one of my Ships; for I love the
Greeks, who have received many Laws from the
Egyp-

Egyptians. I am not ignorant of the Virtues of *Her-cules*; the Glory of *Achilles* has reach'd our Ears; and I admire what I have heard of the Wisdom of the unhappy *Ulysses.* I have no greater Pleasure than to relieve Virtue in Distress.

The Officer, who was by the King intrusted with the Examination of our Affair, was as corrupt and knavish, as *Sesostris* was sincere and generous. The Name of this Man was *Metophis.* He endeavour'd to ensnare us by artful Questions, and perceiving, that *Mentor* answer'd with more Wisdom than I, he look'd upon him with Aversion and Jealousy; for ill Men are always Enemies to the good. He caus'd us to be separated, and from that Time I knew not what became of *Mentor.* This Separation was to me, as if I had been struck with Thunder. *Metophis* always hoped, that by a separate Examination, we might be drawn to contradict one another. At least, he thought to dazzle my Eyes with his flattering Promises, and make me acknowledge what *Mentor* had conceal'd from him. In a word, he fought not honestly to find out the Truth, but only some Pretence to tell the King we were *Phenicians,* that he might keep us for his Slaves.

And indeed, notwithstanding our Innocence, and all the Wisdom of the King, he found means to deceive him. Alas! how are Kings expos'd! The wisest are often abus'd; cunning and interested Persons continually surround them, while good Men retire from Courts, because they are neither forward, nor Flatterers: They wait till they are fought for; and Princes seldom search for them. On the contrary, ill Men are bold, deceitful, impudent, and insinuating; dexterous at dissembling, and ready to

do

do any thing againſt Honour and Conſcience, to
gratify the Paſſions of the Perſon that reigns. O!
how unhappy is a King, who is open to the Artifices
of bad Men! He is loſt, if he does not ſuppreſs Flattery, and love thoſe who ſpeak the Truth with Confidence. Theſe were the Reflections I made in my
Misfortunes, when I call'd to mind the Things that
I had heard from *Mentor.*

In the mean time, *Metophis* ſent me towards the
Mountains in the Deſart of *Oaſis* with his Slaves,
that I might ſerve with them to look after his numerous Flocks. Here *Calypſo* interrupted *Telemachus,*
and ſaid, Well! and what did you then? You that
in *Sicily* had preferr'd Death before Servitude? *Tele-*
machus anſwer'd, My Misfortunes encreas'd daily ;
I had no longer the wretched Conſolation of chuſing
between Slavery and Death. I was compelled to be a
Slave, and to exhauſt, if I may ſo ſpeak, all the Rigours of Fortune. I had loſt all Hope, and could not
ſay one Word, in order to my Deliverance. *Men-*
tor has ſince told me, that he was ſold to certain E-
thiopians, and that he follow'd them to *Ethiopia.*

As for me, I arriv'd in a horrid Deſart, where
nothing but burning Sands were to be ſeen upon the
Plains ; and Snow that never melted, made an
eternal Winter on the Tops of the Hills : Only
ſome ſcatter'd Paſture for the Cattle, was here and
there found among the Rocks. Towards the Middle of the Declivity of thoſe ſteep Mountains, the
Valleys are ſo deep, that the Sun can ſcarce let fall a
Beam upon them.

I found no other Men in theſe Places, but Shepherds, as ſavage as the Country itſelf. There I
paſs'd the Night in bewailing my Misfortunes, and
the Days in following my Flocks, to avoid the brutal
Rage

Rage of *Butis*, who was Chief among the Slaves, and who, hoping to obtain his Liberty, never ceas'd from calumniating the rest, that he might persuade *Metophis* of his Zeal and Industry in his Service. I could no longer support myself in such Circumstances. In the Anguish of my Heart, I one Day forgot my Flock, and lay down upon the Grass by a Cave, where I expected Death to relieve me from the Evils I was not able to bear. In that instant, I perceiv'd the whole Mountain to tremble, the Oaks and Pines seeming to descend from the Summit of the Hill. The Winds suppress'd their Breathing, and a hollow Voice issuing out of the Cave, pronounc'd these Words: O Son of the wise *Ulysses!* thou art, like him, to become great by Patience. Princes who have always been happy, are seldom worthy to be so: They are corrupted by unmanly Pleasures, and intoxicated with the Pride of Prosperity. Happy shalt thou be, if thou canst surmount and never forget these Misfortunes. Thou shalt see *Ithaca* again, and thy Glory shall ascend to the Skies. When thou shalt come to command other Men, remember that thou hast been, like them, in Poverty, Weakness, and Calamity. Take a Pleasure in relieving them; love thy People; detest Flatterers; and know, that there is no other way to be truly Great, but by Moderation, and Fortitude in subduing thy Passions.

These divine Words penetrated to the Bottom of my Heart, renew'd my Joy, and reviv'd my Courage. I felt none of that Horror, which makes Men's Hair stand upright, and chills the Blood in their Veins, when the Gods communicate themselves to Mortals. I rose from the Ground with a serene Mind; I fell upon my Knees, and, lifting up

my

my Hands to Heaven, ador'd *Minerva*, who, I
doubted not, had fent me this Oracle. In that Moment I found myfelf a new Man; Wifdom enlighten'd my Soul; I felt a gentle Force reftraining
all my Paffions, and checking the Impetuofity of
my Youth. I gain'd the Love of all the Shepherds
in the Defart. My Gentlenefs, Patience and Diligence affwag'd at laft the cruel *Butis*, who commanded the reft of the Slaves, and had made it his
Bufinefs at firft to torment me.

I endeavour'd to procure fome Books, to enable
me to fupport the Tedioufnefs of my Captivity and
Solitude; being opprefs'd with Melancholy for want
of fome Inftructions to nourifh and fuftain the Fa-
culties of my Soul. Happy, faid I, are they, who
being difgufted with all violent Pleafures, know
how to content themfelves with the Sweets of an
innocent Life. Happy are they, who are diverted
at the fame time that they are inftructed, and pleafe
themfelves in enriching their Minds with Knowledge.
Wherefoever they are thrown by adverfe Fortune,
they carry their own Entertainment with them;
and the Uneafinefs which preys upon other Men,
even in the Midft of their Pleafures, is unknown to
thofe, who can employ themfelves in Reading :
Happy are they, who love Books, and are not, like
me, deprived of them. Revolving thefe Thoughts
in my Mind, I penetrated into the thickeft of the
Foreft, and, on a fudden, perceived an aged Man,
holding a Book in his Hand : His Forehead was
large and high, bare of Hair, and a little wrinkled :
His white Beard defcended to his Girdle : His Stature was tall and majeftic : His Complexion was
frefh and fanguine : His Eyes lively and piercing :
His Voice fweet, and his Difcourfe plain, but agreeable.

able. I never faw fo venerable an old Man. His Name was *Termofiris*. He was a Prieſt of *Apollo*; and the Temple where he officiated was of Marble, dedicated in the Foreſt to that God, by the Kings of *Egypt:* The Book he held in his Hand was a Collection of Hymns in Honour of the Gods.

He accoſted me in a friendly manner, and ſo we fell into Diſcourſe. He related Things paſt with ſuch Clearneſs, that they ſeem'd preſent: and yet with ſuch Brevity, that I never was tired with them. He could foreſee Futurity, by his profound Wiſdom, which gave him thorough Knowledge of Men, and of the Deſigns they are capable of forming. With all this prudence, he was chearful and complaiſant; and the graveſt Youth was not ſo graceful as this aged Man. He lov'd thoſe that were young, if he found them docile, and that they had a Taſte for Virtue. He ſoon conceiv'd a tender Affection for me, and gave me Books for my Conſolation. He call'd me his Son; and I often ſaid to him, Father, the Gods that took *Mentor* from me, have pity'd my Solitude, and ſent me, in you, another Support. This Man, like *Orpheus* or *Linus*, was doubtleſs inſpired by the Gods. He would ſometimes read to me the Verſes he had made, and give me the moſt excellent Compoſitions of ſeveral Poets who had been Favourites of the Muſes. When he put on his long Robes of the pureſt White, and took his Ivory Harp in his Hand, the Tigers, the Bears, and the Lions came fawning to him, and lick'd his Feet. The Satyrs abandon'd the Woods, to come and dance around him. The Trees themſelves ſeem'd to move; and you would have thought that the Rocks had been touch'd with the Charms of his melodious Accents, and were going to deſcend from

the

the Tops of the Mountains. He fung nothing but the Majefty of the Gods, the Virtue of the Heroes, and the Wifdom of thofe who prefer Glory before Pleafure.

He often told me, that I ought to take Courage, and that the Gods would not abandon either *Ulyffes*, or his Son. Laftly, he perfuaded me to imitate *Apollo*, and to teach the Shepherds to apply themfelves to the Mufes. *Apollo*, faid he, confidering with Indignation, that the brighteft Days were fre-quently difturbed by *Jupiter*'s Thunder, refolv'd to be reveng'd upon the *Cyclops*, who forged the Bolts; fo he took up his Bow, and pierc'd them with his Arrows. Upon this Mount *Ætna* ceas'd to vomit flaming Hurricanes; and Men no longer heard the terrible Hammers ftriking upon the Anvils, and echoing in Groans from the deep Caverns of the Earth, and the Abyffes of the Sea. The Iron and Brafs, being no longer polifh'd by the *Cyclops*, began to gather Ruft. *Vulcan*, in Fury, quits his Forge, and, notwithftanding his Lamenefs, mounts *Olympus* with Expedition; comes cover'd with black Duft and Sweat into the Affembly of the Gods, and makes a moft bitter Complaint. *Jupiter*, incens'd againft *Apollo*, drives him from Heaven, and preci-pitates him down to the Earth. His empty Chariot performd the ufual Courfe of itfelf, and gave Men Night and Day, with a regular Change of Seafons. *Apollo*, depriv'd of his glorious Beams, was forced to turn Shepherd, and keep the Flocks of King *Admetus*. He plays on the Flute, and all the other Shepherds came down to the fhady Elms, on the cool Margin of a limpid Fountain, to hear his Songs. To that Time they had liv'd a favage and brutal Life: They knew only how to tend their Flocks,

to

to sheer them, milk them, and to render Cheeses.
The whole Country was one frightful Desart.

Apollo, in a short Time, made all the Shepherds
acquainted with the Arts which could render their
Lives agreeable. He sung the Flowers that com-
pose the Garland of the Spring; the Perfume she
diffuses, and the Verdure that attends her Steps.
He sung the delicious Nights of Summer, when the
Zephyrs refresh Mankind, and the Dews allay the
Thirst of the Earth. He mingled in his Song, the
golden Harvest and Autumnal Fruits, which recom-
pense the Toil of the Husbandman, with the Repose
of Winter, when the frolicksome Youth dance before the Fire. In the last place, he describ'd the
gloomy Forest, and shady Groves that cover the
Hills; the hollow Valleys, and the Rivers that with
a thousand Windings seem to sport in the lovely
Meadows. He thus taught the Shepherds what are
the Charms of a Country Life, when Men know
how to relish the Presents of pure and bountiful
Nature. The Shepherds with their Flutes soon
saw themselves more happy than Kings, and their
Cottages were filled with Variety of untainted Pleasures, which fly from gilded Palaces. The Smiles,
the Sports, the Graces, accompanied the innocent
Shepherdesses wheresoever they went. Every Day
was a Festival: nothing was heard, but the warbling
of Birds, or the soft Whispering of the Zephyrs
playing about the Branches of the Trees, or the
Murmur of some transparent Stream falling from a
Rock, or Songs that were inspir'd by the Muse,
and sung by the Shepherds that follow'd *Apollo*. This
God taught them also to be victorious in Races, and
to pierce the Bucks and Stags with their Arrows.
The Gods themselves became jealous of the Shepherds.

herds. This fort of Life appear'd to them more delightful than all their Glory; fo they call'd *Apollo*
back again to Heaven.

My Son, this Story may ferve for your Inftruction,
fince you are in the fame Condition *Apollo* was in.
Break up and manure this uncultivated Ground;
make a Defart flourifh as he did; like him, teach the
Shepherds what are the Charms of Harmony; foften
their fierce Natures; fhew them the Lovelinefs of
Virtue, and make them feel how fweet it is to enjoy,
in Solitude, thofe innocent Pleafures that nothing
can take away from Shepherds. A Time will come,
my Son, a Time will come, when the Toils and
tormenting Cares that encompafs Kings, will make
you, upon a Throne, envy the Paftoral Life.

Termofiris, having faid this, prefented me with a
Flute fo melodious, that the Echoes of the Hills,
which carry'd the Sound on every Side, drew all the
neighbouring Shepherds prefently about me. My
Voice was divinely harmonious; I felt myfelf mov'd,
as by a fuperior Power, to fing the Beauties that
Nature has beftowed upon the Country. We pafs'd
the Days, and Part of the Nights, in finging together. All the Shepherds forgetting their Cottages
and their Flocks, ftood attentive and fix'd in Admiration round me, whilft I gave them Leffons. The
favage Rudenefs of our Defarts feemed to difappear;
all things looked gay and fmiling; and the Polite-
nefs of the Inhabitants feem'd to foften the Rugged-
nefs of the Country.

We frequently met to facrifice in the Temple of
Apollo, where *Termofiris* officiated as Prieft. The
Shepherds went thither crown'd with Laurel, in
honour of the God; and the Shepherdeffes follow'd
after them, dancing along with Garlands of Flowers,
and

and carrying on their Heads Baſkets full of ſacred Gifts. After the Sacrifice we made a Country Feaſt ; and the moſt delicious of our Fare was the Milk of our Goats and Sheep, with various Fruits freſh gather'd with our own Hands, ſuch as Dates, Figs and Grapes. Our Seats were the green Turf ; and the ſpreading Trees afforded us a Shade more pleaſant than the gilded Roofs in the Palaces of Kings.

But that, which above all other things made me famous among our Shepherds, was, that one Day a hungry Lion ruſh'd in upon my Flock : Already he had began a dreadful Slaughter: I had nothing in my Hand but my Crook, yet I advanc'd boldly. The Lion erects his Mane, gnaſhes his Teeth, un-ſheaths his dreadful Claws, and opens his parch'd and inflam'd Throat. His Eyes ſeem'd full of Blood and Fire ; and he laſh'd his Sides with his long Tail. I threw him upon the Ground. The lit-tle Coat of Mail that I wore, according to the Cuſtom of the *Egyptian* Shepherds, hinder'd him from tearing my Body. Thrice I threw him up-on his Back, and thrice he raiſed himſelf again, roaring ſo loud that he made all the Foreſts ring.. At laſt I graſp'd him ſo cloſe that I ſtifled him. The Shepherds, who were Witneſſes of my Vic-tory, oblig'd me to wear the Skin of this terrible Animal.

The Fame of this Action, and the wonderful Alteration that had happen'd among our Shepherds, ſpread through all *Egypt*, and even came to the Ear of *Seſoſtris*. He was informed, that one of the two Captives, who had been taken for *Phenicians*, had reſtor'd the golden Age to his almoſt uninhabitable Deſarts. He reſolv'd to ſee me, for he lov'd the Muſes ;.

Mufes; and his great Soul was affected with what-
foever might be ufeful to Mankind. He faw me,
he heard me with Pleafure, and difcover'd that *Metophis* had deceiv'd him through Covetoufnefs. He
condemn'd him to perpetual Imprifonment, and
feiz'd all the Riches which he unjuftly poffefs'd.
O! faid he, how unhappy is the Man, who is
plac'd above the reft of Men ! He can feldom fee the
Truth with his own Eyes: He is furrounded by
thofe who keep the Truth from approaching him :
Their Intereft leads them to deceive him. Every
one conceals his Ambition under the Appearance of
Zeal. They pretend to love the King, but indeed
love only the Riches he can give: Nay they love him
fo little, that in order to obtain his Favours, they
flatter and betray him.

From this Time, *Sefoftris* treated me with a tender Friendfhip, and refolv'd to fend me back to *Ithaca*, with a powerful Affiftance of Ships and Troops
to deliver *Penelope* from the Perfecutions of her Lovers. The Fleet was ready, and we thought of nothing but embarking. I admir'd the ftrange Viciffi-
tudes of Fortune, which exalts thofe on a fudden
whom fhe has moft depreffed. This Experience
made me hope, that *Ulyffes* might return at laft to
his Kingdom, after his long Sufferings; and I thought
it not impoffible to fee *Mentor* again, tho' he had
been carried into the remoteft and moft unknown
Parts of *Ethiopia*. Whilft I delay'd my Departure
to enquire after him, *Sefoftris*, who was very aged,
died fuddenly, and his Death plunged me again into
new Misfortunes.

All *Egypt* was inconfolable for this Lofs. Every
Family thought they had loft their beft Friend,
their Protector, their Father. The old Men lifting

ing up their Hands to Heaven, cry'd out, *Egypt* never had fo good a King, and never will have one like
him. O! ye Gods, you fhould never have fhew'd
him to Men, or never have taken him away. Why
muft we furvive the great *Sefoftris?* The young
Men faid, the Hope of *Egypt* is no more! Our Fathers were happy in living under fo good a King:
But as for us, we only faw him to be fenfible of the
Lofs of him. His Domeftics wept Night and Day:
And when the King's Funeral was performed,
Multitudes of People from the remoteft Parts, came
running to *Thebes*, during forty Days. Every one
was defirous to fee once more the Body of *Sefoftris*,
to preferve the Idea of him; and many to be bury'd
with him.

But what ftill aggravated their Grief, was, that
his Son *Bocchoris* had neither Humanity for Strangers,
nor Regard for the Sciences, nor Efteem for virtuous
Men, nor Defire of Glory. The Greatnefs of his
Father had contributed to make him unworthy to
reign. He had been educated in an effeminate Softnefs and brutal Pride. He accounted Men as nothing, believing them made only to be his Slaves,
and himfelf to be of a Nature different from them.
He thought of nothing but how he might gratify his
Paffions, wafte the immenfe Treafures his Father
had hufbanded with fo much Care, plague the People, fuck the Blood of the Unfortunate, and follow
the flattering Counfels of young Fools, who furrounded him; whilft he turn'd out with Contempt
all the antient Sages, who had been intrufted by his
Father. In a Word, he was a Monfter, and not a
King. All *Egypt* groan'd under him; and though
the Name of *Sefoftris*, which was fo dear to the
Egyptians, made them bear with the bafe and cruel
Con-

Conduct of his Son, yet he made hafte to Ruin; for a Prince fo unworthy of a Throne could not enjoy it long.

As for me, I loft all Hopes of returning to *Ithaca*; I was confined to a Tower that ftands by the Sea, near *Pelufium,* where I fhould have embark'd, if *Sefoftris* had not dy'd. *Metophis* had the Cunning to get out of Prifon, and to be received into Favour by the new King. 'Twas he that caus'd my Confinement, to revenge the Difgrace I had brought upon him. I paffed the Days and Nights in the profoundeft Melancholy. All the Things which *Termofiris* had foretold, and all that I had heard from the Cave, appear'd to me now only like a Dream. I was overwhelm'd with the moft bitter Grief. I faw the Waves beating at the Foot of the Tower where I was Prifoner. I often employed my Time in obferving the Ships that were tofs'd by Storms, and in Danger of being fplit againft the Rocks upon which the Tower was built; and, inftead of pitying thofe who were threaten'd with Shipwreck, I envy'd their Condition. Their Misfortunes, faid I, to myfelf, will either foon be ended together with their Lives, or elfe they will happily arrive in their own Country; but alas! I can hope for neither.

Whilft thus I confum'd myfelf away in fruitlefs Lamentations; I perceiv'd, as it were, a Foreft of Mafts, the Sea was cover'd with Ships, and the Winds fwell'd all their Sails. The Waters foam'd beneath the Strokes of innumerable Oars. I heard a confus'd Noife on every Side. I faw one Part of the *Egyptians* upon the Shore, terrified and running to their Arms; whilft others feem'd going to receive the Fleet which they faw approaching. I foon perceiv'd, that Part of thefe foreign Ships were

of

of *Phenicia*, and the reft of the Ifland of *Cyprus:* For my Misfortunes began to render me experienc'd in Matters relating to Navigation. The *Egyptians* appear'd to me to be divided among themfelves; and I doubted not, that the unthinking King *Bocchoris*, had, by his Violences, caufed his Subjeĉts to revolt, who had rais'd a Civil War. I was Speĉtator of a bloody Battle from the Top of my Tower.

That Part of the *Egyptians*, who had invited thofe Foreigners to their Affiftance, having favoured their Defeent, fell upon the other *Egyptians*, who had the King at their Head. I faw this King animating his Men by his own Example. He appeared like the God of War. Streams of Blood flowed round about him. The Wheels of his Chariot were died with black, thick, foaming Gore, and could hardly pafs for the Heaps of Dead that lay in the Way.

This young King, comely, vigorous, of a fierce and haughty Mien, had Rage and Defpair in his Eyes. He was like a beautiful, but ungovernable Horfe. His Courage pufhed him on to Danger; but he had no Prudence to direĉt his Valour. He knew neither how to repair a Fault, nor to give neceffary Orders, nor to forefee the Mifchiefs that threaten'd him, nor to fpare his Men, tho' he ftood in the ut-moft need of them. Not that he wanted Genius, for his Knowledge was equal to his Courage; but he had never been inftruĉted by Adverfity. His Ma-fters had poifoned his fine natural Qualities with their Flattery. He was intoxicated with his own Power and Felicity. He thought every thing muft yield to his impetuous Defires, The leaft Refiftance inflamed his Rage; and then he confulted his Rea-fon no longer; he was, as it were, befide himfelf; his furious Pride transform'd him into a wild Beaft; his

innate

innate Good-nature and Equity forsook him in an instant; the most faithful of his Servants were forc'd to
fly from him, and he no longer liked any but those
who flattered his Passions. By this means he always
fell into Extremes against his true Interest, and forced
all honest Men to detest his foolish Conduct. His
Valour sustained him for a long Time against the
Multitude of his Enemies; but at last he was borne
down with Numbers. I saw him perish; the Dart
of a *Phenician* pierc'd his Breast: Not being able to
hold the Reins any longer, he fell from his Chariot,
and was trampled under foot by the Horses. A Sol-
dier of *Cyprus* cut off his Head; and holding it up by
the Hair, shewed it, as it were, in triumph to the
victorious Army.

I shall ever remember the Sight of that Head
smeared with Blood; the Eyes shut and extinguish'd;
the Face pale and disfigured; the Mouth half open,
and seeming desirous of concluding the unfinish'd Sen-
tence; a fierce and menacing Air, which Death itself could not efface. This Image will be always
before my Eyes to the last Day of my Life; and if
ever the Gods permit me to reign, I shall never forget, after this fatal Example, That no King is worthy to command, or can be happy in the Possession
of his Power, unless he himself be governed by Reason. Alas! 'tis the utmost of all Misfortunes, for a
Man, who is created for the public Good, to become
Master of vast Numbers of Men, and then only render them miserable.

The END of the SECOND BOOK.

THE
ADVENTURES
OF
TELEMACHUS.

BOOK III.

The ARGUMENT.

Telemachus *relates how he was set at Liberty by the* Succeſſor *of* Bocchoris, *with all the* Tyrian *Priſoners, and with them carried to* Tyre, *on board the Ship of* Narbal, *who commanded the* Tyrian *Fleet ; that* Narbal *gave him the Character of their King* Pygmalion, *whoſe cruel Avarice was to be dreaded; that afterwards he learn'd from* Narbal *all the Regulations obſerved in the Commerce of* Tyre ; *and that he was juſt going to embark on board a* Cyprian *Ship, in order to go by the Iſland of* Cyprus *to* Ithaca, *when* Pygmalion *diſcover'd him to be a Stranger ; and or-*
                                                                 der'd

*Book.*III.

der'd him to be *feiz'd*; *that he was then upon the point
of being deftroy'd*; *but that* Aftarbe, *that Tyrant's
Miftrefs*, *had faved him in order to put to death, in
his room, a young Man, whofe Difdain had provok'd
her Anger.*

ALYPSO heard with Aftonifhment thefe
wife Reflections; and what charm'd her
moft, was to fee how ingenuoufly the
young *Telemachus* related the Faults he
had committed thro' Precipitation, and
Difregard of the Counfels of the fage *Mentor.* She
was furpriz'd with the Greatnefs and Generofity of
his Mind; who accufed himfelf, and made fo good
Ufe of his own Overfights, as to become wife, provident and temperate.

Go on, faid fhe, my dear *Telemachus*; I long to
know how you got out of *Egypt*, and where you
found again the wife *Mentor*, whofe Lofs you re-
gretted with fo much Reafon.

Telemachus, refuming his Difcourfe, faid, The beft
of the *Egyptians* who were moft faithful to the King,
finding themfelves overpower'd, and the King dead,
were compell'd to fubmit to the reft, and another
King, call'd *Termutis*, was fet up. The *Phenicians*
and the Troops of *Cyprus* departed from *Egypt*, after
they had made an Alliance with the new King. All
the *Phenicians*, that were Prifoners, were fet at Liberty, and as I was accounted one of them, I was
releas'd from the Tower; I embark'd with the reft,
and my Hopes began to revive in the Bottom of my
Heart.

Already a favourable Gale fill'd our Sails; our
Oars cut the foaming Waves; the wide Sea was cover'd with our Ships; the Mariners fhouted for Joy;

the

the Shores of *Egypt* fled from us; the Hills and
Mountains gradually diminished; we began to see
nothing but the Heavens and the Waters, whilst the
rising Sun seem'd to dart his sparkling Flames out of
the Bosom of the Sea ; his Rays gilded the Tops of
the Mountains, which we could still just discover upon
the Horizon, and the whole Face of Heaven, painted with a deep Azure, gave us Hopes of a happy
Voyage.

Though I had been set at Liberty as one of the
Phenicians, yet none of them knew who I was.
Narbal, who commanded the Ship I was in, ask'd me
my Name and my Country.   Of what City, said he,
in *Phenicia*, are you? I am not a *Phenician*, said I,
but the *Egyptians* took me at Sea in a *Phenician* Ship.
I have been a long Time Prisoner in *Egypt* as a *Phe-*
nician; under that Name I have long suffer'd, and
under that Name I am deliver'd.   Of what Country
art thou then, said *Narbal?* I am, said I, *Telemachus*,
Son of *Ulysses*, King of *Ithaca*, in *Greece*.   My Fa--
ther made himself famous among the Kings who be-
sieged the City of *Troy*; but the Gods have not permitted him to return to his own Country.   I have
sought him in many Climates, but Fortune persecutes
me also.   You see an unfortunate Person, who desires
no other Happiness, than to return to his own Country, and to find his Father.

Narbal look'd upon me with Astonishment, and
thought he saw in my Face something *Fortunate*, the
Stamp of Heaven, and which is not common to the
rest of Men.   He was by Nature, sincere and generous.   He was mov'd with my Misfortunes, and
conversed with me, with a Dearness and Intimacy
inspired by the Gods for my Preservation in a mighty
Danger.

Tele-

Telemachus, faid he, I neither do nor can doubt the Truth of what you fay·: The lively Images of Good-nature and Virtue drawn upon your Face, will not give me leave to diftruft you. I even perceive, that the Gods, whom I have always ferv'd, love you, and will have me to love you, as if you were my Son. I will give you fafe and ufeful Advice, and for my Recompence defire nothing of you but to be fecret. Fear not, faid I, for I can, without Difficulty, keep any thing fecret that you fhall be pleas'd to intruft me with. Though I am young, yet I have grown up in the Habit of not difcovering my own Secret, and much more of not betraying, ander any Pretext, the Secret of another. How have you been able, faid he, to accuftom yourfelf to keep Secrets in fuch tender Years? I fhall be glad to know by what means you have acquired this admirable Quality, which is the Foundation of the wifeft Conduct, and without which all other Talents are ufelefs.

When *Ulyffes,* faid I, departed to go to the Siege of *Troy,* he took me upon his Knees, and embraced me, (for thus I have been told the Story) and after he had kifled me in the tendereft manner, he faid thefe Words to me, though I could not then underftand them : O my Son ! may the Gods never let me fee thee again; let rather the fatal Sciffars cut the Thread of thy early Days, while yet it is hardly form'd, as the Reaper cuts down with the Sickle the tender Flower that begins to blow ; let my Enemies dafh thee in Pieces, before the Eyes of thy Mother and me, if ever thou art to be corrupted, and abandon Virtue. Oh ! my Friends, continued he, I leave my Son with you, who is fo dear to me ; take care of his tender Years ; if you love me, banifh all pernicious Flatterers from about him ; inftruct him

E 3   how

how to overcome his Paffions ; and let him be like a
tender Plant, that Men often bend, in order to make
it grow upright.   Above all, forget not to render him
juft, beneficent, fincere, and faithful in keeping a
Secret.   Whoever is capable of a Lie, is unworthy
to be counted a Man ; and whoever knows not how
to be filent, is unworthy to govern.

I am exact in the Repetition of thefe Words ; becaufe Care was taken to repeat them often to me, and
they have made a deep Impreffion in my Heart. I
often repeat them to myfelf.   My Father's Friends
made it their Bufinefs to exercife me early in keeping
Secrets.   I was yet in my Infancy, when they trufted
me with all their Uneafineffes and Difturbances of
Mind, to fee my Mother expofed to the Perfecutions
of fo many bold Suitors, who offer'd to marry her.
Thus they began early to treat me as a Man of Reafon, and one that could be trufted.   They convers'd
with me privately concerning the moft important Affairs, and acquainted me with all the Meafures they
took to remove thofe Pretenders.

I was overjoy'd to be trufted in this manner, for
thereby I look'd upon myfelf as a grown Man. I
never abus'd the Confidence repos'd in me; I never
let fall one fingle Word, that might difcover the leaft
Secret. The Suitors often endeavour'd to make me
talk ; expecting that a Child, who had feen or heard
any Thing of Importance, would not have been able
to conceal it.   But I knew how to anfwer them without lying, and without informing them of any Thing
I ought not to mention.

Upon this *Narbal* faid to me, You fee, *Telemachus*, the Power of the *Phenicians :* They are formidable to all the neighbouring Nations, on account of
their mighty Fleets. The Trade they drive as far

as the Pillars of *Hercules*, procures them Riches fur-
paffing thofe of the moft flourifhing People. The
great *Sefoftris*, who could never have fubdued them
by Sea, did, with great Difficulty, conquer them by
Land, with thofe Armies that had fubjugated all the
Eaft. He impos'd a Tribute upon us, which has not
continued long. The *Phenicians* found themfelves
too rich and too potent, to wear the Yoke of Servitude with Patience. We recover'd our Liberty.
Sefoftris was prevented by Death from finifhing the
War againft us. 'Tis true, we had Reafon to fear
the Event, much more on account of his Wifdom,
than his Power. But, as foon as his Power, without,
his Wifdom, had pafs'd into the Hands of his Son,
we concluded we had nothing to fear. And, indeed,
the *Egyptians* have been fo far from returning in Arms
to make an entire Conqueft of our Country, that
they have been conftrain'd to call us to their Affiftance, to deliver them from the Fury of an impious
and outrageous King. We have been their Delive-
rers, and have added the Glory of this Action to the
Liberty and Riches of our Country.

But, whilft we deliver others, we ourfelves are
Slaves. O *Telemachus!* beware of falling into the
cruel Hands of *Pygmalion*, our King. He has already imbrued them in the Blood of *Sichæus*, his Si-
fter *Dido*'s Hufband. *Dido*, full of Horror and Revenge, is fled from *Tyre*, with many Ships. Moft
of thofe, who are Lovers of Liberty and Virtue, followed her. She has founded a magnificent City upon the Coaft of *Africk*, and call'd it *Carthage*. *Pygmalion*, tormented with an infatiable Thirft of
Wealth, renders himfelf every Day more wretched
and odious to all his Subjects. 'Tis a Crime at *Tyre*
to be rich. His Avarice fills him with Sufpicion, Di-

E 4 . ftruft,

ſtruſt, and Cruelty. He perſecutes the Wealthy,
and fears the Poor. 'Tis ſtill a greater Crime at
Tyre to be virtuous : for *Pygmalion* ſuppoſes that good
Men cannot bear with his Injuſtice and Baſeneſs.
As Virtue condemns him, ſo is he exaſperated and
incenſed at it. Every thing diſturbs him, affrights
him, and preys upon him. He trembles at his own
Shadow ; he ſleeps neither by Night nor by Day.
The Gods, to plague him, load him with Treaſures
he dares not enjoy. The Things he covets to make
him happy, are preciſely thoſe that make him miſerable. He regrets whatever he gives ; dreads to loſe,
and torments himſelf with Hopes of Gain. He is
ſeldom ſeen. He ſhuts himſelf up in the remoteſt
Parts of his Palace, ſad, lonely, and dejeċted. His
very Friends dare not approach him, for fear of be-
ng ſuſpeċted. A Guard, terrible to ſee, continually
ſtands round his Palace, with Swords drawn, and
erecċted Pikes. Thirty Chambers on a Floor, with
Doors of Iron, and ſix huge Bolts on each, make
up the dreadful Apartment where he hides himſelf.
No one ever knows in which of theſe Chambers he
lies. 'Tis ſaid, he never lies in any of them two
Nights together, for fear his Throat ſhould be cut.
He knows no ſweet Enjoyments, nor the ſweeter
Delights of Friendſhip. If any one ſpeaks to him of
Joy, he finds it will not come near him, nor ever
enter into his Heart. His hollow Eyes are full of
a fierce and ſavage Fire, and inceſſantly rolling on
every Side. He hearkens to the leaſt Noiſe, and feels
a dread Alarm ; becomes pale, meagre ; and black
Anxiety ſits piċtur'd upon his ever-wrinkled Face.
He ſighs, is ſilent, and fetches deep Groans from
the Bottom of his Heart. He is unable to conceal
the Remorſe that rends his Soul. He nauſeates the
moſt

moſt delicious Food. His Children, inſtead of being the Hopes of his Age, are the Objects of his Fear. He looks upon them as his moſt dangerous Enemies. He never thought himſelf ſecure one Moment of his Life. He preſerves himſelf only by ſhedding the Blood of every one he fears. Fooliſh Man! who ſees not that his Cruelty, which he ſo much relies upon, will be his Deſtruction! Some domeſtic Servant, as ſuſpicious as he, will ſoon deliver the World from this Monſter.

As for me, I fear the Gods, and will be faithful to the King they have ſet over me, let the Conſequence be what it will. I had rather die, than take away his Life, or even fail to defend him. For your Part, O *Telemachus!* let him not know that you are the Son of *Ulyſſes*; for he would make you a Priſoner, in expectation of a great Ranſom, when *Ulyſſes* returns to *Ithaca.*

When we arriv'd at *Tyre*, I follow'd *Narbal's* Counſel, and found every thing he had ſaid to be true. I could not comprehend how a Man could make himſelf ſo miſerable as *Pygmalion* appear'd to be. Surpriz'd with a thing ſo ſhocking, and ſo new to me, I ſaid thus to myſelf: This Man deſign'd to be happy, and perſuaded himſelf, that Riches and Arbitrary Power would make him ſo. He poſſeſſes all he can deſire, and yet is made miſerable even by his Power and his Riches. If he were a Shepherd, as I lately was, he would be as happy as I have been. He would enjoy the innocent Pleaſures of the Country; nay, enjoy them without Remorſe He would not fear either Dagger or Poiſon. He would love Men, and be belov'd by them. He would not indeed be Poſſeſſor of thoſe vaſt Treaſures, which are as inſignificant to him as Sand, ſince he dares not

touch

touch them ; but he would plenteoufly enjoy the
Fruits of the Earth, and fuffer no real Want. This
Man feems to do whatever pleafes him ; but the Cafe
is far otherwife, for he does all that his fierce Paffions
command. He is continually hurried away by Avarice, Fears, and Jealoufy. He feems to be Mafter
of all other Men, but is not Mafter of himfelf; for
he has as many Mafters and Tormentors, as he has
violent Defires.

Thus I reafoned concerning *Pygmalion*, without
feeling him ; for he was not to be feen. Men only
beheld with Awe thofe lofty Towers that were furrounded Night and Day with dreadful Guards, where
he fhut himfelf up, as it were in a Prifon, with his
beloved Treafures. I compar'd this invifible King
with *Sefoftris*, who was fo good, fo eafy of Accefs,
fo affable, fo curious to fee Foreigners, fo attentive
in giving Audience to all Men, and to find out the
Truth, which is always conceal'd from Kings. *Sefoftris*, faid I, fear'd nothing, and had nothing to fear.
He fhew'd himfelf to all his Subjects, as to his own
Children. This Man fears all, and has all to fear.
This wicked King is always expos'd to the Danger
of a violent Death, even within his inacceffible Palace,
and in the Midft of his Guards. On the contrary,
the good King *Sefoftris* was always feen in the Midft
of the greateft Numbers of his People; like a gentle
Father in his own Houfe, with all his Family about
him.

Pygmalion gave Orders to fend home the Forces of
Cyprus, that came to his Affiftance, by virtue of an
Alliance that was between the two Nations. *Narbal*
took this Occafion to fet me at Liberty. He caus'd
me to be mufter'd among the *Cyprian* Soldiers ; for
the King was jealous even in the minuteft Things.

The

The common Fault of too eafy and lazy Princes, is blindly to give themfelves up to the Conduct of crafty and corrupt Favourites : Whereas, on the contrary, it was this Man's Fault to diftruft the beft and moft virtuous. He knew not how to diftinguifh Men of Probity and Uprightnefs, who always act without Difguife ; fo he had never feen an honeft Man, for fuch will always avoid a corrupt King. Befides, he had found, in all thofe who had ferv'd him fince his Acceffion to the Crown, fo much Diffimulation and Perfidioufnefs, and other horrid Vices, difguis'd under the Appearances of Virtue, that he look'd upon all Men, without Exception, as living under a Mafk, and concluded there was no real Virtue in the World : Therefore he look'd upon all Men to be much alike; and, upon this Suppofition, when he found a Servant tricking and corrupt, he took not the Pains to look out for another, becaufe he reckon'd that he could not better his Choice. Nay, good Men appear'd to him worfe than the barefac'd Wicked, becaufe he thought them as bad, and more deceitful.

But to return to myfelf. I pafs'd in the Mufter for a *Cyprian,* and efcap'd the watchful Jealoufy of the King. *Narbal* trembled for fear I fhould be difcover'd, which would have coft his Life, and mine alfo. It is impoffible to conceive the impatience he was under to fee us embark'd ; but contrary Winds ftill detain'd us at *Tyre.*

I made ufe of this Time to inform myfelf of the Manners of the *Phœccians,* fo famous in all Parts of the known World. I admired the happy Situ tion of their City, which is built upon an Ifland in the midft of the Sea. The neighbouring Coaft is delightful for its Fertility, abounding in exquifite Fruit, and fo

cover'd

4

cover'd with Towns and Villages, that they seem to
be contiguous to one another. The Air is sweet
and temperate ; for the Mountains shelter that Coast
from the scorching Winds which come from the
South ; and the Country is every-where refreshed by
the North Wind that blows from the Sea. It lies at
the Foot of Mount *Libanus*, whose Summit pierces
through the Clouds, and advances to meet the Stars.
His Brow is cover'd with eternal Ice; and Rivers, full
of Snow, fall down like Torrents from the Rocks·
that surround his Head. Beneath is seen a vast Forest
of ancient Cedars, which appear as old as the Earth
on which they grow, and shoot their thick-spreading
Branches to the Clouds. At the Foot of this Forest
are rich Pastures, leaning on the Descent of the
Mountain. Here one may see the bellowing Bulls
wandering up and down, and the bleating Ewes with
their tender Lambs, skipping upon the Grass. A
thousand Streams of the clearest Water run down
these charming Fields. Below these Pastures is the
Foot of the Mountains, which appears like a Garden
on every Side. Here *Spring* and *Autumn* reign together, and join the Fruits of the one to the Flowers of
the other. Neither the pestilent Breath of the South-
Wind, that parches and burns up all, nor the cruel
Blast of the North, have ever dared to deface the
lively Colours that adorn this Garden.

Hard by this beautiful Coast, an Island rises in the
Sea, where the City of *Tyre* is built. This great
City seems to float upon the Waters, and to be
Queen of all the Sea. The Merchants resort thither
from all Parts of the World ; and its Inhabitants are
the most famous Merchants in the Universe. When
Men enter into this City, they cannot think it to be
a Place belonging to a particular People ; but rather

to.

to be a City common to all Nations, and the Center of all Trade. Two great Moles, advancing their Arms into the Sea, embrace a vaſt Port, where the Winds cannot enter. In this Harbour, one may ſee, as it were, a Foreſt of Maſts ; and the Ships are ſo numerous, that the Sea which carries them, can hardly be diſcover'd. All the Citizens apply them-ſelves to Commerce, and their vaſt Riches never ren-der them averſe to that Labour which is neceſſary to increaſe their Treaſure. In every Part of the City, one may ſee the fine Linen of *Egypt*, and the *Tyrian* Purple, twice dy'd, and of a marvellous Luſtre. This double Tincture is ſo lively, as not to be effaced by Time. 'Tis us'd upon the fineſt Cloth, ſet off with Embroidery of Gold and Silver. The *Pheni-cians* drive a Trade with all People, as far as the Straits of *Gades :* Nay, they have penetrated into the vaſt Ocean that encompaſſes the Earth. They have made long Voyages upon the *Red-Sea*, and viſited unknown Iſlands, from whence they bring Gold and all ſorts of Perfumes, with various Animals, no where elſe to be ſeen.

I could not ſatiate my Eyes with the Sight of this great City, where every Thing was in Motion. I did not ſee there, as in the Cities of *Greece*, idle and inquiſitive Perſons, going about to hear News in the public Places, and to gaze upon Strangers as they ar-rive in the Ports. The Men are employed in un-loading their Ships, ſending away, or ſelling their Goods, putting their Warehouſes in order, and keeping an exact Account of what is due to them from foreign Merchants. The Women are always buſy in ſpinning of Wool, or in forming various Patterns of Embroidery, or in folding up the richeſt Stuffs.

Whence

Whence comes it, said I to *Narbal*, that the *Phenicians* are Masters of the Trade in all Parts of the World, and enrich themselves thus at the Expence of all other Nations? You see, said he, the Situation of *Tyre*, how conveniently it lies for Trade: Our Country has the Honour of having invented Navigation; the *Tyrians* were the first (if we may believe what is told us by the most obscure Antiquity) who tam'd the boisterous Waves, long before the Times of *Typhis* and the *Argonauts*, so boasted of in *Greece*. They were the first who, in a feeble Ship, durst commit themselves to the Mercy of the Waves and Storms; who founded the Depths of the Sea; who observ'd the Stars at a Distance from the Land, according to the Knowledge they had learn'd from the *Egyptians* and *Babylonians*; and who, by these means, re-united so many People that the Sea seem'd to have separated for ever. The *Tyrians* are industrious, patient, laborious, cleanly, sober, and frugal; exact in their civil Government, and perfectly united among themselves. No Nation has ever been more constant, more sincere, more faithful, more honest, and more kind to all Strangers.

This, without seeking any other Cause, is what gives them the Empire of the Sea, and makes so advantageous a Trade to flourish in their Port. If they should fall into Divisions and Jealousies; if they should emasculate themselves with Pleasures and Idleness; if the principal Citizens should come to despise Labour and Frugality; if Arts should cease to be accounted honourable among them; if they should violate their Faith with Strangers, and in the least transgress the Rules of free Trade; if they neglect their Manufactures, and cease to give due Encouragement to Artificers, in order to enable them to make their

Goods

Goods perfect, each in its Kind, you would foon fee the Ruin of that Power you admire.

But pray, faid I, inftruct me how I may hereafter eftablish the like Commerce in *Ithaca.* Do, faid he, as you fee done here. Receive all Strangers kindly; let them find Safety in your Ports, with Conveniency, and entire Liberty. Suffer not yourfelf to be poffef-fed with Covetoufnefs or Pride. The true way to gain much, is never to defire to gain too much, and to know how and when to lofe; acquire the Love of all Strangers, and even fuffer fmall Wrongs from them; beware of exciting their Sufpicions by info-lent Behaviour; be conftant to the Rules of Trade, which fhould be plain and eafy; accuftom your Sub-jects to obferve them inviolably; punish Fraud with Severity, nay even Negligence or Pride in Mer-chants, who ruin Trade by ruining thofe who carry it on: Above all, never go about to reftrain Trade, or to turn its Courfe according to your own Fancy. The Prince fhould never intermeddle with it, for fear of difcouraging his People; who, as they have the Pains, ought to have all the Profit. He will find fufficient Advantages by the vaft Riches that will be brought into his Kingdom. Commerce is like cer-tain Springs, if you force them to alter their Courfe, you dry them up. 'Tis only Profit and Conveniency that attract Strangers to you. If you render their Trade lefs eafy and lefs beneficial, they will infen-fibly withdraw themfelves, and return no more; be-caufe other Nations, taking Advantage of your Im-prudence, will invite them thither, and accuftom them to live without you. I muft own, that for fome Time paft, the Glory of *Tyre* hath been much clouded. O! if you had feen it, my dear *Telema-chus,* before the Reign of *Pygmalion,* you would have

have been much more fu:prized. Now, you only
find here the difmal Remains of a Grandeur that
tends to its Ruin. O unhappy *Tyre!* into what
Hands art thou fallen! The Sea formerly brought
thee the Tribute of all the Nations in the World.
Pygmalion is afraid of all, both Strangers and Subjects. Inftead of opening his Ports, according to
our ancient Cuftom, with an entire Liberty to all
People, however remote, he requires conftantly to
be informed what Number of Ships arrive, and from
what Country, the Names of the Men on board,
the Trade they drive, the Nature and Price of their
Merchandize, and the Time they defign to ftay. He
does yet worfe; for he ufes all manner of Artifices to
infnare the Merchants, and to confifcate their Goods.
He harrafles the Merchants whom he thinks the
moft wealthy : He burdens Trade under various Pretences with new Impofts : He will be a Merchant
himfelf, while all Men are afraid to deal with him.
Thus our Commerce languifhes : Foreigners, by degrees, forget the Way to *Tyre*, which was once fo
well known to them ; and if *Pygmalion* will not alter
his Conduct, our Glory and our Power muft in a
fhort Time be transferr'd to fome other People who
are under a better Government.

I then demanded of *Narbal*, by what means the
Tyrians had render'd themfelves fo powerful at Sea ;
for I was not willing to be ignorant of any thing that
might contribute to the good Government of a Kingdom. We have, faid he, the Forefts of *Libanus*,
which furnifh us with Timber for the building of
Ships, and we preferve them with Care, for that
Ufe. We never fell the Trees, but for the public
Service ; and, as for the building of Ships, we are
provided with very able Shipwrights. How came
you,

you, faid I, to find thefe excellent Artifts? They
grew up, faid he, by degrees in the Country. When
thofe who excel in Arts are liberally rewarded, Men
will quickly be found, who fhall carry them to the
utmoft Perfection : For Men of the beft Talents and
Underftanding never fail to apply themfelves to thofe
Arts that are attended with the greateft Recompences.
In this City, we honour all fuch Perfons as excel in
any of thofe Arts and Sciences which are ufeful to
Navigation. We refpect a Man fkilled in Geome-
try; we highly efteem an able Aftronomer; and
bountifully reward a Pilot who furpaffes the reft of
his Profeffion. We defpife not a good Carpenter ;
on the contrary, he is well paid, and well us'd.
Even Men dextrous at the Oar, are fure of a Reward proportion'd to their Service : They are fed
with wholfome Provifions ; they are carefully attended when fick ; Care is taken of their Wives and
Children in their Abfence ; if they perifh by Shipwreck, their Families are recompenfed for their Lofs ;
and every Man is fent home to his Habitation, after
he has ferv'd a certain Time. By thefe means, the
Tyrians have as many Seamen as they will. Fathers
are glad to bring up their Children to fo good an Employment, and haften to teach them in their tender
Years to handle an Oar, manage the Tackle, and
fcorn a Storm. Thefe Rewards, and this good Order, lead Men to be ufeful to the Public, without
Compulfion. Authority never does well alone ; the
Submiffion of Inferiors is not enough ; their Hearts
muft be won, and they ought to find their own Account in ferving the State.

After this Difcourfe, *Narbal* conducted me to fee
all the Magazines, the Arfenals, and the feveral
Trades that ferve for the building and fitting out of
Ships.

Ships. I enquired into all Particulars, even the minuteſt Things, and wrote down all that I had learn'd, for fear of forgetting any uſeful Circumſtance.

In the mean time *Narbal,* who knew *Pygmalion,* as well as he lov'd me, was impatient for my Departure, fearing I might be diſcovered by the King's Spies, who went up and down the Town, Day and Night ; but the Winds would not permit us yet to embark. One Day, as we ſtood viewing the Port, and aſking Merchants divers Queſtions, an Officer of *Pygmalion* came up to us, and ſaid to *Narbal,* The King is juſt now inform'd, by a Captain of one of thoſe Ships which return'd with you from *Egypt,* that you have brought a certain Stranger, who paſſes for a *Cyprian.* 'Tis the King's Pleaſure to have him ſeiz'd, and examin'd, that he may know who he is: And for this you are to anſwer with your Head..

In that Moment, I was at ſome Diſtance from *Narbal,* in order to take a nearer View of the Proportions which the *Tyrians* had obſerv'd in building a Ship, that was then almoſt new, and accounted, by reaſon of the exact Proportion of all its Parts, the beſt Sailer that had ever been ſeen in the Harbour. I aſk'd the Builder, who he was that had drawn the Plan of that Ship ?

Narbal, ſurpriz'd and terrified with this Meſſage, anſwered, I will make it my Buſineſs to find out that *Cyprian* Stranger ; but, as ſoon as the Officer was out of Sight, he ran to me, and inform'd me of the Danger I was in. I too well foreſaw, ſaid he, what would happen, my dear *Telemachus,* we are both undone ; the King, who is Night and Day tormented with Diffidence, ſuſpects you not to be a *Cyprian.* He will have you ſeiz'd, and will take away my Life, if I do not put you into his Hands. What ſhall we do?

Q.

O Gods! give us Wifdom to efcape this Danger!
I muft, *Telemachus*, carry you to the King's Palace,
where you fhall affirm, that you are a *Cyprian* of the
City of *Amathus*, and Son to a Statuary of *Venus*. I
will declare, that I formerly knew your Father; and
perhaps the King may let you depart without any
further Examination. I fee no other Way to fave
your Life and mine.

I anfwer'd, O *Narbal!* fuffer a miferable Man to
perifh, fince Fate has decreed my Deftruction. I
know how to die, and am too much indebted to you,
to draw you into my Misfortune. I cannot perfuade
myfelf to tell a Lie; I am not a *Cyprian*, nor can I
affirm myfelf to be fuch. The Gods fee my Sincerity; to them it belongs to preferve my Life, if they
pleafe, by their Power, but I will not fave it by
Falfhood.

Narbal anfwer'd me, This Falfhood, O *Telemachus!* is in all refpects innocent; it cannot be difap-
prov'd by the Gods themfelves; it does no Injury to
any one; it faves the Lives of two innocent Perfons,
and deceives the King only to prevent him from committing a great Crime. You carry the Love of Virtue too far, and are too fcrupulous in your Fears of
offending Religion.

But, faid I, Falfhood is Falfhood ftill; and on
that account unworthy of a Man who fpeaks in the
Prefence of the Gods, and owns the higheft Reverence to Truth. He that offends the Truth, offends
the Gods, and wounds his own Mind, becaufe he
fpeaks againft his Confcience. Propofe no more, O
Narbal! that which is unworthy of us both. If
the Gods have any Pity for us, they know how to
deliver us; but if they fuffer us to perifh, we fhall
fall the Victims of Truth, and leave an Example to

in-

inftruct Men to prefer unblemifh'd Virtue before
long Life. My own is already too long, fince it is
thus unhappy. 'Tis for you alone, my dear *Narbal*,
that my Heart is melted; why fhould your Kindnefs
to an unfortunate Stranger, prove fo fatal to you?

We continued long in this kind of Conflict, till at
laft we faw a Man quite out of Breath, running towards us. He was another of the King's Officers,
and fent to *Narbal* by *Aftarbe*. This Woman was
beautiful as a Goddefs : To the Charms of her Body
were added thofe of a refined Wit; fhe was gay, infinuating, flattering; but under the Appearance of
Gentlenefs, fhe, *Syren*-like, had a Heart fill'd with
Malice and Cruelty. Yet fhe knew how to conceal
her corrupt Defigns with the profoundeft Art. She
had conquer'd the Heart of *Pygmalion*, by her Wit
and Beauty, and by the Charms of her fweet Voice,
and the Harmony of her Lute : And *Pygmalion*,
blinded by the Violence of his Paffion, had abandon'd
Topha, his lawful Confort. He fought of nothing,
but how to gratify the Defires of the ambitious *Aftarbe*. His Love for this Woman was little lefs pernicious to him, than his infamous Covetoufnefs.
But tho' he had fo great a Paffion for her, fhe defpis'd
and loath'd him in her Heart; yet underftood fo well
how to cover her true Sentiments, that fhe feem'd to
defire to live only for him, at the fame time that fhe
could not endure him. There was at *Tyre*, a *Lydian*
Youth, call'd *Malachon*, of admirable Beauty, but
voluptuous, effeminate, and immerfed in Pleafures.
His only Study was to preferve the Delicacy of his
Complexion; to comb his flaxen Hair that flowed
down in waving Curls upon his Shoulders; to perfume himfelf; to make his Robes fit in eafy Folds
with a graceful Air; and to fing amorous Songs to

his

his Lute. *Aftarbe* faw him, fell in Love with him, and became furioufly tranfported with her Paffion. He flighted her, becaufe he was in love with another Woman: And befides, he dreaded to expofe him-felf to the cruel Jealoufy of the King. *Aftarbe*, find-ing fhe was fcorn'd, abandon'd herfelf to Refent-ment. In her Defpair, fhe imagin'd it .poffible to make *Malachon* pafs for the Stranger whom the King had fent for, and who was faid to have come with *Narbal*. Accordingly fhe foon perfuaded *Pygmalion*, as fhe defir'd, and corrupted all thofe who were able to undeceive him. For having no Affection for vir-tuous Men, whom he neither knew, nor valued, he was always furrounded by fuch only: as were merce-nary, crafty, and ready to execute his unjuft and bloody Orders. Thefe Men fear'd the Authority of *Aftarbe*, and help'd her to deceive the King, that they might not offend this haughty Woman, who en-tirely poffefs'd his Confidence. Thus the young *Malachon*, though known by all the City to be of *Crete*, pafs'd for the young Stranger that *Narbal* had brought from *Egypt*. He was feiz'd, and fent away to Prifon.

Aftarbe, who fear'd *Narbal* might go to the King, and difcover her Impofture, had diligently difpatch'd this Officer to him with the following Meffage: *Af-tarbe* forbids you to difcover your Stranger to the King; fhe requires nothing of you but Silence, and will fo manage the Affair, that the King fhall be fa-tisfied with your Conduct. In the mean time, take care that the young Stranger, who came with you from *Egypt*, may embark among the *Cyprians* with all Expedition, and be no more feen in the City. *Narbal*, overjoy'd to fave his own Life and mine, promis'd to be filent; and the Officer, pleas'd with

having

I

having obtain'd what he demanded, immediately return'd to *Aftarbe*, with an Account of his Commiffion.

Narbal and I admir'd the Goodnefs of the Gods,
who had rewarded our Sincerity, and taken fuch tender Care of thofe who had hazarded all for the Sake
of Virtue. We reflected with Horror upon a King
given up to Voluptuoufnefs and Avarice. He deferves to be deceiv'd, faid we, who dreads it fo excef-
fively : And he is fo, moft frequently and grofsly;
for he truffs not Men of Honefty, but abandons himfelf to Villains. He is the only Perfon who knows
nothing of what is doing. See how *Pygmalion* is
made the Sport of a fhamelefs Woman, whilft the
Gods make ufe of the Falfhood of the Wicked to
fave the Good, who chufe to part with Life, rather
than tell a Lie. As we were making thefe Reflections, we perceiv'd the Wind to turn, and become
favourable to the *Cyprian* Fleet. The Gods declare
themfelves, faid *Narbal*; they refolve, my dear *Telemachus*, to provide for your Security : Fly from this
cruel and accurfed Land. Happy he who could follow you to the remoteft Parts of the Earth ! Happy
he, who might live and die with you ! But my hard
Fate ties me to my unhappy Country. I muft fuffer
with her, and perhaps be buried in her Ruins. No
matter, provided I may always fpeak the Truth, and
my Heart love nothing but Juftice. As for you, O
my dear *Telemachus* ! I pray the Gods, who lead you
as it were by the Hand, to grant you the moft precious of all their Gifts, a pure and unblemifh'd Virtue to the laft Moment of your Life. Live, return
to *Ithaca*, comfort *Penelope*; deliver her from the
Perfecutions of her rafh Lovers. May your Eyes
fee, and your Arms embrace the wife *Ulyffes*; and
may

may he find in you, a Son equal to him in Wifdom. But, in the midft of your Felicity, remember the unhappy *Narbal*, and continue always to love me.

When he had finifh'd thefe Words, my Tears ran down fo faft, that I was not able to anfwer him. My Sighs, which I drew from the Bottom of my Heart, would not fuffer me to fpeak. We embrac'd in filence: He brought me to the Ship. He ftaid upon the Shore; and when the Veffel put off, we continu'd looking towards each other, till we loft Sight of one another.

The END *of the* THIRD BOOK.

T H E

THE

ADVENTURES

OF

TELEMACHUS.

BOOK IV.

The ARGUMENT.

Calypſo *interrupts* Telemachus's *Narrative, that he may repoſe himſelf.* Mentor *blames him, when alone, for having undertaken the Recital of his Adventures; but, however, ſince he has begun, he adviſes him to go through.* Then Telemachus *relates, that in his Voyage from* Tyre *to the Iſland of* Cyprus, *he had a Dream wherein he ſaw* Venus *and* Cupid, *againſt whom he was protected by* Minerva; *that afterwards he thought he ſaw* Mentor *likewiſe, who exhorted him to fly from the Iſle of* Cyprus; *that when he awoke, they fell into a Storm, in which they muſt*

have

*Book.*IV.

have perish'd, had he not himself seized the Rudder, the Cyprians *being overcome with Wine, and unable to steer the Ship; that upon his Arrival in the Island, he saw with Horror the Voluptuousness and Effeminacy of the Inhabitants; but that* Hazael, *the* Syrian, *to whom* Mentor *was sold as a Slave, happening to be then in* Cyprus, *taking a Liking to* Telemachus, *brought together the two* Greeks, *and put them on board his Ship, to carry them to* Crete; *and that, in their Passage, they saw the glorious Shew of* Amphytrite, *drawn in her Chariot by Sea-Horses.*

A L Y P S O, who all this while had continued motionlefs and tranfported with Pleafure, liftening to the Adventures of *Telemachus,* interrupted him here, that fhe might perfuade him to take fome Reft. It is Time, faid fhe, after fo many Toils, that you fhould tafte the Sweetnefs of Sleep. In this Place, you have nothing to fear: All here is favourable to you: Abandon your Heart then to Joy; relifh that Peace, and all thofe other Bleffings which Heaven is going to fhower down upon you. To-morrow, when *Aurora* has open'd the golden Gates of the Eaft with her rofy Fingers, and the Horfes of the Sun, fpringing from the briny Main, fpread the Flames of Light, and drive away the Stars before them, we will, my dear *Telemachus,* refume the Hiftory of your Misfortunes. No, your Father never equall'd you in Wifdom and Courage. Neither *Achilles,* who conquer'd *Hector;* nor *Thefeus,* who return'd from Hell; nor even the great *Alcides* himfelf, who purg'd the Earth from fo many Monfters, ever fhew'd fo much Conftancy and Virtue

F   as

as you.   May the fofteft and profoundeft Sleep make
the Night feem fhort to you.   But, alas ! how tedious will it be to me ! How I fhall long to fee you
again ! to hear your Voice ! to make you repeat
what I know already, and afk you what I know not
yet ! Go, my dear *Telemachus*, with the wife *Mentor*, whom the Favour of the Gods has reftor'd to
you ; go into that retired Grotto, where every thing
is prepar'd for your Repofe.   May *Morpheus* fhed
the fweeteft of his Charms upon your clofing Eye-
lids ; may he infufe a divine Vapour through all
your wearied Limbs, and fend you eafy Dreams,
which, hovering about you, may foothe your Senfes
with the moft pleafing Images, and drive far away
whatever might difturb your Reft, or awaken you too
foon.

The Goddefs herfelf brought *Telemachus* to the
Grotto, which was feparated from her own, but not
lefs agreeable, nor lefs rural.   A Fountain of liquid
Cryftal ran down in one Corner, and fweetly murmuring, feem'd contriv'd to invite Sleep.   The
Nymphs had prepar'd there two Beds, compofed of
the fofteft Green, upon which they had fpread two
large Skins, the one of a Lion for *Telemachus*, and
the other of a Bear for *Mentor*.

Before they fuffer'd Slumber to clofe their Eyes,
Mentor fpoke to *Telemachus :* The Pleafure of relating your Adventures, has carry'd you too far ; you
have charm'd the Goddefs with the Hiftory of thofe
Dangers, from which your Courage and Induftry
have deliver'd you.   By this means, you have only
inflam'd her Heart the more, and are preparing for
yourfelf a more dangerous Captivity.   How can you
hope fhe fhould now fuffer you to depart from her
Ifland ; you, who have enchanted her with the Re-

lation

lation of your Story? The Love of empty Glory has caufed you to fpeak without Prudence. She had promifed to acquaint you with the Fate of *Ulyffes*; fhe has found the Way to fpeak much without telling you any thing, and has engaged you to acquaint her with every Thing that fhe defires to know. Such is the-Art of flattering and wanton Women! When will you be fo wife, O *Telemachus!* as never to fpeak out of Vanity? And when will you know how to conceal thofe Things which may raife your Reputation, when it is of no Ufe to mention them. Others admire your Wifdom at fuch Years as may want it without Blame; but for me, I can forgive you nothing: I alone know and love you enough to tell you of all your Faults. How far yet do you come fhort of your Father's Wifdom!

But, faid *Telemachus*, could I refufe to relate my Misfortunes to *Calypfo?* No, reply'd *Mentor*, 'twas abfolutely neceflary; but you ought fo to have related them, as might only have excited her Compaffion. You might have told her, that you had been fometimes wandering in Defarts, then a Prifoner in *Sicily*, and afterwards in *Egypt*. This had been enough, and all the reft has only ferv'd to inflame the Poifon, that has already fcorch'd her Heart. May the Gods grant that your's may be untouch'd!

But what fhall I do now? faid *Telemachus*, in a modeft and fubmiffive manner. It is now in vain, reply'd *Mentor*, to conceal from her the reft of your Adventures; fhe knows enough to fecure her from being deceiv'd in that which is to come; any Referve on your Part would only ferve to provoke her. Finifh therefore, your Relation to-morrow; tell her all that the Gods have done for you, and learn for the future to fpeak with more Referve of all Things that

F 2 may

may tend to your own Praife. *Telemachus* kindly received this good Advice; and both lay down to fleep.

As foon as *Phœbus* had fpread the firft Rays of his Glory upon the Earth, *Mentor*, hearing the Voice of the Goddefs, who call'd to her Nymphs in the Wood, awaken'd *Telemachus*. It is time, faid he, to him, to fhake off Sleep. Come, let us return to *Calypfo*; but beware of her bewitching Tongue; never open your Heart to her, dread the infinuating Poifon of her Praifes. Yefterday fhe exalted you above your wife Father, above the invincible *Achilles*, the renowned *Thefeus*, or even *Hercules* himfelf, who has obtain'd Immortality by his glorious Actions. Could you not perceive the Excefs of thefe Commendations! Or did you believe what fhe' faid? Know, that fhe believes it not herfelf; fhe only commends you becaufe fhe thinks you weak and vain enough to be deceiv'd with Praifes far exceeding the Merit of your Actions.

After this Difcourfe, they went to the Place where the Goddefs expected them. She fmil'd when fhe faw them approaching, and, under an Appearance of Joy, conceal'd the Fears and Sufpicions that difturb'd her Heart; for fhe forefaw, that *Telemachus*, under the Conduct of *Mentor*, would efcape her Hands, as *Ulyffes* had done. Go on, faid fhe, my dear *Telemachus*, and fatisfy my Curiofity. I thought all the Night, I faw you departing from *Phenicia*, and going to feek a new Deftiny in the Ifland of *Cyprus*. Tell me then the Succefs of this Voyage, and let us not lofe one Moment! They immediately fat down in a fhady Grove, upon the green Turf, enamell'd with Violets.

Calypfo could not refrain from looking inceffantly upon *Telemachus* with Tendernefs and Paffion; nor fee, without Indignation, that *Mentor* obferv'd even the leaft Motion of her Eyes. In the mean time, all the Nymphs in filence ftoop'd forward to liften, forming a half Circle, that they might both hear and fee with more Advantage. The Eyes of the whole Affembly were immovably fix'd upon the young Man. *Telemachus*, looking down, and gracefully blufhing, thus refum'd the Thread of his Difcourfe.

Scarce had the fofteft Breath of a favourable Wind fill'd our Sails, when the Coaft of *Phenicia* entirely vanifh'd from our Eyes: And, becaufe I was with the *Cyprians*, whofe Manners I knew not, I refolv'd to be filent, and to obferve every Thing that pafs'd, keeping myfelf within the ftricteft Rules of Difcretion, that I might acquire their Efteem. But during my Silence, a foft and powerful Slumber feiz'd upon me; my Senfes were bound and fufpended; I found a fweet Serenity and home-felt Joy overflow my Heart. On a fudden, methought, I faw *Venus* cleaving the Clouds in her flying Chariot, drawn by a Pair of Doves. She had the fame fhining Beauty, the fame lively Youth, and thofe blooming Graces that appear'd in her when fhe fprung from the Foam of the Ocean, and dazzled the Eyes of *Jupiter* himfelf. She defcended all at once with extream Rapidity juft by me, laid her Hand upon my Shoulder, call'd me by my Name, and, fmiling, pronounc'd thefe Words: Young *Greek*, thou art going into my peculiar Empire; thou fhalt foon arrive in that fortunate Ifland, where Pleafures, Sports, and wanton Joys attend my Steps: There thou fhalt burn Perfumes upon my Altars: There I will plunge thee into a River of Delights: Open thy Heart to the moft charming Hopes, and beware of refifting the moft powerful of all the Goddeffes, who refolves to make thee happy.

F 3   At

At the fame time, I faw young *Cupid* gently moving his little Wings, and hovering about his Mother. He had the tendereft Graces in his Face, and the Pleafantnefs of an Infant; yet there was fomething fo piercing in his Eyes, as to make me afraid. He fmil'd when he look'd upon me; but his Smiles were malicious, fcornful, and cruel. He took the fharpeft of his Arrows from his golden Quiver; he drew his Bow, and was going to pierce my Heart, when *Minerva* fuddenly appear'd, and cover'd me with her impenetrable Shield. The Face of this Goddefs had not the fame effeminate Beauty, nor that paffionate Languifhing which I had obferved in the Face and Pofture of *Venus*. On the contrary, her Beauty was natural, unaffected, modeft; all was grave, vigorous, noble, full of Force and Majefty. The Arrow, too weak to pierce the Shield, fell down upon the Ground. *Cupid*, in a Rage, figh'd bitterly, and was afham'd to fee himfelf defeated. Be gone, cry'd *Minerva*, rafh Boy, be gone; thou canft conquer none but the Bafe, who prefer difhonourable Pleafures before Wifdom, Virtue and Glory. At thefe Words, *Cupid*, incenfed, flew away; and as *Venus* re-afcended towards *Olympus*, I faw her Chariot and two Doves, a long time rolling in a Cloud of Gold and Azure; at length fhe difappear'd. When I turn'd my Eyes toward the Earth, I could no where fee *Minerva*.

Methought I was tranfported into a delicious Garden, fuch as Men paint the *Elyfian* Fields. There I found *Mentor*, who faid to me, Fly from this cruel Country, this peftilent Ifland, where the Inhabitants breathe nothing but Pleafure. The boldeft Virtue ought to tremble here, and cannot be fafe, but by Flight. As foon as I faw him, I endeavoured to throw

throw my Arms about his Neck, and to embrace
him ; but I found my Feet unable to move, my
Knees funk under me ; and my Hands, attempting to
lay hold on *Mentor*, follow'd an empty Shadow that
ftill mock'd my Grafp. As I was making this Ef-
fort, I awak'd, and perceiv'd, that this myfterious
Dream was no lefs than a, divine Admonition. I
found in myfelf a firm Refolution againft the Allurements of Pleafure, a watchful Jealoufy of my own
Conduct, and a juft Abhorrence of the diffolute
Manners that reign'd in *Cyprus*. But that which
wounded me to the Heart was, that I thought *Mentor* was dead, that he had pafs'd the *Stygian* Lake,
and was become an Inhabitant of thofe happy Man-
fions, where the Souls of the Juft refide.

This Thought made me fhed a Flood of Tears.
The *Cyprians* afk'd me, why I wept ? Thefe Tears,
faid I, are but too fuitable to the Condition of an unhappy Stranger, who wanders, defpairing of ever feeing his Country more. In the mean time, all the
Cyprians that were in the Ship, abandon'd themfelves
to the moft extravagant Pleafures ; the Rowers, who
hated to take Pains, fell afleep upon their Oars.
The Pilot put a Garland of Flowers on his Head,
quitted the Rudder, and held a vaft Flaggon of Wine
in his Hands, which he had almoft emptied. He,
and all the reft of the Crew, inflamed with the Fury
of *Bacchus*, fung fuch Verfes in Honour of *Venus*
and *Cupid*, as ought to ftrike Horror into all that love
Virtue.

Whilft they thus forgot the Dangers of the Sea, a
fudden Tempeft arofe ; the Sky and the Sea were
agitated ; the Winds, unchained, roar'd furioufly in
every Sail; the black Waves beat vehemently againft
the Sides of the Ship, which groan'd under the

F. 4. Weight

Weight of their Strokes. One while, we mounted
upon the Back of the fwelling Billows; another
while the Sea feem'd to flip from under the Veffel,
and to precipitate us into the dark Abyfs. We faw
the Rocks clofe by us, and the angry Waves dafhing
againft them with a dreadful Noife. Then I found,
by Experience, the Truth of what I had often heard
from *Mentor*, that Men of diffolute Lives, and abandon'd to Pleafures, always want Courage in the
Time of Danger. All our *Cyprians* funk into Defpair, and wept like Women. I heard nothing but
piteous Exclamations; bitter Lamentations for the
Lofs of the Delights of Life; vain and infignificant
Promifes of large Sacrifices to the Gods, if they
fhould arrive fafe in the Harbour. No one had fufficient Prefence of Mind, either to give neceffary Orders, or to work the Ship. In this Condition, I
thought myfelf obliged to fave my own Life, and the
Lives of thofe that were with me. I took the Rudder into my Hand, becaufe the Pilot, diforder'd with
Wine like a raving *Bacchanal*, was utterly incapable
of knowing the Danger the Ship was in. I chear'd
the aftonifh'd Mariners; I made them take down the
Sails; they ply'd their Oars vigoroufly; we fteer'd
by the Rocks and Quick-fands, and faw all the Horrors of Death ftaring us in the Face.

This Adventure feem'd like a Dream to all thofe
who ow'd the Prefervation of their Lives to my Care:
They look'd upon me with Aftonifhment. We
landed at *Cyprus* in that Month of the Spring which
is confecrated to *Venus*. This Seafon, fay the *Cyprians*, is moft fuitable to this Goddefs, becaufe it
feems to revive the whole Syftem of Nature, and
to give birth to Pleafures and Flowers at the fame
time.

As

As foon as I arriv'd in the Ifland, I perceiv'd an unufual Mildnefs in the Air, rendering the Body floth-
ful and unactive, but infufing a jovial and wanton
Humour. I obferv'd the Country, though naturally
fruitful and delightful, to be almoft every where uncultivated, through the ftrong Averfion of the Inhabitants to Labour. I faw great Numbers of Maids
and Women, vainly and fantaftically drefs'd, finging
the Praifes of *Venus*, and going to devote themfelves
to the Service of her Temple. Beauty, Graces,
Joy and Pleafure, were equally confpicuous in their
Countenances; but their Graces were too much affected; there was not that noble Simplicity, nor that
lovely Modefty, which makes the greateft Charm of
Beauty. A certain Air of Wantonnefs, an artful
Way of adjufting their Looks, their vain Drefs, their
languifhing Gait, their Eyes that feem'd to be in
queft of the Eyes of Men, their mutual Jealoufy
who fhould raife the greateft Paffions; in a word,
all that I faw in thefe Women appear'd vile and con-
temptible to me. By endeavouring to pleafe me im-
moderately, they excited my Averfion.

I was conducted to a Temple of the Goddefs, who
has feveral in this Ifland; for fhe is particularly ador'd
at *Cythera*, *Idalia*, and *Paphos*; it 'was to that of
Cythera I was brought. The Temple is all built
with Marble; it is a perfect *Periftyllium*; the Pillars
are fo lofty, and fo large, that they give a majeftic
Air to the whole Fabric. At each Front of the
Temple, above the Architrave and Frize, are large
Pediments, in which the moft agreeable Adventures
of the Goddefs are curioufly reprefented in *Baffo Re-
lievo*. Great Numbers of People are always at the
Gate, attending to make their Offerings. No Vic-
tim is ever flain within the Precinct of the facred.

Ground. The Fat of Bulls and Heifers is not burnt here, as in other Places. No Blood is ever fhed here. The Victims to be offer'd, are only prefented before the Altar; and no Beaft may be offer'd, unlefs it be young, white, without Blemifh or Defect. They are adorn'd with purple Fillets, embroider'd with Gold ; their Horns are gilded, and garnifh'd with Nofegays of the moft fragant Flowers; and when they have been prefented at the Altar, they are led to a private Place without the Wall, and kill'd for the Banquet of the Priefts that belong to the Goddefs.

Here alfo are offer'd all forts of perfum'd Liquors, and Wines, more delicious than Nectar. The Priefts are cloath'd in long white Robes, with Girdles of Gold, and Fringes of the fame round the Bottom of the Garment. The moft exquifite Perfumes of the Eaft are burnt Night and Day upon the Altars, and form a curling Cloud as they mount up to the Sky. All the Pillars are adorn'd with Feftoons of wreathed Flowers ; all the Veffels for the Service of the Altar are of pure Gold; a facred Grove of Myrtle encompaffes the Building ; none but Boys and Girls of fingular Beauty may prefent the Victims to the Priefts, or kindle the Fire upon the Altars. But Diffolutenefs and Impudence difhonour this magnificent Temple.

At firft I was ftruck with Horror at what I faw, but it infenfibly began to grow familiar to me. I was no longer afraid of Vice ; all Companies infpir'd me with I know not what Inclination to Intemperance. They laugh'd at my Innocence ; and my Referved-nefs and Modefty became the Sport of this impudent People. They forgot nothing that might enfnare me, excite my Paffions, and awaken in me an Appetite to
Plea-

Pleafure. I found myfelf lofing Strength every Day. The good Education I had receiv'd, could fcarce fupport me any longer; all my virtuous Refolutions vanifh'd away; I had no longer any Power to refift the Temptations that prefs'd me on every Side; I grew even afham'd of Virtue. I was like a Man fwimming in a deep and rapid River: At firft, he cuts the Waters, and rifes vigoroufly againft the Stream; but if the Banks are fo fteep that he can find no Place to reft on either Side, he, at laft, tires by Degrees; his Force abandons him; his exhaufted Limbs grow ftiff, and the Torrent carries him down. So my Eyes began to grow dim, my Heart fainted, I could no longer recal either my Reafon, or the Remembrance of my Father's Virtues. The Dream that fhew'd me the wife *Mentor* in the *Elyfian* Fields utterly difcourag'd me. A foft and fecret Languifhing feiz'd upon me; I already began to love the flattering Poifon that had crept into my Veins, and penetrated through the Marrow of my Bones. Yet, for all this, fometimes I would figh deeply; I fhed bitter Tears; I roar'd like a Lion in his Fury. O! unhappy State of Youth! faid I. O Gods! that divert yourfelves fo cruelly with the Fate of Men! Why do you caufe them to pafs through that Age, which is a Time of Folly, or rather a burning Fever? O! Why am not I cover'd with grey Hairs, bowed down and finking into the Grave, like my Grandfather *Laertes?* Death would be more welcome to me, than the fhamelefs Weaknefs I now feel.

Scarce had I had utter'd thefe Words when my Grief began to abate, and my Heart, intoxicated with a foolifh Paffion, fhook off almoft all Shame. After this, I found myfelf plung'd into an Abyfs of Remorfe. Whilft I was under thefe Diforders, I ran

ftraying

ſtraying up and down the ſacred Wood, like a Hind that has been wounded by the Huntſman ; ſhe croſſes vaſt Foreſts to aſſwage her Pain, but the fatal Arrow ſticks faſt in her Side, and follows her whereſoever ſhe flies. Wherever ſhe goes, ſhe carries the murderous Shaft. Thus I endeavour'd to run away from myſelf, but nothing could allay the Affliction of my Heart.

In that very Moment, I perceived, at ſome Diſtance from me, in the thick Shade of the Wood, the Figure of the wiſe *Mentor* ; but his Face appear'd to me ſo pale, ſo ſad, and ſo ſevere, that I felt no Joy at the Sight of him. Is it you then, O my dear Friend ? My only Hope, is it you ? Is it you yourſelf ? Or, is it a deceitful Image come to abuſe my Eyes ? Is it you, O *Mentor ?* Or, is it your Ghoſt, ſtill ſenſible of my Misfortunes ? Are you not among the bleſſed Spirits that poſſeſs the Reward of their Virtue, and, by the Bounty of the Gods, enjoy an eternal Peace, and uninterrupted Pleaſures in the *Elyſian* Plains ? Speak, *Mentor*, do you yet live ? Am I ſo happy as to poſſeſs you ? Or is it only the Shadow of my Friend ? With theſe Words, I ran to him, ſo tranſported, that I was quite out of Breath. He ſtood ſtill unmov'd, and made not one ſtep towards me. O Gods ! you know with what Joy I felt him in my Arms. No, 'tis not an empty Shadow, I hold him faſt ; I embrace him ; my dear *Mentor !* Thus I cry'd out ; I ſhed a Flood of Tears upon his Face ; I hung about his Neck, and was not able to ſpeak. He look'd ſadly upon me, with Eyes full of tender Compaſſion.

At laſt I ſaid to him. Alas ! where have you been ? To what Dangers have you expoſed me, by your Abſence ? And what ſhall I now do without you ?

you? But he, without anfwering my Queftions, with
a terrible Voice, cry'd out, Fly, fly, without Delay :
This Soil produces nothing but Poifon : The Air you
breathe is infected with the Plague : The Men are
contagious, and converfe with each other only to
fpread the fatal Venom : Bafe and infamous Voluptuoufnefs, the worft of all thofe Evils that iffued out
of *Pandora's* Box, enervates their Souls, and fuffers
no Virtue in this place. Fly, ftay not a Moment ;
look not once behind you; and, as you run, fhake off
the very Remembrance of this execrable Ifland.

He fpoke, and immediately I felt as it were a thick
Cloud difperfing from about my Eyes, and perceiv'd
a more pure and beautiful Light. A fweet Serenity,
accompanied with an invincible Refolution, reviv'd in
my Heart. This Joy was very different from that
loofe and wanton Pleafure which had before poifon'd
my Senfes. The one is a drunken and tumultuous
Joy, interrupted with furious Paffions and ftinging
Remorfe; the other is a Joy of Reafon, attended
with a kind of celeftial Happinefs. 'Tis always pure,
equal, inexhauftible. The deeper we drink, the
more delicious is the Tafte. It ravifhes the Soul,
and never difcompofeth it. Then I began to fhed
Tears of Joy, and found that nothing was more
fweet than fo to weep. Happy, faid I, are thofe Men,
to whom Virtue reveals herfelf in all her Beauty ! Is
it poffible to fee her without loving her ? Is it poffible
to love her without being happy ?

Here *Mentor* faid, I muft leave you : I muft depart
this Moment : I am not allow'd to ftay any longer.
Where, faid I, are you going ? Into what uninhabitable Defart will I not follow you ? Don't think you
can efcape from me ; for I will rather die at your Feet
than not attend you. In fpeaking thefe Words, I
graiped

grafped him clofe, with all my Strength. It is in vain, faid he, for you to hope to detain me. The cruel *Metophis* fold me to certain *Æthiopians*, or *Arabs*. Thefe Men, going to *Damafcus*, in *Syria*, on the Account of Trade, refolv'd to fell me, fuppofing they fhould get a great Sum of Money for me of one *Hazael*, who wanted a *Greek* Slave to inform him of the Cuftoms of *Greece*, and inftruct him in our Arts and Sciences. Indeed *Hazael* purchas'd me at a great Price. What he has learn'd from me concerning our Manners, has given him a Curiofity to go into the Ifland of *Crete*, to ftudy the wife Laws of *Minos*. During our Voyage, the Weather has forc'd us to put in at *Cyprus*; and in expectation of a favourable Wind, he is come to make his Offerings in the Temple : See, that is he, who is now coming out of it : The Winds call us; our Sails are hoifted : Adieu, my dear *Telemachus* ; a Slave that fears the Gods, ought faithfully to ferve his Mafter. The Gods do not permit me to difpofe of myfelf : If I might, they know it, I would be only yours. Farewel; remember the Labours of *Ulyffes*, and the Tears of *Penelope :* Remember that the Gods are juft. O ye Gods! the Protectors of Innocence! in what a Country am I, conftrain'd to leave *Telemachus !*

No, no, faid I, my dear *Mentor*, it fhall not be in your Power to leave me here; I'll rather die, than fee you depart without me. Is this *Syrian* Mafter inexorable? Was he fuckled by a Tygrefs? Would he tear you out of my Arms? He muft either kill me, or fuffer me to follow you. You yourfelf exhort me to fly, and will not permit me to fly with you. I'll go to *Hazael*, perhaps he may compaffionate my Youth and my Tears. Since he loves Wifdom, and goes fo far in fearch of it, he cannot have a favage

and.

and infenfible Heart. I will throw myfelf at his Feet, I will embrace his Knees, I will not let him go till he has given me leave to follow you. My dear *Mentor*, I will be a Slave with you; I will give my-felf to him; if he refufes me, it is decreed, I will eafe myfelf of this burthenfome Life.

In this very Moment, *Hazael* call'd *Mentor:* I proftrated myfelf before him; he was furpriz'd to fee an unknown Perfon in this Pofture. What is it you defire of me, faid he? Life, reply'd I; for I cannot live, unlefs you fuffer me to follow *Mentor*, who be-longs to you. I am the Son of the great *Ulyffes*, the moft wife of all thofe *Grecian* Kings that deftroy'd the ftately City of *Troy*, renown'd throughout all *Afia*. It is not out of Vanity that I acquaint you with my Birth, but only to infpire you with fome Pity for my Misfortunes. I have fought my Father in all the Seas, accompanied by this Man, who has been to me another Father. Fortune, to complete my Mife-ries, deprived me of him; fhe has made him your Slave; permit me to be fo too. If it be true, that you are a Lover of Juftice, and that you are going to *Crete*, to learn the Laws of the good King *Minos*, harden not your Heart againft my Sighs and Teais. You fee the Son of a King reduc'd to defire Servi-tude as his only Refuge. Formerly I would have chofen Death in *Sicily* to avoid Slavery; but my firft Misfortunes were only the weak Effays of Fortune's Outrages; now I tremble left I fhould not be receiv'd among Slaves. O Gods! fee my Calamity! O *Ha-zael!* remember *Minos*, whofe Wifdom you admire, and who will judge us both in the Kingdom of *Pluto*.

Hazael, looking upon me with Mildnefs and Hu-manity, ftretch'd forth his Hand and rais'd me up I am not ignorant, faid he, of the Wifdom and Virtue of
Ulyffes.

Ulyſſes. *Mentor* has often told me what Glory he acquir'd among the *Greeks*; and beſides, ſwift-wing'd Fame has not been wanting to ſpread his Name over all the Nations of the Eaſt. Follow me, O Son of *Ulyſſes*, I will be your Father, till you find him again who gave you Life. Though I were not mov'd with the Glory of your Father, his Misfortunes, and your own; yet the Friendſhip I have for *Mentor* would engage me to take care of you. It is true I bought him as a Slave, but I keep him as a faithful Friend; the Money he coſt, has acquir'd me the deareſt and moſt valuable Friend that I have in the World. In him I have found Wiſdom; I owe all the Love I have for Virtue to his Inſtructions. From this Moment he is free, and you ſhall be ſo too; all I aſk of either of you is your Heart.

In an inſtant, I paſs'd from the bittereſt Grief, to the moſt lively Joy that Mortals can feel; I ſaw myſelf deliver'd from the worſt of Dangers; I was drawing near to my Country; I had found one to aſſiſt me in my Return; I had the Comfort of being with a Man, who lov'd me already for the ſake of Virtue alone. In a word, I found every thing in finding *Mentor* again; whom I reſolv'd to loſe no more.

Hazael advances to the Shore; we follow; we embark with him; our Oars cut the gentle Waves; a ſoft Zephyr wantons in our Sails; it animates the whole Ship, and gives it an eaſy Motion; the Iſland of *Cyprus* ſoon diſappears. *Hazael*, impatient to know my Sentiments, aſk'd me, what I thought of the Manners of that Iſland? I told him ingenuouſly to what Dangers my Youth had been expos'd, and the Conflict I had ſuffer'd within me. He was tenderly mov'd with my Abhorrence of Vice, and ſaid theſe Words: O *Venus!* I acknowledge your Power,

and

and that of your Son ; I have burnt Incenfe upon
your Altars ; but give me leave to deteft the infamous
Effeminacy of the Inhabitants of your Ifland, and
the brutal Impudence with which they celebrate your
Feftivals.

After this, he difcourfed with *Mentor* of that firft
Being, which form'd the Heavens and the Earth ; of
that pure, infinite, and unchangeable Light, which
communicates itfelf to all, without being divided; of
that fupreme and univerfal Truth, which enlightens
the fpiritual World, as the Sun enlightens the corpo-
real. He who has never feen this pure Light, added
he, is as blind as one born without Sight ; he paffes
his Life in a difmal Night, like that of thofe Regions,
where the Sun never fhines for many Months of the
Year ; he thinks himfelf wife, and is a Fool ; he fan-
cies he fees all, and fees nothing ; he dies, without
having ever feen any thing ; at the moft he perceives
only falfe and obfcure Glimmerings, empty Shadows,
Phantoms that have no Reality. Of this kind are all
thofe, who are carried away by fenfual Pleafures,
and the Enchantments of Imagination. There are
no true Men upon the Earth, but thofe who confult,
love, and obey this eternal Reafon. It is fhe that infpires us when we think well : It is fhe that reproves
us when we think ill. Our Reafon, as well as our
Life, is her Gift. She is like a vaft Ocean of Light;
the Reafon of Men is like little Rivulets which flow
from her, and which Return and lofe themfelves in
her again.

Though I did not as yet perfectly comprehend the
Wifdom of this Difcourfe, I tafted, neverthelefs,
fomething in it fo pure and fo fublime, that my
Heart grew warm with it, and Truth feemed to fhine
in every Word he utter'd. They continued to fpeak
of

of the Original of the Gods, of the Heroes, of the
Poets, of the Golden Age, of the Deluge, of the
firſt Hiſtories of Mankind, of the River of Oblivion,
into which the Souls of the Dead are plung'd, of
the eternal Puniſhments prepar'd for the Impious in
the black Gulph of *Tartarus,* and of that bleſſed
Tranquillity which the Juſt enjoy in the *Elyſian*
Fields, without any Apprehenſions of ever loſing
it.

Whilſt *Hazael* and *Mentor* were converſing together, we ſaw great Numbers of Dolphins, cover'd
with Scales that ſeem'd to be of Gold and Azure.
They play'd in the Sea, and laſh'd the Floods into
a Foam. After them came the *Tritons,* ſounding
their wreathed Trumpets, made of Shells : They
ſurrounded the Chariot of *Amphytrite,* drawn by Sea-
horſes, whiter than Snow, and which, cutting the
briny Flood, left vaſt Furrows in the Sea far behind
them. Their Eyes darted Fire, and Smoke iſſued
from their Noſtrils. The Chariot of the Goddeſs
was a Shell of a wonderful Figure ; it was more
white than the fineſt Ivory, and the Wheels were all
of Gold. This Chariot ſeem'd to fly upon the Surface of the gentle Waters. A Shoal of Sea-Nymphs,
crown'd with Garlands, came ſwimming after the
Chariot : Their lovely Hair hung looſe upon their
Shoulders, and wanton'd with the Winds. In one
Hand the Goddeſs held a Golden Sceptre, to command the Waves ; with the other, ſhe held upon her
Knee the little God *Palæmon,* her Son, who hung
upon her Breaſt. Her Face was ſo ſerene, and ſo
ſweetly majeſtic, that the black Tempeſts, and all
the ſeditious Winds, fled from before her. The *Tritons* guided the Horſes, and held the Golden Reins.
A large Sail of the richeſt Purple hung floating in
the

the Air, above the Chariot; a Multitude of little
Zephyrs hover'd about it, and labour'd to fill it with
their Breath. In the Midft of the Air, *Æolus* appear'd, diligent, reftlefs, and vehement ; his ftern
and wrinkled Face, his menacing Voice, his thick
over-hanging Eye-brows, his Eyes full of a dim and
auftere Fire, repell'd the Clouds, and kept the fierce
and boifterous Winds in Silence. The vaft Whales,
and all the Monfters of the Sea, came in hafte out
of their profound Grottos to gaze upon the Goddefs, and with their Noftrils made the briny Waters
ebb and flow.

The END *of the* FOURTH BOOK.

THE

THE
ADVENTURES
OF
TELEMACHUS.

BOOK V.

The ARGUMENT.

Telemachus *relates, that upon his Arrival in* Crete, *he learn'd, that* Idomeneus, *the King of that Ifland, had facrificed his only Son, to perform a rafh Vow; that the* Cretans, *in order to avenge the Son's Blood, had compell'd the Father to fly their Country; and that, after various Confultations, they were actually affembled in order to elect a new King.* Telemachus *adds, that being admitted into that Affembly, he carried the Prize of feveral Games, and explain'd the*

Que-

Book V

Queries left by Minos, *in the Book of his Laws, whereupon the old Men, the Judges of the Island, and all the People, admiring his Wisdom, would have made him their King.*

FTER we had admir'd this wonderful Sight, we began to difcover the Mountains of *Crete,* tho' yet we could hardly diftinguifh them from the Clouds of Heaven, and the Billows of the Sea. We foon faw the Summit of Mount *Ida,* rifing above all the other Mountains of the Ifland, as an ancient Stag carries his branching Head above the young Fauns that follow him in the Foreft. By degrees we faw more diftinctly the Coafts of the Ifland, which refembled the Form cf an Amphitheatre. As we found the Land of *Cyprus* neglected and uncultivated, fo that of *Crete* appear'd fertile, and inriched with all manner of Fruits by the Induftry of the Inhabitants.

On all Sides we perceiv'd well built Villages, Towns equalling Cities, and magnificent Cities. We obferv'd no Spot of Ground where the Hand of the diligent Hufbandman was not ftamp'd; the Plough had left deep Furrows in every Place. Thorns, Briars, and all fuch Plants as are a ufelefs Burthen to the Earth, are utterly unknown in this Country. We contemplated with Pleafure the hollow Vallies, where Troops of Oxen go lowing in their rich Paftures, along the Banks of refrefhing Streams; the Sheep every where feeding upon the Defcent of the Hills; the vaft Fields cover'd with golden Ears of Corn, the liberal Bleffings of bountiful *Ceres:* In a word, the Mountains adorn'd with Vines, whofe cluftering Grapes, already purpled,

pro-

promis'd a plentiful Vintage of the delicious Prefents of *Bacchus*, which charm away the anxious Cares of Men.

Mentor told us, he had been formerly in *Crete*, and inform'd us of all he knew of it. This Island, faid he, admir'd by all Strangers, and famous for its hundred Cities, is more than fufficient to nourifh all the Inhabitants, though they are innumerable; for the Earth never fails to pour forth her Fruits to the induftrious Hand that manures her; her fertile Bofom can never be exhaufted. The more numerous Men are in a Country, provided they be laborious, the more Plenty they enjoy. They need not be jealous of one another; the Earth, like a tender Mother, multiplies her Gifts according to the Number of her Children, if they deferve her Favours by their Diligence. The Ambition and Covetoufnefs of Men are the only Springs of their Unhappinefs. They covet all; and make themfelves miferable, by defiring what is fuperfluous. If they would be moderate, and contented with a Competency, we fhould fee Plenty, Joy, Union and Peace diffus'd throughout the World.

Minos, the wifeft and the beft of Kings, underftood this well. All the admirable Things you fhall fee in this Island, are owing to the Excellency of his Laws. The Education he appointed for Children, renders their Bodies ftrong and healthful: They are accuftom'd, from their Infancy, to a plain, frugal, laborious Life: It is a receiv'd Maxim among them, that all Pleafure enervates both the Body and Mind. No other Pleafure is ever propos'd to them, but the Acquifition of an invincible Virtue and folid Glory. This People do not meafure Mens Courage only by defpifing Death in the Hazards of War, but by the

Con-

Contempt of fuperfluous Riches and ignoble Pleafures. Three Vices are punifh'd here, which remain
unpunifh'd in all other Nations; Ingratitude, Diffimulation and Avarice.

They have no need of Laws to fupprefs Luxury,
and Diffolution of Manners; for fuch things are unknown in *Crete*. Every Man works, yet no Man
defires to be rich. They think all their Labour fufficiently recompenced with an eafy and regular Life,
in which they enjoy, plentifully and quietly, all that
is truly neceffary to Men. Coftly Furniture, gor-
geous Apparel, delicious Feafts, and gilded Palaces,
are not permitted in this Country. Their Cloaths are
of fine Wool, beautiful in Colour, but all plain,
and without Embroidery. Their Repafts are fober;
they drink little Wine; good Bread with excellent
Fruits, which the Trees almoft fpontaneoufly yield,
and the Milk of Cattle, make the principal Part of
their Meals. At the moft, their Meat is plain,
drefs'd without Sauce or Ragout; and they always
take care to referve the beft and ftrongeft of the Cattle for the Advancement of Agriculture. Their
Houfes are neat, commodious, pleafant; but without
Ornaments. They are not ignorant of the moft magnificent Architecture; but that's referv'd for the
Temples of the Gods: They dare not live in
Houfes like thofe of the immortal Powers.

The great Riches of the *Cretans*, are Health,
Strength, Courage; Peace and Union in Families,
the Liberty of all their Citizens; Plenty of Things
neceffary, and a Contempt of thofe that are fuperfluous; a Habit of Labour, and an Abhorrence of
Sloth; a mutual Emulation of virtuous Actions; Submiffion to the Laws, and a Reverence of the juft Gods.

I afk'd him, wherein the Authority of the King
confifted? And he anfwer'd thus: The King is above
all

all the People but the Laws are above the King. He has an abfolute Power to do Good; but his Hands are tied, fo foon as he attempts to do Ill. The Laws intruft him with the Care of the People, as the moft valuable of all Trufts, on Condition that He fhall be the Father of his Subjeƈts. The Laws require, that one Man fhall, by his Wifdom and Moderation, ferve to make a whole Nation happy, and not that fo many Men fhall, by their Mifery and abjeƈt Slavery, ferve to flatter the Pride and Luxury of one Man. The King ought to have nothing more than other Men, but what's neceffary either to relieve him in difcharge of his painful Funƈtions, or to imprint on the Minds of the People that Refpeƈt which is due to him who is to maintain the Vigour of the Laws. On the other hand, the King ought to be more fober, more averfe to Luxury, more free from Haughtinefs and Oftentation than any other Man. He is not to have more Riches and Pleafure, but more Wifdom, Virtue and Glory, than the reft of Men. Abroad, he is to be the Defender of his Country, at the Head of their Armies; at home, he is to diftribute Juftice to the People, to make them good, wife and happy. It is not for his own fake that the Gods have made him King, but only for the Service of the People. He owes to the People all his Time, all his Care, all his Affeƈtion; and he is no otherwife worthy of his Crown, than as he forgets his own perfonal Interefts, to facrifice himfelf to the public Good. *Minos* appointed, that his Children fhould not reign after him, unlefs they would reign by thefe Rules; for he lov'd his People more than his Family. By this Wifdom, he render'd *Crete* fo powerful and fo happy. By this Moderation he has

effac'd

effac'd the Glory of all Conquerors, who make their People fubfervient to their own Grandeur, that is, to their Vanity. In a word, by his Juftice, he merited the Office of fupreme Judge of the Dead in the Regions below.

While *Mentor* was thus fpeaking, we arrived in the Ifland. We faw the famous Labyrinth, built by the Hands of the ingenious *Dædalus*, in Imitation of the great Labyrinth which we had feen in *Egypt.* As we were confidering this curious Fabrick, we beheld the Shore cover'd with People, and Multitudes preffing towards a Place that was near the Sea. We afked the Reafon of their Hafte, and receiv'd this Account from one *Nauficrates*, a Native of *Crete.*

Idomeneus, faid he, the Son of *Deucalion*, and Grandfon to *Minos*, went with the reft of the *Grecian* Kings to the Siege of *Troy*. After the Deftruction of that City, he fet fail in order to return to *Crete*; but was furpriz'd by fo violent a Storm, that the Pilot, and the moft experienced Mariners in the Ship thought they fhould inevitably be caft away. Every one had Death before his Eyes; every one faw the Abyfs open to fwallow him up; every one deplor'd his Misfortune, and had not fo much as the wretched Hope of that imperfect Reft, which the Souls enjoy, who crofs the River *Styx* after their Bodies have receiv'd Burial. *Idomeneus*, lifting up his Eyes and Hands to Heaven, invok'd *Neptune* in thefe Words: O powerful God! who commandeft the Empire of the Sea, vouchfafe to hear the Prayers of the Diftreffed: If thou delivereft me from the Fury of the Winds, and bringeft me again fafe to *Crete*, the firft Head I fee, fhall fall by my own Hands a Sacrifice to thy Deity.

G   In

In the mean time his Son, impatient to fee his Father again, made hafte to meet and embrace him at his Landing. Unhappy Youth! who knew not that he was running to his own Deftruction! The Father, who had efcap'd the Storm, arriv'd fafe in the wifh'd-for Haven. He return'd Thanks to *Neptune* for hearing his Prayers, but foon found how fatal they had been to him. A black Prefage of his Misfortune made him bitterly to repent his rafh Vow. He dreaded his coming amongft his own People; he turn'd his Eyes to the Ground, and trembled for fear of feeing whatever was dearest to him in the World. But the inexorable Goddefs *Nemefis*, who is ever watchful to punifh Men, and efpecially haughty Kings, pufh'd him on with a fatal and invifible Hand. *Idomeneus* arrives, hardly daring to lift up his Eyes. He fees his Son: he ftarts back with Horror; his Eyes, in vain, look about for fome other Head, lefs dear to him, to ferve for his vow'd Sacrifice. Mean while his Son approach'd, and threw his Arms about his Neck, aftonifhed to fee his Father diffolving in Tears, and making fo ftrange a Return to his Tendernefs.

O my Father! faid he, whence comes this Sadnefs? After fo long Abfence, are you difpleas'd to fee your Kingdom again, and to be the Joy of your Son? What have I done? You turn your Eyes away for fear of feeing me. The Father, overwhelm'd with Grief, made no Anfwer. At laft, after many deep-fetch'd Sighs, he faid, Ah! *Neptune*, what have I promis'd thee? At how dear a Rate haft thou preferv'd me from Shipwreck! Reftore me to the Waves, and to the Rocks, which ought to have dafh'd me in pieces, and finifh'd my wretched Life. Let my Son live! O thou cruel God,

God, here, take my Blood, and spare his. As he spoke, he drew his Sword to pierce his own Heart; but those that were about him stay'd his Hand. The aged *Sophronymus*, the Interpreter of the Will of the Gods, assur'd him that he might satisfy *Neptune* without the Death of his Son. Your Promise, said he, was rash and indiscreet: The Gods will not be honour'd by Cruelty: Beware of adding to the Fault of your Promise, the Crime of accomplishing it against the Laws of Nature: Let a hundred Bulls, whiter than Snow, be offer'd up to *Neptune*; let their Blood stream about his Altar crown'd with Flowers; let the sweetest Incense smoke in honour of the God.

Idomeneus heard this Discourse, bending his Head towards the Earth, and answer'd not one Word: Fury sat glaring in his Eyes; his pale and disfigur'd Face chang'd Colour every Moment; and all his Limbs shook with Horror. In the mean time his Son said to him, My Father, here I am; your Son is ready to die, to appease the God of the Sea. Do not provoke his Anger. I die contented, since my Death will have prevented yours. Strike, O my Father, and fear not to find in me the least Dread of Death, or any thing unbecoming your Son.

In that Moment *Idomeneus*, grown mad, and push'd on by the infernal Furies, acted a thing that astonish'd all that stood about him. He thrust his Sword into the Heart of the Youth; and drew it out again all reeking and drench'd in Blood, to plunge it into his own Bowels; but he was once more prevented by those that were present. The Youth sunk down in his own Blood; the Shades of Death cover his Eyes; he half-open'd them to the Light, but scarcely had he found it, when, unable to bear it, he clos'd them

for

for ever. As a beautiful Lilly in the midst of the
Field, cut up from the Root by the sharp Plow-share,
lies down and languishes on the Ground ; it receives
no more Nourishment from the Earth, and the
Springs of Life are intercepted; yet the glory
Whiteness and that Glory which charm'd the Eye still
remain : So the Son of *Idomeneus*, like a young and
tender Flower, is cruelly mow'd down in the Bloom
of his Age. The Father, through Excess of Grief,
is become insensible, he knows not where he is, nor
what he does, nor what he ought to do ; he walks
with tottering Steps towards the City, and demands
his Son.

In the mean time, the People being touch'd with
Pity for the Son, and full of Horror at the barbarous
Action of the Father, cry out, That the just Gods
had abandon'd him to the Furies. Their Rage fur-
nishes them with Arms ; they lay hold on Sticks and
Stones ; Discord breathes a deadly Venom into every
Breast. The *Cretans*, the wise *Cretans*, forget their
beloved Wisdom ; they will no longer acknowledge
the Grandson of sage *Minos* ; *Idomeneus's* Friends
know not how to consult his Safety, otherwise than
by conducting him back to his Ship ; they embark
with him, and commit their Flight to the Mercy of
the Waves. *Idomeneus*, being come to himself, returns them Thanks for Snatching him away from a
Land he had besprinkled with his Son's Blood, and
which he could no longer inhabit. The Winds waft
them over to *Hesperia*, where they go to lay the
Foundation of a new Kingdom in the Country of the
Salentines.

In the mean time, the *Cretans*, being destitute of
a King to govern them, resolve to chuse such a one
as will preserve the Purity of the establish'd Laws.
And

And thefe are the Meafures they take for that Purpofe : all the chief Men of an hundred Cities are
now met at this Place; they have already begun with
offering Sacrifices; they have affembled all the moft
renowned Sages of the neighbouring Countries, to
examine the Wifdom of thofe who fhall be thought
worthy of the Supreme Command; they have order'd
public Games, where all the Competitors are to contend ; the Crown is the Prize which they propofe to
confer on him who fhall be found to excel, both as to
Strength of Body and Endowments of Mind. They
will have a King, whofe Body is ftrong and active,
and his Soul adorn'd with Wifdom and Virtue : They
invite all Strangers to this grand Affembly.

Naufterates having recounted to us this wondrous
Story, faid to us : Hafte therefore, O Strangers, to
our Affembly; you fhall contend with the reft, and
if the Gods decree the Victory to either of you, he
fhall reign in this Country. We follow'd him, not
out of any Defire of being victorious, but only out
of a Curiofity to fee fo extraordinary an Election.

We arriv'd at a Place refembling a very large *Circus,* furrounded with a thick Wood. The Middle of
this *Circus* was an *Arena,* or Pit, prepar'd for the
Combatants ; it was furrounded by a large Amphi-
theatre of green Turf, whereon was feated and ranged
an innumerable Multitude of Spectators. As foon
as we came there, we were honourably receiv'd ; for
the *Cretans,* of all Nations in the World, are the
moft noble and religious Obfervers of Hofpitality :
They defir'd us to take our Places, and invited us to
enter the Lifts. *Mentor* excufed himfelf, upon account of his Age, and *Hazael* on the Score of his ill
State of Health. My Youth and Vigour left me
without Excufe ; however, I caft a Look upon *Mentor*

to difcover his Mind, and I perceived he defir'd that I
fhould engage: I therefore accepted their Propofal,
and ftripp'd myfelf of my Cloaths: They pour'd
Streams of fweet and fhining Oil on all my Limbs;
and I mixed among the Combatants. It was faid on
every Side, that the Son of *Ulyffes* was come to contend for the Prize; and feveral *Cretans*, who had been
at *Ithaca* during my Infancy, knew me again.

The firft Exercife was Wreftling. A *Rhodian*,
about five and thirty Years of Age, furmounted all
thofe who dared to encounter him. He had ftill all
the Vigour of Youth; his Arms were nervous and
brawny; at the leaft of his Motions you might difcover all his Mufcles, and he was no lefs nimble than
ftrong. He did not think me worthy to be conquer'd
by him; and looking with Pity upon my tender Age,
he was about to retire, when I challeng'd him.
Hereupon we laid hold on each other; we almoft
fqueez'd the Breath out of one another's Bodies; we
ftood Shoulder to Shoulder; Foot to Foot; all our
Nerves were diftended; and our Arms interwoven
like twining Serpents; each of us ftriving to lift his
Antagonift from the Ground. Sometimes he endeavoured unexpectedly to throw me, by pufhing me to
the right Side; fometimes he ftrove to bend me on
the left: But whilft he was plying me in this manner,
I gave him fuch a violent Pufh, as bent his Loins;
fo he tumbled down upon the Stage, and dragg'd me
after him; in vain he us'd all his Strength to get
uppermoft, I kept him immoveably under me. All
the People cry'd, Victory to the Son of *Ulyffes*, and
fo I help'd the difmay'd *Rhodian* to get up again.

The Combat of the *Ceftus* was more difficult:
The Son of a rich Citizen of *Samos* having acquired
a great Renown in this Exercife, all the reft yielded
to him, and I alone offer'd to difpute the Victory
with

with him, At firſt he dealt me ſuch fierce Blows
on my Head and Breaſt, as made me caſt up Blood,
and ſpread a thick Cloud over my Eyes: I ſtagger'd ;
he preſs'd me: I was almoſt out of Breath ; but I
was re-animated by *Mentor*'s Voice, who cry'd to
me, O Son of *Ulyſſes !* will you ſuffer yourſelf to be
vanquiſh'd ? Anger ſupply'd me with freſh Strength,
and I avoided ſeveral Blows which would have cruſh'd
me to the Earth. As ſoon as the *Samian* had made a
falſe Blow at me, and that his Arm was ſtretch'd out
in vain, I ſurpriz'd him in that ſtooping Poſture, and
as he had began to ſtep back, I lifted up my *Cæſtus*,
that I might fall upon him with greater Force ; he
endeavour'd to avoid me, and loſing his proper Balance, he gave me an Opportunity to throw him
down. He had ſcarce meaſur'd the Ground with his
Length, when I reach'd him my Hand to raiſe him
up. He got up of himſelf, cover'd with Duſt and
Blood, full of Confuſion and Diſorder, but he durſt
not renew the Fight.

Immediately after began the Chariot-Races : The
Chariots were diſtributed by Lot ; mine happened to
be the worſt, both as to the Lightneſs of the Wheels,
and the Mettle of the Horſes : We ſtarted ; a Cloud
of Duſt flew about us, that darken'd the very Sky.
At firſt, I let all my Competitors go before me ; a
young *Lacedemonian*, named *Crantor*, preſently out-
ſtript all the reſt ; a *Cretan*, *Polycletus*, by Name,
follow'd him cloſe ; *Hippomachus*, a Relation of *Idomeneus*, who aſpir'd to ſucceed him, giving the Reins
to his Horſes, reeking with Sweat, leaned on their
flowing Mains, and his Chariot-Wheels turned ſo
very ſwift, that they ſeem'd to be without Motion,
like the Wings of an Eagle that cuts the Air. My
Horſes being animated, and having gather'd Breath

by

by degrees, I out-ftripped moft of thofe who ftarted with fo much Ardour. *Hippomachus*, *Idomeneus*'s Kinfman, driving his Horfes too faft, the moft mettlefome of them fell down, and by his Fall depriv'd his Mafter of the Hopes of the Crown.

Polycletus, leaning too much upon his Horfes, and having no firm Sitting, tumbled down as his Chariot gave a Jolt, loft his Reins, and it was great Luck that he efcap'd Death. *Crantor* feeing, with Eyes full of Indignation, that I was got up clofe to him, redoubled his Eagernefs: Now, he invoked the Gods, promifing them rich Offerings; then he chear'd up his Horfes with his Voice: He was afraid left I fhould pafs between him and the Bounds; for my Horfes, which I fpared at firft, were now able to beat his; fo that the only Remedy he had left was, to flop up my Paffage: In order to this he ran the Rifk of breaking his Wheel againft the Bound, and broke it accordingly. I turn'd about prefently to avoid his broken Chariot, and a Moment after he faw me at the Goal. Again the People fhouted, and cry'd out, Victory to the Son of *Ulyffes*; 'tis he the Gods have deftin'd to reign over us.

Then the moft illuftrious, and the wifeft amongft the Cretans, conducted us into an antient facred Wood, remote from the Sight of prophane Men, where the Elders whom *Minos* had eftablifhed to be the Judges of the People, and Guardians of the Laws, convened us who had contended at the Exercifes, no other being admitted. The Sages opened the Books wherein all the Laws of *Minos* are collected. As I drew near thofe old Men, whom Age had render'd venerable, without impairing the Vigour of their Minds, I felt myfelf feiz'd with an awful Refpect and Confufion. They fat in order, and motionlefs in their Places; their Hair was hoary, fome of them

had

had scarely any ; a calm and serene Wisdom was con-
spicuous in their grave Countenances; they did not
strive who should speak first ; they spoke with Deliberation, and said nothing but what they had well
weigh'd before. When they happen'd to differ in Opinion, they were so moderate in maintaining their Sentiments, that one would be apt to think they were all
of one Mind. Their long Experience of past Trans-
actions, and their constant Application to Labour and
Study, gave them extensive Views in all Affairs. But
what most conduc'd to perfect their Reason, was the
Tranquillity of their Minds, freed from the fond
Paffions and wild Caprices of Youth : They were
actuated by Wisdom alone, and the Advantage they
reap'd from their accomplish'd Virtue was such a perfect Mastery over their Passions, that they enjoy'd,
without Disturbance, the pleasant and noble Delight
of being govern'd by Reason. As I was admiring
them, I wish'd my Life contracted, that I might arrive suddenly at so valuable an old Age. I counted
Youth unhappy, for being so impetuous, and at so
great Distance from that calm and enlighten'd Virtue.

The Chief among these old Men opened the Volume of *Minos's* Laws, which was a great Book
usually kept among Perfumes in a golden Box. Each
of them kifs'd it with great Respect ; for they said,
That next the Gods, from whom good Laws are de-
riv'd, nothing ought to be more sacred among Men,
than those Laws themselves, which tend to make
them good, wise and happy : Those who have in
their Hands the Administration of the Laws for the
Government of the People, ought themselves to be
govern'd by those very Laws upon all Occasions:
'Tis the Law, and not the Man, that ought to reign.
Such was the Discourse of these Sages. Afterwards

he

he who prefided at the Affembly, propounded three
Queftions, which were to be decided by the Maxims
of *Minos*.

The firft Queftion was, *Of all Men, who is moft
free ?* Some anfwer'd, 'Twas a King, who had an
abfolute Power over his People, and had conquer'd
all his Enemies. Others maintain'd, that 'twas a
Man who had fufficient Riches to gratify all his
Defires. Others faid, 'twas a Man, who being
never married, travell'd all his Life-time thro' divers
Countries, without being ever fubject to the Laws
of any Nation. Others fancied, that it was a *Barbarian*, who living upon Hunting in the Midft of
the Woods, was independent upon any Government,
and fubject to no manner of Want. Others thought,
it was a Man newly made free, becaufe coming out
of the Rigours of Servitude, he enjoy'd more than
any other the Sweets of Liberty. Others, at laft,
bethought themfelves to fay, That it was a dying
Man, becaufe Death freed him from all Troubles,
and all Men put together had no longer any Power
over him.

When it came to my Turn, I was not puzzled how
to anfwer, becaufe I ftill remembered what *Mentor*
had often told me : The moft free of all Men, anfwer'd I, is he who can be free, even in Slavery itfelf
In what Condition or Country foever a Man may be,
he is moft free when he fears the Gods, and none but
them : In fhort, that Man is truly free, who, difen-
gag'd from all manner of Fear, or anxious Defire,
is fubject to the Gods, and his Reafon only. The
Antients looked upon one another fmiling, and were
furpriz'd to find that my Anfwer was exactly the
fame with that of *Minos*.

After-

Afterwards, they propofed the fecond Queftion, in thefe Words, *Who is the moft unhappy of all Men?* Every one anfwered as he thought. One faid, 'Tis a Man who has neither Eftate, Health, nor Honour. Another faid, 'Tis a Man who is friendlefs. Others maintained, That 'tis a Man who has difobedient, ungrateful, and unworthy Children. There came a Sage of the Ifland of *Lesbos*, who faid, That the moft unhappy of all Men, is he who thinks himfelf fo; for Unhappinefs doth not entirely proceed from what we fuffer, but rather from our own Impatience and Uneafinefs, which aggravate our Misfortunes. This Speech was highly commended and applauded by the whole Affembly, and every one thought that the *Lefbian Sage* would carry the Prize, in thus folving this Queftion. But being afk'd my Opinion, I anfwer'd according to *Mentor's* Maxims, The moft unhappy of all Men, is a King, who thinks himfelf happy, when he makes other Men miferable: His Blindnefs makes him doubly unhappy; for not knowing his Mifery, he cannot apply Remedies to it, nay, is even afraid to know it: Truth cannot pierce thro' the Crowd of his Flatterers, to reach him; his Paffions tyrannize over him; he is a Stranger to his Duty; he never tafted the Pleafure of doing Good, nor felt the Charms of untainted Virtue; he is unhappy, and deferves to be fo; his Unhappinefs increafes daily; he runs to his own Ruin, and the Gods prepare an eternal Punifhment to confound him. All the Affembly confeffed I had overcome the wife *Lefbian*, and the old Men declared I had hit upon the true Senfe of *Minos.*

The third Queftion they afked, was, *Which of the two is to be preferred, a King victorious and invincible in War, or a King unexperienced in War, but able to*
rule

rule his People wisely in Peace? The Majority answer'd, That the King invincible in War was to be
preferred. What are we the better, said they, for
having a King who knows how to govern well in
Peace, if he knows not how to defend his Kingdom
when a War breaks out? For then his Enemies will
overcome him, and make his People Slaves. Others
on the contrary maintain'd, That the peaceful King
was better, because he would be afraid of War, and
consequently take care to avoid it. Others said,
That a conquering King would consult and advance
as well the Glory of his People as his own, and make
his Subjects Matters of other Nations; whereas a
peaceful King would sink their Courage into a
shameful Effeminacy. They desir'd to know my
Opinion, and I answer'd thus:

A King, who knows how to govern, only in
Peace, or only in War, and is incapable to rule his
People in both those Circumstances, is but half a
King; but if you compare a King, who is only
skilled in War, to a wise King, who, without being
acquainted with War, is able to maintain it upon
Occasion, by his Generals, I think he is to be preferred to the other. A King, whose Mind shall be
entirely bent upon War, would always be for making war, in order to extend his Dominion, and advance his own Glory, and not care if all his People
were ruined. What are a People the better for the
Conquests their King makes over other Nations, if
they themselves are miserable under his Reign.
Moreover, long Wars are always attended with great
Disorders; the Conquerors themselves grow licen-
tious in those Times of Confusion. See at what a
dear Rate *Greece* has triumph'd over *Troy:* she was
depriyed of her Kings for above ten Years. Whilst
all

all is ruined by War, the Laws grow faint, Agriculture is neglected, all Arts languifh and decay; even
the beft Princes, when they have a War to carry on,
are forced to commit the greateft of Ills, which is, to
tolerate Licentioufnefs, and make ufe of wicked Men.
How many profligate Villains would be punifhed in
Times of Peace, whofe Audacioufnefs muft be rewarded during the Diforders of War ? Never had
any Nation a conquering Sovereign, but they fuffer'd much upon account of his Ambition. A Conqueror, intoxicated with his Glory, is almoft as
ruinous to his own victorious People as to the
Nations he has vanquifh'd. A Prince, who wants
the neceffary Qualifications for Peace, cannot make
his Subjects relifh the Fruits of a War happily ended.
He is like a Man who could defend his own Field
againft his Neighbour, and ufurp even that of his
Neighbour himfelf, but could neither plow nor fow
his Grounds, in order to reap the Harveft. Such a
Man feems to be born to deftroy, lay wafte, and turn
the World topfy-turvy, and not to make the People
happy by a wife Government.

Now let us confider a peaceful King : 'Tis true,
he is not fit for great Conquefts ; that is to fay, he is
not born to difturb the Tranquillity of his own People, by endeavouring to fubdue thofe other Nations
who are not his lawful Subjects ; but if he be truly
fit to govern in Peace, he is Mafter of all the Qualifications neceffary to fecure and protect his People
againft their Enemies. The Reafon of it is plain : '
For he is juft, moderate, and eafy, with refpect to
his Neighbours ; he never attempts to do any thing
againft them that may difturb the public Peace ; he
is religioufly faithful in all his Alliances : his Allies
love him, they are not in fear of him, but rather repofe

pofe an entire Confidence in him. If he happens to
have fome reftlefs, haughty, ambitious, and troublefome Neighbour, all the other Kings, who fear that
turbulent Neighbour, and in no manner d ftruft the
peaceful King, join themfelves in Confed.racy with
that good King, and keep him from being oppres'd.
His Integrity, Honefty and Moderation, make him
the Arbiter of all the States that furround his.
Whilft the enterprizing King is odious to all the reft,
and ever expos'd to their Leagues, the peaceful Prince
has the Honour of being, as it were, the Father and
Guardian of all the other Kings. Thefe are the Advantages he has abro d : Thofe he enjoys at home are
ftill more folid. Sin he is fit to govern in Peace, 'tis
certain he governs according to the wifeft Laws; he
difcountenances Pomp, Luxury, and all thofe Arts
that ferve only to cherifh and foment Vice; he pro-
motes and encourages thofe that are ufeful, and can
fupply Mankind with the real Wants of Life; more
particularly he caufes his Subjects to apply themfelves
to Agriculture, and by that means he procures them
Plenty of all Neceffaries. This laborious People,
plain in their Manners, and accuftom'd to a thrifty
Way of Living, get an eafy Livelihood by tilling of
their Lands, and multiply every Day. This Kingdom contains not only an infinite Multitude of People, found in Body, vigorous, and ftrong : not foften'd by Pleafure, but exercis d and inur'd to Virtue;
not addicted to the Enjoyment of an effeminate,
luxurious Life : A Peop that know how to defpife Death, and had rar r part with their Lives,
than with the Liberty they enjoy under a wife King,
who reigns only by the Dictates of Reafon and Juftice. Let now a neighbouring Conqueror attack
this People, perhaps he may find them not fo well

fkill'd

ſkill'd in pitching a Camp, or drawing up an Army in Order of Battle, or in erecting Machines for the Befieging of a Town; but he will find them invincible by their Numbers, their Courage, their Patience upon hard Duty, their Familiarity with Want and Poverty, their Refolution and Obſtinacy in Fight, and their conſtant Virtue, not to be ſhaken even by ill Succeſs and Diſaſters. Moreover, if the King has not Experience enough to command his Armies in Perfon, he will caufe them to be commanded by thofe who are capable of it; and will underſtand how to make uſe of ſuch Generals without loſing his Authority. In the mean time, his Allies will furniſh him with Supplies; his Subjects will rather die, than undergo the Yoke of another unjuſt and tyrannical King; nay, the Gods themſelves will fight for him. See how many Helps and Advantages he will find amidſt the greateſt Dangers. I therefore conclude, That a peaceful King, who is unſkill'd in War, is a very imperfect King, ſince he cannot diſcharge one of his moſt important Functions, which is to overcome his Enemies: but, at the ſame time, I add, he is infinitely ſuperior to a conquering King, who wants the neceſſary Qualifications to govern in Peace, and is only fit for War.

I perceiv'd a great many in the Affembly, who feem'd to diſlike my Opinion; for the Generality of Men, dazzled by glittering Things, ſuch as Victories and Conqueſts, prefer them before what is plain, calm, and ſolid; ſuch as Peace, and the good Government of a Nation. But, however, all the old Men declared I had ſpoken the Sentiments of *Minos.*

The chief of theſe Ancients cry'd out, I fee the fulfilling of one of *Apollo*'s Oracles, which is known through all our Iſland: *Minos,* having confulted the
Gods,

Gods, to know how long his Progeny fhould reign, according to the Laws he had newly eftablifhed, *A- pollo* anfwer'd him, Thy Off-fpring will ceafe to rule, when a Stranger, coming into thy Ifland, fhall caufe thy Laws to reign there. We fear'd left fome Stran- ger fhould come and conquer the Ifle of *Crete* ; but *Idomeneus's* Misfortunes, and the Wifdom of the Son of *Ulyffes*, who beft of any Mortal underftands the Laws of *Minos*, do plainly difcover to us the Mean- ing of the Oracle. Why do we any longer defer crowning of him, whom Deftiny appoints to be our King?

The END *of the* FIFTH BOOK.

THE

Book VI

THE

ADVENTURES

OF

TELEMACHUS.

BOOK VI.

The ARGUMENT.

Telemachus *relates how he refused the Crown of* Crete, *in order to return to* Ithaca : *That the* Cretans *desiring him to name a King, he proposed* Mentor, *who likewise declined the Royal Diadem : That at last the Assembly pressing* Mentor *to chuse for the whole Nation, he told them what he had learn'd of* Aristode-mus's *Virtues, whereupon he was immediately proclaim'd King : That afterwards* Mentor *and he embark'd for* Ithaca ; *but that* Neptune, *to gratify*

Ve-

Venus's Refentment, rais'd the late Storm, and ship-wreck'd their Vessel, after which the Goddess Ca-lypso receiv'd them into her Island.

EREUPON the old Men went out of the Inclofure of the facred Wood, and the Chief of them taking me by the Hand, declar'd to the People, who were impatient to know the Decifion, That I had carry'd the Prize. His Words were fcarce out of his Mouth, when there was heard a confus'd Noife of all the Affembly, every one giving a Shout for Joy; the Shore, and all the neighbouring Hills echoed with this general Acclamation, Let the Son of *Ulysses*, who refembles *Minos*, reign over the *Cretans*.

I waited a while, and making Signs with my Hand, I defir'd to be heard. In the mean time, *Mentor* whifper'd me; What! will you renounce your Country? Will your ambitious Defires of a Crown make you forget *Penelope*, who now expects you as her only Hope; and the great *Ulysses*, whom the Gods have refolv'd to reftore to you? Thefe Words pierced my Heart, and check'd my Ambition of being a King. But now the profound Silence of this tumultuous Affembly gave me Opportunity thus to fpeak: Illuftrious *Cretans*, I am not worthy to command over you. The Oracle you mention'd, fhews indeed that the Offspring of *Minos* fhall ceafe to rule, when a Stranger fhall come into this Ifland, and fhall caufe the Laws of that wife King to reign therein; but it is not faid, That Stranger fhall rule. I will fuppofe I am that Stranger, mark'd out by the Oracle: I have made this Prediction good; I am come into this Ifland; I have difcover'd the true Senfe of the Laws, and I wifh my Explanation may

con-

contribute to make them reign with the Man whom
you fhall chufe. For my own part, I prefer my
Country, the poor little Ifland of *Ithaca*, before the
hundred Cities of *Crete*, and the Glory and Wealth
of this fine Kingdom. Suffer me to purfue what Fate
has deftin'd : If I enter'd your Lifts, 'twas not with
Hopes to reign here, but only to merit your Efteem
and your Pity, and that I might be furnifh'd by you
with Neceffaries for my fpeedy Return into my Native
Country. I would rather chufe to obey my Father
Ulyffes, and to comfort my Mother *Penelope*, than
reign over all the Nations of the Univerfe. Oh
Cretans! you fee the Bottom of my Heart : I muft
leave you ; but Death alone fhall put a Period to my
Gratitude : Yes, *Telemachus* will love the *Cretans*,
and be no lefs concern'd for their Honour than his
own, as long as he has Breath.

I had fcarce done fpeaking, when there arofe
through the whole Affembly a hollow Noife, like
that of the Waves of the Sea dafhing one againft
another in a Storm. Some faid, Is this a God in
human Shape? Others maintain'd, they had feen
me in other Countries, and that they knew me again.
Others cry'd, We muft force him to reign here.
At laft, I refum'd my Difcourfe, and every one was
filent in a Moment, not knowing but I was going to
accept what I had at firft rejected. I fpoke to them
thus.

Suffer me, O *Cretans!* to tell you my Thoughts :
You are the wifeft of all Nations, but methinks
Wifdom requires a Precaution, which you feem to
have forgot. You ought to fix your Election, not
on that Man who beft difcourfes about the Laws,
but on him who with a moft fteady and conftant
Virtue puts them in practice. For my part, I am
young,

young, and confequently unexperienc'd, expos'd to
the Violence of Paffions, and more fit to learn, by
obeying, how to command hereafter, than to command at prefent : Therefore, feek not a Man that
has overcome others in thefe Trials of Wit and
Strength, but one that has overcome himfelf; look
out for a Man that has your Laws deeply engraven
in his Heart, and whofe whole Life is a continued Practice of thofe Laws : Let his Actions,
rather than his Words, recommend him to your
Choice.

All the old Men, charm'd with this Difcourfe,
and feeing the Applaufes of the whole Affembly ftill
increafing, faid to me, fince the Gods will not fuffer
us to hope to fee you reign amongft us, at leaft do us
the Favour to affift us in the finding out a King,
that fhall caufe our Laws to reign. Do you know
any body that can command with that Moderation
you fpeak of? I know a Man, anfwer'd I, to whom
I am beholden for all you have admir'd in me; 'tis
his Wifdom, and not mine, that fpoke to you; 'tis
he, who infpired me with all thofe Anfwers you heard
juft now.

Thereupon the whole Affembly caft their Eyes
upon *Mentor*, whom I fhew'd to them, holding him
by the Hand. Moreover, I told them what Care he
had taken of me from my Infancy; what Dangers
he had refcu'd me from; what Misfortunes had befallen me as foon as I began to neglect his Counfels.
At firft, they took no notice of him, by reafon of
his plain, negligent Drefs, his modeft Countenance,
his being filent almoft all the while, and his cold
and referv'd Demeanour: But, when they view'd
him more attentively, they difcover'd in his Afpect
fomething divinely firm and elevated, they obferv'd
the

the Vivacity of his Eyes, and the Vigour with which he perform'd every, even the leaft action. They afk'd him feveral Queftions, which he anfwer'd to the Admiration of all; upon which they refolv'd to make him their King, but he excus'd himfelf without any Concern. He told them, he preferr'd the Sweets of a private Life before the Pomp of a Crown; that even the beft of Kings were unhappy, in that they fcarce ever did that Good they had a Defire to do; and that thro' Surprize, and the Infinuations of Flatterers, they often did that Mifchief they never intended. He added, That if Slaves be miferable, the Condition of a King is no lefs wretched, fince 'tis but Servitude in a Difguife. When a Man, faid he, is King, he is ftill dependent upon all thofe whom he has Occafion for, in order to make others obey. Happy is he, who is not oblig'd to command! 'Tis only to his own Country, when fhe invefts a Man with Power, that he ought to offer the dear Sacrifice of his Liberty, in order to toil for the Public Good.

At thefe Words, the *Cretans*, not being able to recover from their Surprize, afk'd him. What Man they ought to chufe? A Man, reply'd he, that knows well every one of you, fince he muft govern you; and fuch a one as is fhy of governing you. Whoever defires Sovereignty, is not acquainted with it; and how then will he perform the Duties incumbent upon his Dignity, if he be a Stranger to them? He courts a Crown for himfelf; but you ought to have fuch a one, as only accepts it for your Sake, and not his own.

All the *Cretans* being ftrangely furpriz'd to fee thefe two Strangers refufe a Crown, which many others feek after with eager Ambition, they enquir'd who

came

came along with them. *Naufcrates*, who had conducted them from the Port to the *Circus*, where
the Games were celebrated, shew'd them *Hazael*,
who was come with *Mentor* and myself, from the
Isle of *Cyprus*; but their Wonder still increased,
when they heard that *Mentor* had been *Hazael*'s
Slave; that *Hazael*, deeply affected with the Wifdom and Virtue of his Slave, had made him his
Counfellor and intimate Friend; that That Slave
made free, was the fame who just now refus'd to be
King; and that *Hazael* was come from *Damafcus* in
Syria, to inftruct himfelf in the Laws of *Minos*; fo
much was his Heart poffefs'd with the Love of Wifdom.

The old Men faid to *Hazael*, We dare not defire you to rule over us, for we fuppofe your
Thoughts are the fame with thofe of *Mentor*; you
defpife Men too much, to be willing to take upon
you the Conduct of them. Befides, Riches, and
the Pomp of Royalty, attract not you fo ftrongly, as
to make you defirous to purchafe them at the Expence of thofe painful Anxieties which are infepara-
bly annex'd to Dominion. *Hazael* anfwer'd, Do
not think, O *Cretans!* that I defpife Men. No,
I know too well what a great and noble Employment it is to make them good and happy; but that
Employment is full of Trouble and Danger; the
Splendor that attends it is but a falfe Brightnefs,
which can only dazzle the Eyes of vain-glorious
Men. Life is fhort; Greatnefs and Exaltation do
more provoke the Paffions, than they can fatisfy
them. My Defign in coming fo far, was not to
purchafe thefe falfe Goods, but only to learn to be
eafy without them. I muft bid you farewel; I have
no other Thoughts than to return to a peaceful and
                                                    retired

retired Life, where Wifdom fhall fill my Heart, and nourifh my Soul; and where the Hopes, fupply'd by Virtue, of a better Life after Death, fhall comfort me under the Miferies of old Age. If I were to wifh for any thing, it fhould not be, to be a King; it fhould be, Never to be parted from thefe two Men you fee here before you.

At laft, the *Cretans*, addreffing themfelves to *Mentor*, cry'd out, You, the wifeft and greateft of all Mortals, tell us then, who it is we muft chufe to be our King, for we will not let you go till you have directed us where to fix our Choice? To which he anfwer'd: Whilft I was among the Crowd of Spectators, I took notice of a vigorous old Man, who fhew'd no manner of Eagernefs or Concern; I afk'd who he was? and Anfwer was made, He was call'd *Arijlodemus*. Afterwards, I heard fome body telling him, that his two Sons were among the Combatants; at which he exprefs'd no manner of Joy: He faid, That as for the one, he did not wifh him the Dangers which attend a Crown; and as for the other, he lov'd his Country too well, ever to confent that he fhould be King. By that I underftood, that the Father had a rational Love for one of his Sons, who is good and virtuous, and that he did not indulge the other in vicious Exceffes. My Curiofity ftill increafing, I enquir'd into the Life and Character of this old Man; one of your Citizens anfwer'd me: He bore Arms a long time; his Body is cover'd with Wounds and Scars; but his plain and fincere Virtue, entirely averfe to Flattery, render'd him troublefome to *Idomeneus*, which is the Reafon that King did not employ him in the *Trojan* War. He fear'd a Man who would give thofe wife Counfels, which he was not inclin'd

to

to follow; he was even jealous of the Honour and
Reputation which that Man would infallibly have
acquir'd in a little Time; he forgot all his paft Services, and left him here poor, and expos'd to the
Scorn of thofe fordid, bafe Men, who value nothing
but Riches; but contented in his Poverty, he lives
a pleafant Life, in a retir'd Place of this Ifland,
where he tills and manures his Ground with his
own Hands. One of his Sons helps him in his
Work; they have a tender Love for each other;
their Frugality and Labour make them happy, and
fupply them with an Abundance of all Things neceffary for a plain way of Living. That wife old Man
diftributes to the Sick and the Poor of his Neighbourhood, all that he can fpare from his own Wants,
and his Son's: He fets all young People to work,
and encourages, admonifhes, and inftructs them.
He decides all Controverfies amongft his Neighbours,
and is, as it were, the Father of all Families. His
own Misfortune is, that he has a fecond Son, who
would never follow his Advice in any thing: The
Father having borne with him a long Time, with
hopes to reclaim him from his Vices, has at laft
turn'd him out of his Houfe; fince which he has
abandon'd himfelf to fond Ambition, and all extravagant Pleafures.

This, O *Cretans!* is what I have been inform'd;
you can beft tell whether that Relation be true;
but if that Man be fuch as he is 'defcrib'd to be,
what need you celebrate any Games? Why do you
affemble together fo many unknown Perfons? You
have amongft you a Man who knows you, and
whom you know; one who underftands War,
who has fhewn his Courage not only againft
Darts and Arrows, but againft dreadful Poverty,
and

4

and has defpis'd Riches gain'd by Flattery; one who
loves Labour; who knows how ufeful Agriculture is
to a Nation; who abhors Pomp and Luxury; who
fuffers not himfelf to be unmann'd by a blind Fondnefs
for his Children, and loves the Virtue of the one, and
condemns the Vices of the other. In a word, a Man
who is already the Father of the People. This muft
be your King, if you truly defire to fee the Laws of
wife *Minos* reign amongft you.

All the People cry'd out: 'Tis true, *Ariftodemus*
is fuch as you defcribe him; 'tis he that deferves the
Crown. The old Men order'd he fhould be call'd;
he was fetch'd from among the Crowd, where he
was mingled with the meaner Sort, and, having appeared before them, calm and unconcern'd, they
declare to him, That they had made him King.
He anfwer'd, I cannot confent to it, but upon thefe
three Conditions: Firft, that I fhall lay down my
Dignity in two Years time, in cafe I can't make
you better than you are at prefent, and if you remain
refractory to the Laws. Secondly, That I fhall be
free to maintain my plain and frugal Way of living.
And thirdly, That my Children fhall have no Rank
or Precedence; and that after my Death they fhall
be treated without any other Diftinction, than
according to their Merit, like the reft of the
Citizens.

At thefe Words, the Air was fill'd with joyful
Acclamations; the Chief of thofe old Men, who
were the Guardians of the Laws, put the Crown
upon *Ariftodemus*'s Head; and afterwards they offer'd Sacrifices to *Jupiter*, and the other great Gods.
Ariftodemus gave us Prefents, not with that Magnificence which is ufual to Kings, but with a noble
Simplicity. He gave to *Hazael* the Laws of *Minos*,

Vol. I.   H   vritten

written with *Minos*'s own Hand; he likewife gave
him a Collection of the whole Hiftory of the Ifle of
Crete, from *Saturn* and the Golden Age, down to
that Time : He fent aboard his Ship all kinds of the
choiceft Fruits that grow in *Crete*, but are unknown
in *Syria*, and offer'd him all the Affiftance he had
occafion for.

Now, becaufe we prefs'd for our Departure, he
ordered a Ship to be fitted up, and manned with a
great Number of ftrong Rowers, and armed Men ;
he gave us likewife Changes of Cloaths, and all
manner of Provifions. At that very Inftant there
arofe a fair Wind for *Ithaca* ; this Wind, being contrary to *Hazael*, oblig'd him to ftay behind. He faw
us go away, and embrac'd us as dear Friends, whom
he fear'd he fhould fee no more : However, faid he,
the Gods are juft ; they know our Friendfhip is founded on Virtue alone ; they will one Day bring us together again ; and thofe happy *Elyfian* Fields, where
the Good and Juft are faid to enjoy an eternal Peace
after Death, fhall fee our Souls meet, never to be
parted any more. Oh ! that my Afhes may be gathered into the fame Urn with yours ! As he fpoke
thefe laft Words, he fhed a Flood of Tears, and his
Voice was ftifled by deep Sighs : We wept no lefs than
he ; and in this folemn Woe he conducted us to our
Ship.

As for *Ariftodemus*, he faid to us : 'Twas you
made me King ; remember what Dangers you have
expofed me to, and therefore requeft the Gods that
they may vouchfafe to infpire me with true Wifdom, and make me as much fuperior to other Men
in Moderation, as I am above them in Authority.
For my part, I befeech them to conduct you fafe
into your Country, to confound the Infolence of
　　　　　　　　　　　　　　　　　　　　your

your Foes, and bleſs you with the Sight of *Ulyſſes*, reigning in Peace with his dear *Penelope*. *Telemachus*, I give you a good Ship, full of able Mariners and Soldiers, who may ſerve you againſt thoſe unjuſt Men who perſecute your Mother. O *Mentor!* your all-ſufficient Wiſdom leaves me no room even to wiſh you any thing! Go both in Peace, and live together happy; remember *Ariſtodemus*; and if ever the *Ithacans* have occaſion for the *Cretans*, depend upon me as long as I have Breath. He embrac'd us, and we could not forbear mingling our Tears with our Thanks.

In the mean time, the Wind, which filled our ſpreading Sails, ſeemed to promiſe a pleaſant Voyage. Already Mount *Ida* began to decreaſe in our Sight, and look'd like a little Hill; the *Cretan* Shore diſappear'd, and the Coaſt of *Peloponneſus* ſeemed to advance into the Sea to meet us. But on a ſudden, a low'ring Storm over-caſt the Sky, and ſtirr'd up all the Billows of the Sea; the Day was turn'd into Night, and ghaſtly Death hovered over us. O *Neptune*, it is you, who with your proud Trident, rouſed up the Rage of your watry Empire! *Venus*, to be revenged upon us for deſpiſing her even in her Temple of *Cythera*, went to that God, and ſpoke to him, full of Grief, and with her beauteous Eyes' diſſolved in Tears; at leaſt, it is what *Mentor*, who is acquainted with Celeſtial Things, has aſſured me. O *Neptune*, ſaid ſhe, will you ſuffer thoſe impious Wretches to mock my Power with Impunity? The Gods themſelves acknowledge it; yet theſe raſh Mortals have dared to condemn all the Cuſtoms of my Iſland; they pretend to a Wiſdom, Proof againſt all Paſſions, and look upon Love as Folly and Madneſs. Have you forgot that I was born in your Do-

minion?

minion? Why do you delay any longer to bury, in your deep Abyſſes, thoſe two Wretches whom I abhor?

She had ſcarce done ſpeaking, when *Neptune* made his boiſterous Waves riſe up to the very Skies, and *Venus* ſmiled, believing our Wreck inevitable. Our Pilot, being now beſide himſelf, cry'd out, That he could no longer oppoſe the Violence of the Winds, which fiercely drove us upon ſome Rocks; a Guſt of Wind broke our Main Maſt; and a Moment after, we heard the Bottom of our Ship ſplit againſt the craggy Points of the Rock. The Water enters at ſeveral Places; the Ship ſinks; all the Crew rend the Sky with lamentable Cries. I embraced *Mentor*, and ſaid to him, Death is come; we muſt receive it with Courage; the Gods have deliver'd us from ſo many Dangers, only to deſtroy us this Day: Let us die, O *Mentor!* let us die! it is a Comfort to me that I die with you; it were in vain to contend for our Lives againſt the Storm.

To this *Mentor* anſwer'd: True Courage finds always ſome Reſource or other; it is not enough to expect Death calmly and unconcerned; we ſhould alſo, without being afraid of it, uſe all our Endeavours to keep it off. Let you and I take one of the Rower's Seats. Whilſt that Multitude of fearful and troubled Men, regret the Loſs of their Lives, without uſing Means to preſerve them; let us not loſe one Moment to ſave ourſelves. Thereupon he took a Hatchet, and cut off the broken Maſt, which hanging into the Sea, made the Ship lean on one Side. The Maſt being thus ſevered from its Stump, he ſhoved it out of the Ship, and leaped upon it amidſt the furious Waves. Then, calling me by my Name, he encouraged me to follow him. As a

great

great Tree, which all the confederate Winds attack
in vain, and which remains unmoved, and fixed to its
deep Roots, fo that the Storm can only fhake its
Leaves : Thus *Mentor*, not only refolute and courageous, but alfo calm and undifturbed, feemed to
command the Winds and Sea. I followed him; for,
who could not have followed, being encouraged by
Mentor ? And now we fteer our ourfelves upon the
floating Maft. It prov'd a great help to us, for we
fat a-ftride upon it; whereas had we been forced to
fwim all the while, our Strength had foon been fpent.
But the Storm did often turn and over-fet this huge
Piece of Timber ; fo that, being plunged into the
Sea, we fwallowed large Draughts of the briny Flood,
which ran afterwards out of our Mouths, Ears and
Noftrils; and we were forc'd to contend with the
Waves, to get uppermoft again. Sometimes alfo we
were over-whelm'd by a Billow as big as a Mountain,
and then we kept faft to the Maft, for fear that violent Shock fhould make us lofe hold of what was now
our only Hope.

Whilft we were in that dreadful Condition,
Mentor, as calm and unconcern'd as he is now
upon this green Turf, faid to me, Do you think,
O *Telemachus !* that your Life is at the Mercy of
the Winds and the Waves ? Do you believe, that
they can deftroy you, unlefs the Gods have order'd
it ? No, no; the Gods over-rule and decree all
Things; and therefore it is the Gods, and not
the Sea, you ought to fear. Were you in the deep
Bottom of the Sea, great *Jove's* Hand were able to
deliver you out of it; and were you on the Top
of *Olympus*, having the Stars under your Feet, he
could plunge you in the deep Abyfs, or hurl you

down

down into the Flames of black *Tartarus*. I liftened to, and admired his Speech, which gave me a little Comfort; but my Mind was not calm enough to anfwer him. We pafs'd a whole Night without feeing one another, trembling, and half dead with Cold, not knowing whither the Storm would drive us. At length the Winds began to relent, and the roaring Sea was like one who having been a long Time in a great Paffion, has almoft fpent his Spirits, and feels only the Remains of a ruffled Motion which draws towards a Calm: Thus the Sea grown weary, as it were, of its own Fury, growled in hollow Murmurs, and its Waves became little higher than the Ridges of Land betwixt two Furrows in a ploughed Field.

In the mean time, bright *Aurora*, with her dewy Wings, came to open the Gates of the Sky, to introduce the radiant Sun, and feemed to promife a fair Day. All the Eaft was ftreaked with fiery Beams; and the Stars, which had fo long been hid, began to twinkle again, but withdrew as foon as *Phœbus* appeared on the lightened Horizon. We defcry'd Land afar off, and the Wind wafted us towards it. Hereupon, I felt Hopes reviving in my Heart, but we faw none of our Companions. It is probable, their Courage failed them, and the Tempeft funk them together with the Ship. Being come pretty near the Shore, the Sea drove us againft the fharp Rocks, which were like to have beat us to pieces; but we endeavour'd to oppofe to them the End of our Maft, which *Mentor* ufed to as much Advantage, as a wife Steerfman does the beft Rudder. Thus we efcap'd

thofe

thofe dreadful Rocks, and found, at laft, a clear and eafy Coaft, where we fwam without any Hindrance, and landed, at laft, on the fandy Shore. There you faw us, O great Goddefs! You who reign over this Ifland; there you vouchfafed to receive and comfort us.

The END *of the* SIXTH BOOK.

THE

THE

ADVENTURES

OF

TELEMACHUS.

BOOK VII.

The ARGUMENT.

Calypſo *admires* Telemachus *in his Adventures, and tries all Means to detain him in her Iſland, by engaging him in an Amour with her.* Mentor, *by his wiſe Counſels, ſupports* Telemachus *againſt the Artifices of that Goddeſs, and againſt* Cupid *himſelf, whom* Venus *had brought to her Aſſiſtance. Neverthelefs,* Telemachus *and the Nymph* Eucharis *ſoon feel a mutual Paſſion, which at firſt raiſes* Calypſo's *Jealouſy, and afterwards her Reſentment againſt thoſe two Lovers. She ſwears by the Sty-gian* Lake, *that* Telemachus *ſhall go out of her Iſland.*

Book VII

Iſland. Cupid *goes to comfort her, and obliges her* Nymphs *to ſet on fire a Ship built by* Mentor, *juſt as the latter was forcing away* Telemachus, *to embark in it.* Telemachus *feels a ſecret Joy at the burning of the Ship; which* Mentor *perceiving, puſhes him headlong into the Sea, and throws himſelf in after him, in order, by ſwimming, to get to another Ship, which he perceiv'd near that Coaſt.*

ELEMACHUS having ended his Speech, all the Nymphs, whoſe deep Attention had kept them motionleſs, with Eyes fix'd upon him, began to look upon one another, and aſk'd among themſelves, with Aſtoniſhment, who are theſe Men ſo cheriſh'd by the Gods? Who did ever hear ſuch wonderful Adventures? The Son of *Ulyſſes* does already ſurpaſs his Father, in Eloquence, Wiſdom and Valour. What a Look! What Beauty! What Sweetneſs! What Modeſty! But withal, What Nobleneſs and Majeſty! If we did not know him to be the Son of a Mortal, we might eaſily take him either for *Bacchus, Mercury,* or even the great *Apollo.* But who is this *Mentor,* who looks like a plain, obſcure, and ordinary Man? When one views him narrowly, there appears in him ſomething more than human.

Calypſo liſten'd to this Diſcourſe, with a Concern which ſhe could not conceal; her Eyes inceſſantly wander'd from *Mentor* to *Telemachus,* and from *Telemachus* to *Mentor.* Sometimes ſhe would have *Telemachus* begin again that long Story of his Adventures; then, on the ſudden, ſhe check'd herſelf; and, at laſt, riſing abruptly from her Seat, ſhe led

Tele-

Telemachus alone into a Grove of Myrtles, where she used all her Arts to know from him, if *Mentor* was not some Deity conceal'd in human Shape? *Telemachus* could not satisfy her; for *Minerva*, who accompanied him under the Shape of *Mentor*, had not discover'd herself to him, by reason of his Youth, for she did not yet trust his Secrecy so far, as to make him the Confidant of her Designs. Besides, she had a mind to try him in the greatest Dangers; and had he known that *Minerva* was his Companion, such a Support would have made him too presuming, and he would have despised the fiercest and most dreadful Accidents, without any Concern. Therefore he all along apprehended *Minerva* to be indeed *Mentor*; and all the Artifices of *Calypso* could not discover what she desir'd to know.

In the mean time, all the Nymphs, gathering round *Mentor*, took great Delight in asking him Questions: One of them ask'd him the Particulars of his Travels into *Ethiopia*; another desir'd to be informed of what he had seen at *Damascus*; and a third ask'd him, Whether he was acquainted with *Ulysses* before the Siege of *Troy?* He answer'd every one with gentle Courtesy; and though his Words were plain, yet were they full of Beauty. It was not long before *Calypso* return'd and interrupted their Conversation; and whilst her Nymphs fell to gathering of Flowers, singing all the while to amuse *Telemachus*, she took *Mentor* aside, in order to make him speak, and discover who he was. As the soft Vapours of Sleep do gently glide into the heavy Eyes, and wearied Limbs, of a Man quite spent with Fatigue; so the flattering Words of the Goddess insinuated themselves, in order to bewitch the

Heart

Heart of *Mentor* ; but ftill fhe met with Something that baffled her Efforts, and mock'd her Charms. Like a fteep Rock, which hides its proud Forehead among the Clouds, and defies the Rage of the infulting Winds ; thus *Mentor*, unfhaken in his wife Refolves, fuffer'd the preffing Importunities of the inquifitive *Calypfo* ; nay, fometimes he gave her a Glimpfe of Hope, that fhe might enfnare him with her Queftions, and draw forth the Truth from the Bottom of his Heart : But in the inftant when fhe thought herfelf almoft fure to fatisfy her Curiofity, her Hopes vanifh'd away ; what fhe imagin'd fhe held faft, gave her prefently the flip ; and one fhort Anfwer from *Mentor* threw her back into her former Uncertainty.

Thus fhe fpent whole Days, now flattering *Telemachus*, and then endeavouring to take him away from *Mentor*, from whom fhe defpair'd of ever getting the Secret. She made ufe of her faireft Nymphs to kindle the Fire of Love in young *Telemachus*'s Heart, and a Deity more powerful than *Calypfo* came to her Affiftance.

Venus, ftill full of Refentment for the Contempt which *Mentor* and *Telemachus* expreffed of the Worfhip that was paid her in the Ifland of *Cyprus*, was enrag'd to fee that thefe two rafh Mortals had efcap'd the Fury of the Winds and the Sea, in the late Storm raifed by *Neptune*. She complain'd bitterly to *Jupiter* ; but the Father of the Gods, unwilling to let her know that *Minerva*, in the Shape of *Mentor*, had preferv'd the Son of *Ulyffes*, told her with a Smile, That he gave her leave to revenge herfelf of thofe two Men. She therefore leaves *Olympus* ; neglects the fweet Perfumes which are burnt on her Altars at *Paphos*, *Cythera*, and *Idalia* ; flies in her

I   Chariot,

Chariot, drawn by Doves ; calls her Son *Cupid,* and, with a Face full of Sorrow, adorn'd with new Charms, she thus bespeaks him :

Dost thou not see, my Son, those two Men, who scorn my Power and thine ? Who for the future will worship us ? Go, and pierce with thy Arrows those two insensible Hearts : Descend with me into that Island, where I will discourse with *Calypso.* She said ; and cutting the yielding Air in a golden Cloud, presented herself to *Calypso,* who, at that Moment, sat alone on the Edge of a Fountain, at some Distance from her Grotto.

Unhappy Goddess, said she to her, the ungrateful *Ulysses* has despis'd and abandon'd you ; his Son, still more cruel than his Father, is preparing to do the same : But Love himself is come to revenge your Cause. I leave him with you ; he may remain among your Nymphs, as heretofore young *Bacchus* was bred among the Nymphs of the Isle of *Naxos.* *Telemachus* will look upon him as an ordinary Child ; and, not mistrusting him, will soon feel his Power. She said ; and re-ascending in the golden Cloud from whence she alighted, she left behind her a sweet Smell of *Ambrosia,* which perfumed all the Woods and Thickets around.

Cupid remain'd in the Arms of *Calypso,* who, tho' a Goddess, began to feel a secret Flame glide thro' her Bosom. To relieve herself, she presently gave him to a Nymph who happen'd to be near her, whose Name was *Eucharis;* but alas! how often did she repent it afterwards ? At first, nothing appear'd more innocent, more gentle, more lovely, more ingenuous, more obliging than this Child. By his sprightly, flattering, and ever-smiling Looks, one would have thought he could bring nothing but Delight ;

light; but as foon as one began to truft his fond
Careffes, there was found in them a ftrange Venom.
That malicious, deceitful Boy never flatter'd, but
with a Defign to betray; and never fmil'd, but
at the cruel Mifchief he had done, or meant to
do. He durft not come near *Mentor*, being
frighted away by his Severity; befides, he was
fenfible, That unknown Perfon was invulnerable,
and not to be pierced by his Arrows. As for the
Nymphs, they foon felt the Flames that were
kindled by this treacherous Boy; but they carefully
concealed the deep Wounds which fefter'd in their
Breafts,

In the mean time, *Telemachus*, feeing the Boy
playing with the Nymphs, was furpriz'd with his
Beauty and Gentlenefs. He embraces him, fometimes he takes him on his Knees, and fometimes in
his Arms. He feels within himfelf a fecret Uneafinefs, the Caufe of which he cannot difcover;
the more he indulges himfelf in his innocent Play,
the more he is diforder'd and foften'd. Do you fee
thofe Nymphs, faid he, to *Mentor?* How different
are they from thofe Women of the Ifle of *Cyprus*,
whofe very Beauty was offenfive. by reafon of their
Immodefty! But thefe immortal Beauties difplay an
Innocency, a Modefty, a Simplicity, all over charming! At thefe Words he blufh'd; but could not tell
why: He could not forbear fpeaking of them; yet
no fooner had he began, but he wanted Power to
proceed. His Words were broken, obfcure, and
fometimes without Senfe or Meaning. Hereupon
Mentor faid to him, O *Telemachus!* the Dangers
you efcap'd in the Ifle of *Cyprus*, were nothing
compar'd with thofe which now you don't miftruft,
bare-fac'd Lewdnefs ftrikes Horror, and brutifh

Im-

Impudence raifes our Indignation; but modeft Beauty is much more dangerous and enfnaring. When we begin to love it, we fancy we are in love with Virtue only; and, by infenfible Degrees, we yield to the deceitful Allurements of a Paffion, which we can fcarce perceive, before it is almoft too fierce to be extinguifh'd. Fly, my dear *Telemachus*, fly from thofe Nymphs, who are fo modeft and difcreet only to decoy you: Fly from the Dangers your Youth expofes you to; but above all, fly from that Boy, whom you do not know. 'Tis *Cupid* himfelf, whom his Mother *Venus* has brought into this Ifland, to revenge the Contempt you teftified for the Worfhip which was paid to her at *Cythera*. He has wounded the Heart of the Goddefs *Calypfo*, and made her paffionately in love with you; he has fir'd all thofe Nymphs that are now about him; and even *Telemachus* himfelf! Oh! wretched young Man, you yourfelf burn, fcarcely perceiving your own fecret Flame!

Telemachus often interrupted *Mentor*, faying, But why fhall we not ftay in this Ifland? *Ulyffes* is no longer among the Living, and muft certainly have been a long time buried in the Waves; and *Penelope*, feeing neither of us return home, can never have been able to refift fo many Lovers; and without doubt her Father *Icarus* has, by this Time, oblig'd her to marry a fecond Hufband. Shall I return to *Ithaca*, to fee her engaged in new Bonds, contrary to the folemn Faith fhe had plighted to my Father? The *Ithacans* have quite forgot *Ulyffes*; and we cannot return thither, without running upon certain Death, fince *Penelope*'s Lovers are already poffefs'd of all the Avenues to the

Port,

Port, to make our Deſtruction more ſure at our Return.

Mentor reply'd : Your Diſcourſe is the Reſult of
a blind Paſſion ; with great Subtilty we ſearch out
all the Reaſons which ſeem to favour it, and with
no leſs Care we turn away our View from thoſe
which condemn it ; we employ all our Wit in deceiving ourſelves, and ſtifling thoſe Remorſes which
give a check to our Deſires. Have you forgot all
that the Gods have done, in order to bring you back
into your own Country ? Which way did you come
out of *Sicily?* Thoſe Misfortunes which befel you
in *Eyypt*, did they not turn on a ſudden to your
Proſperity ? What unſeen Hand ſnatch'd you from
all thoſe impending Dangers which threaten'd your
Head in the City of *Tyre?* After ſo many wonderful Deliverances, can you be doubtful of what
the Gods have in ſtore for you ? But what do I
ſay ? You are unworthy of their Favours.   For
my own part, I will leave you, and ſoon quit this
Iſland. But you, O degenerate Son of ſo wiſe
and noble a Father ! you may lead here a ſoft, inglorious Life among Women ;   and, in ſpite of
Heaven, do what your Father thought unworthy of
him.

Theſe ſcornful Reproofs ſtung *Telemachus* to the
very Soul ; he felt his Heart relenting at *Mentor's*
Words ; his Grief was mingled with Shame ; he
fear'd both the Departure and Indignation of ſo
wiſe a Perſon, to whom he was ſo very much oblig'd ;
but a new-born Paſſion, with which he was but
little acquainted, made him quite another Man.
What, ſaid he to *Mentor*, with Tears in his Eyes,
do you reckon for nothing that immortal Life which
the Goddeſs offers me ? No, anſwer'd *Mentor*, I

make

make no account of any thing that is inconfiftent with Virtue, and againft the fupreme Decrees of Heaven. Virtue calls you back into your own Country, that you may fee and comfort *Ulyffes* and *Penelope:* Virtue forbids you to abandon yourfelf to an extravagant Paffion: The Gods, who deliver'd you from fo many Dangers, in order to make your Glory fhine as bright as your Father's, the Gods, I fay, command you to quit this Ifland. Love alone, that bafe Tyrant Love, can he detain you here? But what will you do with Immortality bereft of Liberty, Virtue and Glory? This Sort of Life would ftill be the more wretched, by being endlefs. *Telemachus* anfwer'd him only with Sighs; fometimes he wifh'd that *Mentor* had forc'd him away in fpite of himfelf from that Ifland; and fometimes he wifh'd that *Mentor's* Departure had rid him of a troublefome rigid Friend, who was ever reproaching him with his Weaknefs. His Soul was continually diftracted by various Thoughts; nor did he continue long in any one of them. His Heart was like the Sea, which is tofs'd by contrary Winds, that fport with its inconftant Waves. He often lay ftretch'd at full Length and motionlefs on the Sea-fhore; fometimes, in the Midft of fome gloomy Wood, he fhed a Flood of bitter Tears, and cry'd like a roaring Lion: He was grown lean; his hollow Eyes were full of a devouring Fire; and by his pale, downcaft Looks, and disfigur'd Face, one could never have thought he had been *Telemachus.* His Beauty, his Gaiety, and his noble Afpect, were fled from him; he was like a Flower, which being blown in the Morning, diffufes its Fragrancy around the Field, but fades infenfibly towards the Evening; its lively Colours decay, it languifhes, it withers,

and

and its fine Top droops, and bears down the feeble Stalk. Thus was the Son of *Ulyſſes* brought to the Gates of Death.

Mentor, perceiving that *Telemachus* was not able to refiſt the Violence of his Paſſion, bethought himſelf of a Stratagem to deliver him from ſo great a Danger. He took notice that *Calypſo* was deſperately in love with *Telemachus*, and that *Telemachus* was no leſs taken with the Charms of the young Nymph *Eucharis*; for cruel *Cupid*, to torment Mortals, makes them ſeldom love the Perſon by whom they are belov'd. Now, upon a Day, when *Telemachus* was to go out a hunting with *Eucharis*, *Mentor*, in order to raiſe *Calypſo*'s Jealouſy, ſpoke to her in theſe Words: I find in *Telemachus* an eager Love for Hunting, which I never perceiv'd in him before; this Recreation makes him ſlight all other Pleaſures; he only delights in Foreſts and wild Mountains: Is it you, O Goddeſs, who have inſpir'd him with this ſtrong Paſſion?

Calypſo was touch'd with cruel Vexation at theſe Words, and was not able to contain herſelf. This *Telemachus*, anſwer'd ſhe, who deſpis'd all the Pleaſures of the Iſle of *Cyprus*, cannot refiſt the faint Charms of one of my Nymphs. How dares he to boaſt of ſo many wonderful Actions, whoſe Heart is ſo ſhamefully ſoftened by effeminate Pleaſures, and who ſeems to be born only to lead an obſcure, inglorious Life among Women? *Mentor*, not a little pleas'd to find that Jealouſy began to diſturb the Heart of *Calypſo*, ſaid no more at that Time for fear ſhe ſhould diſtruſt him; he only expreſs'd his Concern by his ſad and down-caſt Looks. The Goddeſs diſcover'd to him her Uneaſineſs at all thoſe Things ſhe had obſerv'd, and renew'd her

Com-

Complaints every Day : This Hunting-match, of which *Mentor* gave her notice, rais'd her Fury to the Heighth ; she was told, that *Telemachus* had no other Defign in his Sports, than to withraw from the other Nymphs, in order to converfe with *Eucharis* alone. There was alfo a Talk of a fecond Hunting-match, wherein she forefaw he would behave as he had done in the firft. But to break *Telemachus*'s Meafures, she declar'd, that she defign'd to make one amongft them; and then on a fudden, being no more able to contain her Paffion, she fpoke to him in thefe Words :

Is it for this, rafh young Mortal ! that thou art come into my Ifland, efcaping the juft Wreck which *Neptune* prepar'd for thee, and the Vengeance of the Gods ? Didft thou come into this Ifland, which no mortal ever dares to approach, only to defpife my Power, and the Love I have exprefs'd for thee ? O ! all ye powerful Deities of Heaven and Hell, hear the Complaints of an unfortunate Goddefs ! Haften to confound and deftroy this perfidious, this ungrateful, this impious Man ! Since thou art ftill more cruel and unjuft than thy Father, may thy Sufferings be more cruel and lafting than his ; may'ft thou never fee thy Country again, that poor and wretched *Ithaca*, which thou haft not blufh'd bafely to prefer to Immortality ; or rather, may'ft thou be deftroy'd in fight of it, in the middle of the Sea ; and may thy Body become the Sport of the Waves, and be caft on this fandy Shore, without any Hopes of Burial ; may my Eyes fee it devour'd by ravenous Vultures ; may fhe whom you love, fee it alfo ; yes, fhe fhall fee it ; that Sight fhall break her Heart ; and her Defpair fhall be my Blifs and Delight.

Whilft

Whilft *Calypfo* was thus fpeaking, her Eyes glow'd and fparkled with Fire; her wild, diftracted Looks were ever unfteady; they had fomething gloomy and favage in them; her trembling Cheeks were full of livid Spots; her Colour chang'd every Moment; her Face was often over-fpread with a deadly Palenefs; her Tears did not flow fo plentifully as before; their Springs being in a great meafure dry'd up by Rage and Defpair, fo that fcarcely any bedew'd her Cheeks; her Voice was hoarfe, trembling, and broken. *Mentor* obferv'd the different Motions of her Paffion, and fpoke no more to *Telemachus*; he us'd him as we do a Man defperately ill, and given over by the Phyficians; yet would often look upon him with compaffionate Eyes.

Telemachus was fenfible how guilty he was, and unworthy of *Mentor's* Friendfhip; he durft not lift up his Eyes, for fear they fhould meet thofe of his Friend, whofe very Silence condemn'd him. Sometimes he had a mind to embrace him, and confefs to him how deeply he was concern'd for his Fault; but ftill he was withheld, fometimes by a miftaken Shame, fometimes by a Fear of doing more than he intended, to avoid a Danger which feem'd fo pleafing to him; for he could not yet refolve within himfelf to conquer his foolifh Paffion.

The Gods and Goddeffes of bright *Olympus*, were now met together, and with profound Silence kept their Eyes fixed on *Calypfo's* Ifland, impatient to know who would be victorious, *Minerva* or *Cupid*. The God of Love, by his fporting and playing with the Nymphs, had fet all the Ifland on Fire; and *Minerva*, under the fhape of *Mentor*, employ'd Jealoufy, the infeparable Companion of Love, againft Love himfelf. *Jupiter* refolv'd to be only a Spectator of this Conteft, and to ftand neuter. In the mean time, *Eucharis*, who

who was afraid to lose *Temelachus*, used a thousand
Arts to keep him in her Chains. And now she was
just ready to go out a second time a hunting with him;
her Dress was exactly like that of of *Diana*; *Venus*
and *Cupid* had supply'd her with new Charms, infomuch, that her Beauty then eclipsed even that of the
Goddess *Calypso* herself. *Calypso*, seeing her afar off,
presently turn'd her Eyes down to view herself in
one of her clearest Fountains; and, being asham'd
of her own Face, she ran to hide herself in the
remotest Part of her Grotto, and talked thus to
herself:

In vain then have I endeavour'd to disturb the
Joys of these two Lovers, by declaring that I design'd to be one of the Hunters. Shall I go with
them? Shall I be the Occasion of her Triumph?
And shall my Beauty serve only for a Foil to her's?
Shall *Telemachus* at the Sight of my Charms be still
more transported with those of *Eucharis?*   Oh!
wretched me! what have I done? No, I will not
go; neither shall they themselves go; I know well
enough how to prevent them. I'll go to *Mentor.*
I'll desire him to carry away *Telemachus* from this
Island, and convey him to *Ithaca*, But what do I
say? And what must become of forlorn me, when
Telemachus is gone? Where am I? O cruel *Venus!*
what shall I do? O *Venus!* you have deceiv'd me!
What a treacherous Present you gave me! Pernicious Boy! Infectious Love! I gave thee free Entrance into my Heart, only with the Hope of living
happy with *Telemachus*, and thou hast brought into
that Heart nothing but Trouble and Despair. My
Nymphs have rebell'd against me; and my Divinity
serves only to make my Miseries eternal. Oh! that I
could destroy myself, to end my Sorrows! But, O!
                                        Telemachus!

Telemachus! since I cannot die, thou muſt. I will be reveng'd on thy Ingratitude. Thy Nymph ſhall be Eye-witneſs of it; I will ſtrike thee to the Heart, whilſt ſhe ſtands by. But, whither does my raving Paſſion hurry me? O unfortunate *Calypſo!* What meaneſt thou? Wilt thou deſtroy a guiltleſs Youth, whom thou thyſelf haſt plung'd into this Abyſs of Misfortunes! I myſelf have convey'd the fatal Brand into the chaſte Boſom of *Telemachus.* How innocent was he before! How virtuous! How averſe to Vice! reſolute againſt ſhameful Pleaſures! What made me poiſon his Heart?——He would have abandon'd me. ——Well! ſhall he not leave me now? Or ſhall he ſtay to deſpiſe me, and make my Rival bleſs'd?— No, no, I ſuffer nothing, but what I have juſtly deſerved. Go, dear *Telemachus,* go, croſs the Seas; leave *Calypſo* comfortleſs, whoſe Life is a Burden to her, and who cannot meet Death to eaſe her Torments; leave her, diſconſolate, covered with Shame, and full of Deſpair, together with thy proud *Eucharis.*

Thus ſhe ſpoke to herſelf in her Grotto; but ruſhing out on the ſudden, tranſported with impetuous Fury, Where are you, O *Mentor!* ſaid ſhe? Is it thus you ſupport *Telemachus* againſt the Aſſaults of Vice, to which he is juſt ready to yield? You ſleep, whilſt Love is broad awake to undo him. I cannot bear any longer with that ſhameful Indifference you ſhew. Will you always calmly look on, and ſee the Son of *Ulyſſes* diſgrace his Father, and neglect the great Things to which he is deſtin'd? Is it you or me, whom his Parents have entruſted with his Conduct? I endeavour to find Remedies to cure his diſtemper'd Heart, and will you ſtand idle and unconcern'd? There are in

the

the remoteſt Part of this Foreſt, tall Poplars, fit
for the Building of a Ship; there it was *Ulyſſes* built
that in which he ſailed away from this Iſland.
You will find in the ſame Place, a deep Cavern,
wherein are all manner of Inſtruments neceſſary to
cut out and join together all the different Parts of a
Ship.

She had ſcarce utter'd theſe Words, but ſhe re-
pented of them. *Mentor* did not loſe one Moment
of Time; he went down into that Cave, found the
Tools, fell'd the Poplars, and in one Day equipp'd
and fitted out a Ship for Sea; for *Minerva*'s Power
and Induſtry require but very little Time to bring the
greateſt Works to Perfection.

Calypſo, in the mean time, was under the moſt
horrible Agony of Mind. On the one Side, ſhe
was willing to ſee whether *Mentor*'s Work went forward; on the other, ſhe could not find in her heart
to leave the Hunting-match, where *Eucharis* would
have enjoy'd the Company of *Telemachus*, in full Liberty. Her Jealouſy never ſuffer'd her to loſe ſight of
thoſe two Lovers; but at the ſame time, ſhe endeavour'd to turn the Chace towards that Place where ſhe
knew *Mentor* was building the Ship; ſhe heard the
Strokes of the Hatchet, and Hammer; ſhe liſten'd;
and every Blow ſtruck her with Horror. But then,
in the ſame Moment, ſhe was afraid leſt the buſying
her Mind with *Mentor*, ſhould make her miſs ſome
Look or Wink from *Telemachus* to the young
Nymph.

In the mean time, *Eucharis* ſaid to *Telemachus*,
in a jeering Tone, Are not you afraid of being re-
proved by *Mentor*, for going out a hunting without
him? Oh! how you are to be pity'd for living under ſo rigorous a Maſter, whoſe ſevere Auſterity
nothing

nothing can mitigate ! He profeſſes himſelf an Enemy
to all manner of Pleaſure, and will not ſuffer you to
enjoy any ; he condemns, as a Crime, the moſt innocent Actions. You might be ruled by him, indeed, when you was not able to govern yourſelf ;
but after you have ſhew'd ſo. much Wiſdom, you
ſhould no longer ſuffer yourſelf to be us'd as a
Child. Theſe crafty Words ſunk deep into *Telemachus's* Heart, and fill'd it with Indignation againſt
Mentor, whoſe Yoke he was willing to ſhake off.
He fear'd to ſee him again, and was ſo perplex'd,
that he return'd *Eucharis* no Anſwer. After they had
ſpent the Day in Hunting, and in perpetual Conſtraint ; at laſt, towards the Evening, they return'd
home through that Part of the Foreſt, near which
Mentor had been working all Day. *Calypſo* ſaw
afar off the Ship compleatly built, and at that Sight
her Eyes were overſpread with a thick Cloud, like
that of gloomy Death. Her trembling Knees gave
way, and ſunk beneath her Body: A cold, damp
Sweat ſeiz'd all her Limbs : She was forc'd to lean on
the Nymphs that ſtood about her ; and, as *Eucharis*
reach'd her Hand to ſupport her, ſhe put it back with
a dreadful Frown.

Telemachus, who ſaw the Ship, but did not ſee
Mentor, who was already gone home, having juſt
finiſh'd his Work, aſk'd the Goddeſs, who it
was that own'd that Ship, and for what Uſe it
was deſign'd ? She was at firſt puzzled for an
Anſwer ; but, a-while after, ſhe ſaid, I caus'd it to
be built to ſend away *Mentor* ; you'll not be troubled any longer with that ſevere Friend, who
thwarts your Happineſs, and would grow jealous of
you, if you ſhould become immortal. *Mentor* for-
ſake me ! I am undone ! cry'd *Telemachus*. O *Eucharis*,

charis, if *Mentor* abandons me, I have no Friend
left but you. Having let thefe Words fall in the
Tranfport of his Paffion, he faw prefently how
much his Rafhnefs was to blame ; but he was not
at liberty enough to think on their Meaning at
firft. All the Company was filent, and full of Sur-
prife. *Eucharis* blufh'd, and caft her Eyes down ;
fhe ftaid behind the reft fpeechlefs, not daring to
fhew herfelf : Yet, whilft her Face was overfpread
with Trouble and Confufion, fhe felt a fecret Joy
in her Heart. As for *Telemachus*, he could not underftand himfelf, nor think he had fpoke fo indif-
creetly ; what he had done feem'd to him as a Dream,
but fuch a Dream as fill'd him with Perplexity and
Uneafinefs.

Calypfo, more fierce and wild than a Lionefs that
has her Whelps taken from her, ran up and down
the Foreft, without knowing whither fhe was going. At laft, fhe found herfelf at the Entrance
of her Grotto, where *Mentor* expected her. Go
out of my Ifland, faid fhe, you Strangers, who
came hither to trouble my Repofe : Away with
that young Fool : And you, old Dotard, fhall feel
the Power of an enrag'd Goddefs, unlefs you carry
him away this very Moment. 1 will fee him no
more ; nor fhall any of my Nymphs fpeak to him,
or fo much as look upon him. I fwear it by the
Stygian Lake ; an Oath which makes the Gods
themfelves tremble. But know, *Telemachus !* that
thy Misfortunes are not at an end : No, ungrateful
Wretch, if *I* turn thee out of my Ifland, 'tis only
that thou may'ft become a Prey to new Difafters.
I fhall be reveng'd ; thou fhalt repent the Lofs of
Calypfo, but all in vain ; *Neptune*, ftill angry at
thy Father who offended him in *Sicily*, and follicited

4   by

by *Venus*, whom thou did'ft defpife in the Ifle of *Cyprus*, prepares new Storms for thee. Thou fhalt fee thy Father, who is ftill alive; but thou fhalt fee him without knowing him. Thou fhalt not fee him at *Ithaca*, until thou haft been the Sport of moft cruel Fortune. Depart ————— I conjure the celeftial Powers to revenge me! May'ft thou, in the Middle of the raging Sea, hang thunder-ftruck on the fharp Point of a Rock, invoking in vain *Calypfo*, whom thy juft Punifhment will fill with Joy.

Having fpoke thefe Words, her troubled and perplexed Mind was ready to recall what fhe had faid, and put her upon Refolutions quite oppofite to the former. Love reviv'd in her Heart the fond Defire of ftaying *Telemachus:* Let him live, faid fhe to herfelf; let him ftay here; perhaps he may at laft be fenfible how much I have done for him. *Eucharis* cannot beftow Immortality upon him as I can. Oh! too blind *Calypfo*, thou haft betray'd thyfelf by thy hafty Oath; thou ftandeft now' en-gag'd, and the *Stygian* Waves, by which thou haft fworn, leave thee no manner of Hope. Thefe Words were heard by no-body; but one might fee the Picture of a Fury in her ghaftly Face, and all the peftilential Venom of black *Cocytus* feem'd to reek out of her Heart.

Telemachus was feiz'd with Horror: She perceiv'd it; for, what can be hid from jealous Love? *Tele-machus*'s Diforder redoubled the Tranfports of the Goddefs. Like a furious Prieftefs of *Bacchus*, who fills the Air with frightful Roarings, and makes the *Thracian* Mountains refound with her Shrieks: Thus *Calypfo* roves about the Woods with a Dart in her Hand, calling all her Nymphs, aad threatning to pierce

I   any

any one that shall refuse to follow her. Frightned by these Threats, they all crowd after her; even *Eucharis* advances with Tears in her Eyes, keeping her Looks fix'd at a Distance upon *Telemachus*, but not daring to speak to him any more. The Goddess shivered when she saw her near her, and far from relenting upon that Nymph's Submission, she felt a new Fury when she perceiv'd, that even Grief and Affliction served to heighten the Beauty of *Eucharis*.

In the mean time, *Telemachus* continued alone with *Mentor :* He grasps his Knees, not daring either to embrace him, or look upon him; he shed a Flood of Tears; he offers to speak, but his Voice fails him; Words fail him yet more; he knows neither what he is doing, nor what he ought to do, nor what he would do. At last, he cries out, Oh my true Father! Oh *Mentor !* deliver me from my Miseries! I cannot leave you, neither can I follow you, Oh! deliver me out of all these Troubles; rid me of myself; and give me present Death.

Mentor embraces him, comforts him, encourages him, teaches him how to support himself, without indulging his fond Passion, and says to him, O! Son of the wise *Ulysses*, whom the Gods have loved so much, and whom they love still, 'tis that very Love that makes them expose you to such terrible Miseries. Whoever is unacquainted with his own Weakness, and the Violence of his Passions, cannot be called wise; for he is still a Stranger to his own Heart, and has not learned to distrust himself. The Gods have conducted you, as it were, by the Hand, to the very Brink of a Precipice, to let you see the immense Depth of it, without suffering you to fall into it; therefore, conceive now what you
cou

could never have comprehended, unlefs you had experienc'd it yourfelf. You would in vain have been told of the Treacheries of Love, who flatters in order to deftroy ; and who, under an outward Sweetnefs, conceals the moft dreadful and unplea-fant Bitternefs. That lovely Boy, all over Charms, is come hither, attended by the Sports, the Smiles, and the Graces ; you have feen him, he has robbed you of your Heart, and yourfelf were pleafed with this Robbery. You laboured to find Pretences to conceal from yourfelf the feftering Wound of your Heart ; you endeavoured to deceive me and yourfelf ; you feared nothing ; fee now the Effect of your Rafhnefs : You now call upon Death as the only Remedy of your Ills. The diftemper'd Goddefs is like one of the infernal Furies ; *Eucharis* is confum'd by a Fire, a thoufand times more cruel than all the racking Pangs of Death ; all thofe jealous Nymphs are ready to tear one another to Pieces ; and lo ! this is the Work of that Traytor, Love, for all he appears fo gentle and inoffenfive. Summon all your Courage to your Affiftance. O how highly are you belov'd by the Gods, fince they furnifh you with fo fair an Opportunity to fly from Love, and to return to your dear native Country. *Calypfo* herfelf is forced to fend you away ; the Ship is quite ready ; why do we delay to quit an Ifland where Virtue cannot dwell ?

As he fpoke thefe laft Words, *Mentor* took him by the Hand, and pull'd him along toward the Sea-fhore. *Telemachus* follow'd him unwillingly, ftill looking behind him. He kept his Eyes fixed upon *Eucharis,* who went away from him ; and though he could not fee her Face, yet he view'd with Admi-ration her fine Hair, ty'd behind, her loofe Gar-

ments

ments playing with the Wind, and her noble Gait.
He would gladly have kiffed the very Ground on
which fhe went; and, even when he loft fight of
her, he ftill liften'd, thinking that he heard her Voice.
Tho' abfent, he faw her ftill; her living Picture was
prefent to his Eyes; he even imagined he fpoke to
her, not knowing where he was, nor heeding what
Mentor faid to him.

At laft, when he began to recover, as if waked
out of a profound Sleep, he faid to *Mentor*, I am
refolv'd to follow you, but I have not yet taken my
Leave of *Eucharis*. I had rather die, than thus un-
gratefully to forfake her: Stay, I befeech you, till I
have feen her once more, and bidden her an eternal
Farewel; at leaft, fuffer me to fay to her, Oh
Nymph! the cruel Gods, the Gods jealous of my
Happinefs, force me away from you, but they may
fooner put a Period to my Life, than ever blot you out
of my Memory. Oh Father! either grant me this
laft and juft Confolation, or tear away my Life from
me this Moment. No, I will neither ftay in this
Ifland, nor abandon myfelf to Love; I have no fuch
Paffion in my Breaft, I only feel the Impulfe of Friendfhip and Gratitude for *Eucharis :* I only defire to bid.
her once more adieu, and then I'll follow you without
delay.

How much I pity you! anfwer'd *Mentor*; your
Paffion is fo fierce and violent, that you are not
fenfible of it. You think you are calm and com-
pos'd, and yet you call upon Death; you boaft
that you are not conquer'd by *Cupid*, and yet you
cannot leave the Nymph you love; you fee and
hear nothing but her, and are blind and deaf to
every thing elfe. You are like a Man, who, being
delirious through a violent Fever, cries he is not
fick.

fick. Oh blind *Telemachus!* you were ready to renounce your Mother *Penelope,* who expects you;
Ulyſſes, whom you ſhall ſee again; *Ithaca,* where
you ſhall be a King; and finally, thoſe great Honours, and that high Fortune, which the Gods
have promiſed you by thoſe many Wonders they
have done in your favour: All theſe Advantages
you were going to renounce, to lead an inglorious
Life with *Eucharis.* Will you ſtill pretend, that it
is not Love that binds you to her? What is it then
that diſcompoſes you? What makes you be willing
to die? Why did you ſpeak with ſo much Tran-
ſport before the Goddeſs? I do not charge you with
Diſſimulation, but I lament your Blindneſs. Fly,
oh *Telemachus!* fly; for Love is not to be conquer'd, but by Flight: With ſuch an Enemy, true
Courage conſiſts in fearing and in flying, without any Deliberation, or ſo much as looking behind
one. You have not forgot what Care I have taken
of you from your Infancy, and what Dangers you
have eſcaped by my Counſels; either be ruled by
me, or ſuffer me to leave you. Oh! if you knew
how much I grieve to ſee you thus ruſh on your
own Ruin, and how much I have ſuffer'd during
the time that I durſt not ſpeak to you! the Pangs
your Mother felt when ſhe brought you forth, were
nothing in compariſon of mine. I held my Tongue;
I fed upon my own Grief, and ſtifled my Sighs, to ſee
whether you would return to me again. O my Son,
my dear Son, eaſe my oppreſs'd Heart; reſtore to
me what I hold dearer than my own Bowels; reſtore to me my loſt *Telemachus!* reſtore yourſelf to
yourſelf. If Wiſdom can prevail over Love in
your Breaſt, I ſhall then live and be happy: But if

Love

Love hurries you away in defpite of Wifdom, *Mentor* can no longer live.

Whilft *Mentor* was thus fpeaking, he went on his Way towards the Sea; and *Telemachus*, who was not confirm'd enough in his new Refolution to follow him of his own Accord, was yet willing to fuffer himfelf to be led away without Refiftance. *Minerva*, who ftill conceal'd herfelf under the Shape of *Mentor*, covering *Telemachus* with her invincible Shield, and fpreading round him Beams of divine Light, made him feel a refolute Courage, the like of which he had not experienced during his Abode in that Ifland. At laft they arriv'd at a very fteep Rock on the Seafhore, which was continually buffetted by the foaming Waves. From this Height they look'd to fee whether the Ship *Mentor* had built was in the fame Place, but beheld a difmal Spectacle.

Cupid was highly incenfed, not only at the unknown old Man's Infenfibility, but alfo at his robbing him of *Telemachus*; his Vexation wrung Tears from him, and made him run to *Calypfo*, who wander'd up and down the gloomy Forefts. She could not behold him without groaning, and felt her wounded Heart bleeding afrefh. *Cupid* thus accofts her: You are a Goddefs, and yet you fuffer yourfelf to be conquer'd by a feeble Mortal, who is a Prifoner in your Ifland! Why do you let him go? Oh unlucky Boy, anfwer'd fhe, I will no more give ear to thy deftructive Counfels; it is thou haft broken my foft and profound Tranquillity, and caft me into a bottomlefs Abyfs of Mifery. It is now paft recall; fince I have fworn by the *Stygian* Flood to let *Telemachus* go. *Jove* himfelf, Almighty *Jove*, the Father of the Gods, dares not to break that
dreadful

dreadful Oath. But as *Telemachus* goes out of my
Ifland, go thou away too, pernicious Boy, for thou
haft done me more Mifchief than he.

Cupid, having wip'd away his Tears, with a
fcornful, malicious Smile, faid, Truly, this is a
might Bufinefs to be puzzled at! leave all to my
Management ; keep your Oath, and do not oppofe
Telemachus's Departure. Neither your Nymphs nor
I have fworn by the *Stygian* Flood to let him go. I
will infpire them with the Defign of burning that
Ship which *Mentor* hath built fo expeditioufly. His
Diligence, which fill'd you with Wonder, will be
altogether vain ; he fhall have Reafon to wonder
himfelf in his Turn, and fhall have no Means left to
take away *Telemachus* from you.

This flattering Speech convey'd pleafing Hopes
and Joys into the very Bottom of *Calypfo*'s Heart,
and allay'd the wild Fury and Defpair of the Goddefs ; juft as a cooling Breeze, which blows on the
graffy Margin of a purling Stream, refrefhes the
languifhing Flocks, fcorch'd by the Summer's fultry
Heat. Her Afpect became clear and ferene ; the
Fiercenefs of her Eyes was foftened ; thofe black
Thoughts, and carking Cares, which prey'd upon
her Heart, fled from her for a Moment; fhe ftopt,
fhe fmil'd, fhe carefs'd the wanton *Cupid*, and, by
careffing him, prepar'd new Torments for herfelf.

Cupid, well pleas'd with having perfuaded *Calypfo*,
flew inftantly in order to perfuade the Nymphs,
who were wandering and difpers'd up and down the
Mountains, like a Flock of Sheep, which the Rage
of ravenous Wolves hath frighted away from their
Shepherd. *Cupid* gathers them together, and tells
them, *Telemachus* is ftill in your Hands ; hafte, and
let devouring Flames confume the Ship which the rafh

I 4

Men-

Mentor has built to favour his Efcape. Immediately they light Torches, run towards the Sea-fhore, and they tremble, fill the Air with dreadful Howlings, tofs about their difhevel'd Hair, like frantic *Baccha-nals*. And now the greedy Flames devour the Ship, which burns the more fiercely, as fhe is made of dry Wood, daub'd over with Rofin; and rolling Clouds of Smoke, ftreak'd with Flame, afcend the Skies.

Telemachus and *Mentor* beheld this Conflagration from the Top of the Rock; and as *Telemachus* heard the Shoutings of the Nymphs, he was almoft tempted to rejoice at it, for his wounded Heart was not yet cured; and *Mentor* perceiv'd that his Paffion was like a Fire not quite extinguifh'd, which breaks out by Fits, from beneath the Afhes that cover it, and cafts forth bright Sparks. Now, faid *Telemachus*, muft I return to my former Engagements, fince we have no Hopes left of quitting this Ifland.

Mentor plainly perceiv'd, that *Telemachus* was going to relapfe into all his Follies, and that he had not one Moment to lofe. He efpy'd afar off, in the main Sea, a Ship that ftood ftill, not daring to approach the Shore, for all Pilots knew that the Ifle of *Calypfo* was inacceffible to Mortals. At that very inftant, the wife *Mentor* pufhing *Telemachus*, who fat on the Edge of the Rock, caft him down into the Sea, and threw himfelf after him. *Telemachus*, amaz'd and ftunn'd by his violent Fall, drank large Draughts of briny Water, and was for a while tofs'd about by the Waves; but at laft coming to himfelf, and feeing *Mentor*, who reach'd him his Hand to help him to fwim, he thought of nothing but flying from the fatal Ifland.

The Nymphs, who expected to have kept them Prifoners, burft forth into the moft furious Exclama-tions,

tions, being enraged at the Difappointment in not being able to prevent their Flight. The difconfolate
Calypfo return'd to her Grotto, which fhe fill'd with
hideous Shrieks. *Cupid,* who faw his Triumph,
turn'd into a fhameful Defeat, fhook his Wings, and
through the yielding Air flew to the facred Grove of
Idalia, where his cruel Mother expected him. The
Son, ftill more cruel than the Mother, comforted
himfelf with laughing with her at all the Mifchief he
had done.

As *Telemachus* went farther off from the Ifland, he
felt, with fecret Pleafure, both his Courage and his
Love for Virtue reviving in his Heart. I am fenfible,
cry'd he to *Mentor,* of what you told me, and which
I could not believe for want of Experience : There's
no way to conquer Vice, but by flying from it. Oh
Father ! how kind were the Gods to me, when they
gave me your Affiftance ! I deferve to be depriv'd of
it, and to be left alone to myfelf. I fear now, neither
Sea, nor Winds nor Storms ; I am only afraid of my
own Paffions ; Love alone is more dangerous than a
thoufand Wrecks.

The *END of the* SEVENTH BOOK.

THE

THE
ADVENTURES
OF
TELEMACHUS.

BOOK VIII.

The ARGUMENT.

Adoam, *Brother to* Narbal, *proves to be the Commander of the* Tyrian *Ship, where* Mentor *and* Telemachus *are kindly receiv'd: That Captain knowing* Telemachus *again, related to him the Tragical Death of* Pygmalion *and* Aftarbe, *and the Advancement of* Baleazar, *whom the Tyrant his Father had difgrac'd at the Inftigation of that lewd Woman. During a Repaft made for* Telemachus *and* Mentor, *Achitoas, by the Melody of his Voice and Harp, draws the* Tri-

Book VIII

Tritons, Nereids, and other Sea-Deities around the Ship. Mentor taking a Lute into his Hand, strikes it much finer than Achitoas. Adoam afterwards relates the Wonders of Bœtica, and describes the mild Temperature of the Air, and the other Beauties of that Country, whose Inhabitants lead a peaceable Life with great Simplicity of Manners.

HE Ship that stood still, and towards which they swam, was a *Phenician* Vessel bound to *Epirus.* Those who were aboard her, had seen *Telemachus,* in his Voyage to *Egypt,* but but could not know him again in the Midst of the Waves. As soon as *Mentor* came within hearing, he raised his Head above the Water, and with a strong Voice cry'd to them, O *Phenicians!* you, who are ever ready to afford Succour to all Nations, do not refuse to give Life to two Men, who expect it from your Humanity. If you have any Respect for the Gods, receive us into your Ship; we will go along with you where-ever you go. The Commander of the Ship answer'd, We will receive you with Joy, for we are not ignorant how we ought to relieve Strangers in your unfortunate Condition. So they instantly took them up into the Ship.

They were scarce got into her, but their Breath being quite spent, they sunk motionless; for they had swam a long while, and struggled hard with the fierce Waves. By degrees they recovered their Spirits; they had other Cloaths given them, for their own were soak'd thro' by the briny Water, which ran down on every side. As soon as they were able to speak all the *Phenicians* crowded eagerly about them, desiring to know their Adventures. The Com-

Commander afk'd them, How could you enter the
Ifland from whence you came? It is faid to be poffefs'd by a cruel Goddefs, who never fuffers any Mortal to land there; befides it is encompaffed with
frightful Rocks, againft which the Sea rages in vain,
and cannot be approach'd without fuffering Shipwreck.

Mentor anfwer'd, We were drove upon that
Coaft by a Storm; we are *Grecians*; the Ifle of
Ithaca, which lies near *Epirus* (whither you are
bound) is our Country. If you are unwilling to
touch at *Ithaca*, which is in your Way, we are
contented to be carried into *Epirus*, where we fhall
find Friends who will take care to furnifh us with
all Neceffaries for our fhort Paffage from thence to
Ithaca; and we fhall for ever be oblig'd to you for
the Happinefs of feeing again what we hold moft
dear in the World.

All this while *Telemachus* was filent, and let *Mentor* fpeak; for the Errors he had committed in the
Ifle of *Calypfo* had made him much wifer; he di-
ftrufted his own felf; he was fenfible how much he
continually wanted the prudent Counfels of *Mentor*; and, when he could not fpeak to him to afk his
Advice, he confulted his Eyes, and endeavoured to
guefs at his Thoughts.

The *Phenician* Mafter of the Ship, looking fted-
faftly upon *Telemachus*, fancied he had feen him fomewhere, but 'twas a confufed Remembrance, which
he knew not how to clear. Give me leave, faid he
to *Telemachus*, to afk you whether you remember you
have feen me before; for methinks I recollect my
having feen you elfewhere; I am no Stranger to
your Face; it made an Impreffion on me at firft
fight; tho' I cannot tell where I have feen you.
Perhaps your Memory will help out mine.

Tele-

Telemachus anfwer'd him, with Surprize blended with Joy; when firft I look'd upon you, I was as much puzzled about your Face as you are about mine, I'm fure I have feen you; I know you again, but cannot call to mind, whether 'twas in *Egypt* or at *Tyre*. Thereupon, the *Phenician*, like a Man who wakes in the Morning, and, who, by degrees, calls back the fugitive Dream that vanifhed away at his waking, cry'd out on a fudden, You are *Tele-lemachus*, whom *Narbal* took into his Friendfhip when we return'd from *Egypt:* I am his Brother of whom he has undoubtedly fpoken to you often. I left you with him, after the Expedition into *Egypt*. I was under a Neceffity of going to the fartheft Seas, into the famous *Bœtica*, near the Pillars of *Hercules*; fo that I did but juft fee you, and 'tis no wonder I was fo puzzled to know you again at firft fight.

I perceive, anfwer'd *Telemachus*, that you are *Adoam:* I had but a Glimpfe of you at that time, but I knew you again by the Difcourfe I had with *Narbal*. Oh! how am I fill'd with Joy to hear News of a Man who fhall ever be fo very dear to me! Is he ftill at *Tyre?* Is he expos'd to the bar-barous Treatment of the fufpicious and barbarous *Pygmalion?* *Adoam*, interrupting him, faid, Know, oh *Telemachus!* that Fortune has entrufted you with one who will take all the Care imaginable of you. I will carry you back to *Ithaca*, before I go to *Epirus*, and *Narbal's* Brother will love you no lefs than *Narbal* himfelf. Having thus fpoken, he took notice that the Wind, for which he waited, began to blow; whereupon he gave Orders for weighing Anchor, and unfurling of the Sails; which done, the Rowers ply'd their Oars amain, and cut

the

the yielding Flood.   After that he took *Telemachus*
and *Mentor* afide.

I am going, faid he, addreffing himfelf to *Telemachus*, to fatisfy your Curiofity: *Pygmalion* is no
more ; the juft Gods have rid the World of him;
as he trufted no Man, no Man could truft him:
The Good were contented to groan in Silence,
and fly his Cruelties, without endeavouring to do
him any Hurt ; the Wicked thought they had no
other way to fecure their Lives, than by putting a
Period to his.   There was not one *Tyrian* but who
was every Day expofed to fall a Sacrifice to his Diftruft.   His very Guards were more expofed than
any body elfe ; for his Life being in their Power,
he fear'd them more than all the reft of Mankind,
and, upon the leaft Sufpicion, he facrific'd them to
his Safety ; feeking Security thus violently, he could
no-where find it ; fince thofe who were the Truftees of his Life, being in continual Danger from his
Diftruftfulnefs, could not deliver themfelves from
fuch an horrible Situation, but by preventing
the Tyrant's cruel Jealoufies, and putting him to
Death.

The impious *Aftarbe*, whom you have fo often
heard mention'd, was the firft who refolv'd upon
the Death of the King.   She was paffionately in
love with a young *Tyrian*, *Joazar* by Name, a
Màn of great Wealth, whom fhe hoped to place on
the Throne.   The better to fucceed in her Defign,
fhe perfuaded the King, that the eldeft of his two
Sons, nam'd *Phadael*, impatient to wear the Crown,
had confpir'd againft his Life, and procur'd falfe
Witneffes to prove the Confpiracy, fo that the unhappy Father put to death his innocent Son.   The
fecond, named *Balcazar*, was fent to *Samos*, under
pretence

pretence of learning the Manners, Cuftoms, and
Sciences of *Greece*; but, indeed, becaufe *Aftarbe*
fuggefted to the King, that his Safety requir'd he
fhould be removed from Court, for fear he fhould
enter into Combinations with the Malecontents.
As foon as he had put to Sea, thofe who commanded
the Ship, being corrupted by that cruel Woman,
contrived it fo as to be fhipwreck'd in the Night;
and having caft the young Prince overboard, they
faved their Lives by fwimming to other Barks that
attended them.

In the mean time, *Pygmalion* was the only Perfon
that was unacquainted with *Aftarbe's* Amours; for
he fancied fhe would never love any Man but him;
and that diftruftful Prince was blinded by Love to
fuch a degree, that he repofed an entire Confidence
in that wicked Woman. At the fame time, his
extreme Avarice put him upon feeking Pretences
to make away with *Joazar*, whom *Aftarbe* loved
with fo much Paffion. All his Thoughts were
how to feize upon the vaft Riches of that young
Man

But while *Pygmalion* was thus a Prey to his
Diftruft, his Love, and his Avarice, *Aftarbe* thought
it convenient to put him to death with all Speed.
She was apprehenfive of his having difcover'd her
infamous Amours with this Youth; and befides,
fhe knew the King's covetous Temper was a fufficient Motive to put him upon exercifing his Cruelty
upon *Joazar*; and therefore fhe concluded fhe had
not one Moment to lofe to prevent him. She faw
the chief Officers of his Houfhold willing to imbrue their Hands in the King's Blood; fhe heard
every Day of fome new Confpiracy or other. but
fhe was afraid of trufting any body, left fhe fhould
be

be betray'd.   At laſt, ſhe thought it moſt ſafe to poi-ſon *Pygmalion*.

He uſed moſt commonly to eat in private with her; and dreſs'd all his Victuals with his own Hands, not daring to truſt any body elſe ; he locked him-ſelf up in the remoteſt Part of his Palace, the bet-ter to conceal his Diſtreſs, and that he might not be obſerv'd whilſt he was dreſſing his Victuals.   He depriv'd himſelf of all Dainties and Delicacies, be-ing afraid to taſte of any thing which he could not dreſs himſelf.   Thus, not only all manner of Meats dreſs'd by his Servants, but alſo Wine, Bread, Salt, Oil, Milk, and other ordinary Aliments, were no longer of any uſe to him.   He lived only upon Fruit, which he gathered with his own Hands in his Garden, or Pulſe and Roots, which he had ſow'd and cook'd himſelf.   Finally, his Drink was nothing but Water, which he drew out of a Foun-tain within his Palace, and of which he always kept the Key.   Although he ſeem'd to confide ſo entirely in *Aſtarbe*, yet he uſed all poſſible Precau-tions againſt her ; he always cauſed her to taſte of every thing that was ſerv'd at his Table, that he might not be poiſon'd without her, and that all Hopes of ſurviving him might be taken away from her.   But, to baffle this Precàution, ſhe took an Antidote, which an old Woman, ſtill more wicked than herſelf, and the Confidant of her Amours, furniſh'd her with : After which, ſhe poiſon'd the King without any Dread, in this Manner :

Juſt as they were going to ſit down to take their Repaſt, the old Woman, of whom I ſpoke before, came on a ſudden, and made a great Noiſe at one of the Doors : The King, who was ever in fear of being aſſaſſinated, ſtarts up in Diſorder, and runs to
that

that Door, to fee whether it was faſt enough : The old Woman makes off, the King remains full of dreadful Apprehenſions ; and though he knew not what to think of the Noiſe he had heard, yet he durſt not open the Door to be informed. *Aſtarbe* cheers him up, and with fond Careſſes perſuades him to eat : Now, whilſt the King was gone to the Door, ſhe had put Poiſon into his golden Cup, and ſo when he bid her drink firſt, according to his Cuſtom, ſhe obey'd without any Fear, truſting to the Antidote. *Pygmalion* drank alſo, and a little while after ſwoon'd away. *Aſtarbe*, who knew his cruel Temper, and that he would kill her upon the leaſt Suſpicion, begins to rend her Cloaths, tears off her Hair, and bemoans herſelf in a moſt hideous manner ; ſhe claſped and hugged the dying King in her Arms, and bathed him in a Flood of Tears ; for this cunning Woman had always Tears at command. At laſt, when ſhe perceiv'd that the King's Strength and Spirits were exhauſted, and that he was even in the Agonies of Death, for fear he ſhould recover and force her to die with him, ſhe gave over her endearing Fondneſs, and the tendereſt Marks of Love, and, having put on the moſt horrid Cruelty, ruſh'd upon him with Fury, and ſtifled him. Afterwards ſhe pluck'd the Royal Signet off his Finger, took the Diadem from his Head, and called in *Joazar*, to whom ſhe gave them both. She fancied that all thoſe who had been attach'd to her before, would not fail to countenance her Paſſion, and that her Lover would be proclaim'd King ; but thoſe who had been moſt forward in humouring her, were mean and mercenary Souls, and therefore incapable of a ſincere and conſtant Affection. Beſides, they wanted Courage and

and Refolution; and fear'd not only *Aftarbe*'s Enemies, but ftill more the Haughtinefs, Diffimulation, and Cruelty of that impious Woman; fo
that all wifh'd her Death to fecure their own Lives.
In the mean time, a dreadful Tumult fills the
whole Palace; The King is dead! The King is
dead! is the general Cry: Some are frighted, others
run to Arms; all feem apprehenfive of the Confe-
quences, but yet overjoy'd at the News; bufy
Fame carries it from Mouth to Mouth, throughout
the great City of *Tyre*; but not one Man is found
that laments the King. His Death is at once the
Deliverance, and the general Comfort of all his Subjects.

Narbal, deeply affected with fo terrible an Accident, deplor'd, like a good Man, *Pygmalion*'s Misfortune, who had betray'd himfelf by committing
his Safefty to the impious *Aftarbe*; and had chofen
to be an inhuman Tyrant, much rather than the
Father of his People, which is a Duty incumbent
on a King. He therefore confulted the Good of
the State, and haften'd to affemble all good and
public-fpirited Men to oppofe *Aftarbe*, under whom
they were like to fee a more cruel Government, than
that to which fhe had put a period.

Narbal knew, that *Baleazar* was not drown'd,
when he was thrown into the Sea; and thofe who
affur'd *Aftarbe* that he was dead, did it only upon a
mere Conjecture: But, by the Favour of the Night,
he fav'd himfelf by Swimming; and certain *Cretan*
Merchants, mov'd with Compaffion, receiv'd him
into their Bark. He durft not return into his Father's Kingdom, fufpecting with Reafon, that his
Shipwreck was contriv'd by his Enemies; and fearing no lefs the cruel Jealoufy of *Pygmalion*, than
the

the Artifices of *Aſtarbe.* He remain'd a long while wandering in Diſguiſe on the Sea-Coaſt of *Syria,* where the Merchants of *Crete* had left him : And, to get a Livelihood, he was reduc'd to the Condition of a Shepherd. At laſt he found means to let *Narbal* know what Condition he was in, for he could not but think his Secret and his Life ſafe with a Man of his untainted Virtue and Integriety. *Narbal,* though ill-us'd by the Father, had neverthelefs a Love for the Son, over whoſe Intereſts he conſtantly kept a watchful Eye ; but he took care of them only to hinder him from failing in his Duty to his Father, and he perſuaded him to bear patiently his evil Fortune.

Baleazer had writ to *Narbal,* that if he thought it ſafe to come to him to *Tyre,* he ſhould ſend him a Gold Ring, upon the Receipt of which, he would immediately come and join him. *Narbal* did not judge it convenient to invite *Baleazer* to come whilſt *Pygmalion* was alive, for by that means he would have brought both that Prince's Life, and his own, into certain Danger ; ſo difficult a thing it was to guard againſt *Pygmalion's* rigorous Inquiries. But, as ſoon as that wretched Prince had met with a Fate ſuitable to what his Crime deſerv'd, *Narbal* ſent the gold Ring to *Baleazer* with all ſpeed. Upon the Receipt of it, *Baleazer* came away immediately, and arriv'd at the Gates of *Tyre,* when all the City was in an Uproar about *Pygmalion's* Succeſſor. *Baleazar* was ſoon acknowledg'd by the chief Citizens of *Tyre,* and by the whole Populace. He was belov'd, not upon the Account of the late King his Father, who had the univerſal Hatred, but becauſe of his own Moderation, and Sweetneſs of Temper. Even his long Sufferings endued him

with

with a fort of Glory which heighten'd all his good Qualities, and foften'd the Hearts of all the *Tyrians* in his Favour.

Narbal aſſembled all the chief Men among the People, the old Men of the City-Council, and the Prieſts of the great Goddeſs of *Phenicia*. They ſaluted *Baleazer* as their King, and caus'd him to be proclaim'd by the Heralds. The People anſwer'd them with repeated Acclamations, which reach'd the Ears of *Aſtarbe*, in the remoteſt Part of the Pa-lace, where ſhe was lock'd in with her baſe and in-famous *Joazar*. All·thoſe wicked Men, whom ſhe had made uſe of during *Pymalion's* Life, had already forſaken her; for the Wicked do naturally hate and fear the Wicked, and never wiſh to ſee ſuch in Au-thority, becauſe they know what wrong Uſe they would make of their Power, and how tyrannically they would exert it. As for good Men, the Wicked think them better for their Turn, becauſe they hope at leaſt to find in them Indulgence and Moderation. *Aſtarbe* had no-body left about her, but ſome noto-rious Accomplices of her enormous Crimes, who were continually in fearful Expectation of their de-ſerved Puniſhment.

The Gates of the Palace being broke open, thoſe profligate Wretches durſt not make a long Reſiſtance, and only endeavour'd to run away. *Aſtarbe*, in the Habit of a Slave, would have made her Eſcape through the Crowd; but, being diſcover'd by a Sol-dier, ſhe was preſently ſecur'd, and it was with much ado that *Narbal* kept her from being torn to Pieces by the enrag'd Multitude, who began already to drag her along in the Dirt. In this Extremity ſhe deſir'd to ſpeak with *Baleazar*, hoping ſhe might dazzle him by her Charms, and excite an Expectation that ſhe

she would difcover fome important Secrets to him. *Baleazar* could not but admit her, to hear what she had to fay ; and at firft, befides her Beauty she difplay'd fuch Sweetnefs, and gentle Modefty, as would have melted the fierceft Anger. She flatter'd *Baleazar* with the moft delicate and moft infinuating Praifes ; she reprefented to him how much *Pygmalion* loved her ; she conjur'd him by his Father's Afhes, to take pity on her : She invok'd the Gods, as if she had paid a fincere Adoration to them ; she shed Floods of Tears ; she grafp'd the Knees of the new King ; but afterwards she ufed all poffible Arts to render his beft-affeéted Servants fufpeéted and odious to him. She accufed *Narbal* of having enter'd into a Confpiracy againft *Pygmalion*, and endeavouring to draw in the People to make himfelf King, in prejudice of *Baleazar :* She added, that he defign'd to poifon that young Prince. She forged the like Calumnies to afperfe all the reft of the *Tyrians*, who were addiéted to Virtue. She hop'd to have found the Heart of *Baleazar* fufceptible of the fame Diftruft and Sufpicion, which she had found in the King his Father : But *Baleazar* not being able to bear any longer with the black Malice of that wicked Woman, he interrupted her, and call'd for a Guard to fecure her. She was fent to Prifon ; and the wifeft among the ancient Men were commiffion'd to examine into all her Actions.

They difcover'd with Horror, that she had poifon'd and ftified *Pygmalion* ; and the whole Courfe of her Life appear'd to be a continued Series of monftrous Crimes. They were ready to fentence her to fuffer the Punifhment which is infliéted on the greateft Criminals in *Phenicia*, that is, to be burnt alive by a lingering Fire ; but, when she found she had no

manner

manner of Hopes left, she became fierce and mad
like a Fury come from Hell, and swallow'd down
a Poison which she us'd to carry about her, with
design to make away with herself, in case they
should put her to lingering Torments. Those who
guarded her, took notice that she was in violent
Pain, and offer'd to give her Ease; but she would
never return them any Answer, only by Signs she let
them understand that she would receive no Relief.
They mention'd to her the just and avenging Gods,
whom she had provok'd; but instead of shewing
any Trouble or Sorrow, as her Crimes required,
she look'd up to Heaven with Scorn and Arrogance,
as it were to insult the Almighty Powers. The
Image of Rage and Impiety was impressed on her
agonizing Countenance; nor was there the least Remainder of that excellent Beauty which had been
the Destruction of so many Men; all her Graces
were blotted out; her Eyes, divested of their Lustre,
rolled about in their Orbits, with wild and savage
Looks; a convulsive Motion shook her Lips, and
kept her Mouth open hideously wide; all her Face,
shrivell'd and contracted, exhibited the most ghastly
Grimaces; a livid Paleness and a mortal Chilness
had seiz'd all her Limbs; sometimes she seem'd to
gather fresh Spirits, and come to herself again, but
it was only a faint Struggle of Nature, which spent
itself in hideous Howlings; at last she expir'd,
leaving all the Spectators full of Horror and Fear.
Without doubt, her impious Ghost went down into
those Places of Sorrow, where the cruel *Danaids*
do eternally draw Water in bored Vessels; where
Ixion perpetually turns his Wheel; where *Tantalus*,
parch'd with Thirst, can never catch the wanton
Water that flies his eager Lips; where *Sisyphus* vainly
rolls

rolls up to the Top of a Mountain, a Stone which tumbles down again continually; and where *Titius* will for ever feel a Vulture preying upon his growing Liver.

Baleazar, being deliver'd from this Monster, return'd the Gods Thanks by immediate Sacrifices. His Conduct, at the Beginning of his Reign, was the Reverse of *Pygmalion's*; he applies himself to the reviving of Trade, which languish'd and decay'd more and more every Day; he confults with *Narbal* about the most important Affairs, and yet is not govern'd by him; for he will fee every thing with his own Eyes; he hears every-body's Opinion, and afterwards determines according to that which appears to him to be best. He is generally beloved by his People, and, being Master of their Hearts, he enjoys more Riches than ever his Father heaped up with his infatiable and cruel Avarice; for there is not a Family, but what would part with all they have, if he happen'd to be reduc'd to a pressing Necessity. Thus, what he suffers them to enjoy is more at his command, than if he should forcibly take it from them. He needs not ufe any Precaution, or to be follicitous to fecure his Life; for he has always the fafest Guards about him, which is the Love of all his Subjects; every one of them being afraid to lofe him, and therefore willing to hazard his own Life to preferve that of fo good a King. He lives happy with his People; and all his People live happy under him. He is tender of burdening his People; and they are afraid of giving him too fmall a Part of their Estates. He lets them live in Plenty, and yet this Plenty makes them neither refractory nor infolent; for they are laborious, addicted to Trade, and stedfaft in preferving the Purity of their ancient Laws.

3

Laws. *Phenicia* has now recover'd the utmoſt Height of her Greatneſs and Glory; and it is to her young King ſhe owes ſo much Proſperity. *Narbal* governs under him. O *Telemachus!* were he now to ſee you, with how much Joy would he load you with Preſents! What a Pleaſure would it be to him to ſend you back into your own Country in State and Magnificence! Am I not then very fortunate in doing what he could wiſh to do himſelf, in going to the Iſle of *Ithaca*, there to place on the Throne the Son of *Ulyſſes*, that he may reign there, as wiſely as *Baleazar* reigns at *Tyre?*

Adoam having thus ſpoken, *Telemachus*, charm'd with his Story, and much more with the Marks of Friendſhip he had received from that *Phenician* in his Misfortunes, embrac'd him with great Tenderneſs and Affection. Afterwards, *Adoam* aſk'd him, what extraordinary Adventure had brought him into the Iſland of *Calypſo!* *Telemachus*, in his Turn, gave him the Story of his Departure from *Tyre*, and his going over to the Iſle of *Cyprus:* He related to him, his meeting again with *Mentor*; their Voyage into *Crete*; the public Games for the Election of a new King after *Idomeneus*'s Flight; the Reſentment of *Venus*; their Shipwreck; the Pleaſure with which *Calypſo* received them; the Jealouſy of that Goddeſs againſt one of her Nymphs; and *Mentor*'s throwing his Friend into the Sea, as ſoon as he eſpy'd the *Phenician* Ship.

After theſe Diſcourſes, *Adoam* caus'd a magnificent Entertainment to be ſerv'd up; and the better to expreſs his exceſſive Joy, he procur'd all the Diverſions that could be had. Whilſt they were at Table, attended by young *Phenician* Boys, clad in white, with Garlands of Flowers on their Heads, the moſt exquiſite

4   Perfumes

Perfumes of the Eaſt were burnt.   All the Rowers
Seats   were   fill'd   with   Muſicians,   playing   on   the
Flute.   *Achitoas* now   and   then   interrupted   them,
by the ſweet Harmony of his Voice and his Lyre,
fit to entertain the Gods at their Revels, and even
to raviſh the Ears of *Apollo* himſelf.   The *Tritons,*
the *Nereids,* all the Deities who obey the Command
of *Neptune,* and the Sea-Monſters themſelves forſook
their deep watry Grottos, and came in Shoals round
the Ship, charm'd by this divine Melody.   A Company of young *Phenician* Boys, of excellent Beauty,
and clad in fine Lawn, whiter than the driven Snow,
danc'd for a long time ſeveral Dances of their own
Country ; afterwards they danc'd after the *Egyptian* Manner, and laſt of all after the *Grecian.*   At
proper Intervals the loud Trumpets made the Waves
reſound with their Clangor as far as the diſtant
Shore.   The Silence of the Night,   the Stilneſs of
the Sea, the trembling Light of the Moon, which
play'd on the Surface of the Waves, and the ſhaded
Azure of the Skies, ſtudded with glittering Stars,
ſerv'd to heighten the Nobleneſs and Majeſty of the
Scene.

Telemachus, being of a ſprightly Diſpoſition, and
very perceptive, reliſh'd all thoſe Pleaſures with Delight ; but he durſt not indulge himſelf too far in the
Enjoyment of them.   Ever ſince he had experienc'd,
with ſo much Shame, in *Calypſo's* Iſland, how ready
Youth is to be inflam'd, he was ſhy and afraid, even
of the moſt innocent Pleaſures, and ſuſpected every
thing.   He look'd upon *Mentor,* and conſulted his
Face and his Eyes, to know what he ought to think
of all theſe Pleaſures.

K   *Mentor*

Mentor was not a little pleas'd to see him in that Perplexity, but made as if he did not take notice of it. At laft, mov'd with *Telemachus*'s Moderation, he faid to him with a Smile, I perceive what you are afraid of, and cannot but commend your Fear; but, however, you muft not carry it too far. No Man can wifh you more earneftly than I the Enjoyment of Pleafure, provided it be fuch Pleafure as will not hurry you to Excefs, nor emafculate your Nature. You muft have Diverfions; but they fhould be fuch as recreate and delight you, not fuch as enflave you: I would recommend to you foft and gentle Diverfions, fuch as will never degrade the reafonable Soul, and transform you into a wild beaft. It is now very proper that you fhould refrefh yourfelf, after all your Trouble and Fatigues; relifh, with a grateful Complaifance to *Adoam*, all thofe Enjoyments he offers you. Rejoice, O *Telemachus*, and be merry. Wifdom is neither morofe, auftere, nor affected: It is fhe yields true Pleafures; fhe alone knows how to feafon and temper them, fo as to make them pure and lafting; fhe knows how to mix Mirth and Sports with the moft important and ferious Affairs. She prepares us for Pleafure by Labour, and refrefhes the Hardfhips of Labour by Pleafure. Wifdom is not afham'd to be gay, when it is needful.

Having fpoke thefe Words, *Mentor* took up a Harp, and touch'd it with fuch exquifite Art, that *Achitoas*, ftung with Jealoufy, let his drop out of his Hands; his Eyes flafh'd Fire; his troubled Countenance changed Colour; and every body would have taken notice of his Pain and Confufion, but that at the fame Moment *Mentor's* Harp ravifh'd the Souls of all that were prefent. No Man hardly durft

draw

draw Breath, for fear of breaking in upon the profound Silence; and fo lofing fomething of the divine Melody; all were ftill in Pain, left he fhould end it too foon. *Mentor*'s Voice had no effeminate Softnefs, but was flexible, ftrong, and movingly exprefs'd the minuteft Things.

He fung, at firft, the Praifes of mighty *Jove*, the Father and King of Gods and Men, who with a Nod fhakes the whole Univerfe: Afterwards, he reprefented *Minerva* coming out of his Head, that is, Wifdom, which that God moulds within himfelf, and which iffues from him, to inftruct thofe who are willing to be taught. *Mentor* fung all thefe Truths in fuch pathetic, and lofty Strains, and with fuch divine Devotion, that the whole Affembly thought themfelves tranfported to the very Top of *Olympus*, in the Prefence of *Jupiter*, whofe Looks are more piercing than his Thunder. Next to that. he fung the Misfortune of young *Narciffus*, who, being fondly enamour'd with his own Beauty, which he was continually viewing in a Fountain, confum'd himfelf with Grief, and was chang'd into a Flower that bears his Name. Laftly, he fung the fatal Death of fair *Adonis*, torn in pieces by a wild Boar, and whom *Venus*, tho' paffionately doating on him, could never bring to Life again, with all the bitter Complaints fhe put up to Heaven.

None of thofe who heard him were able to contain their Tears; and every one felt a fecret Pleafure in Weeping. When he had done finging, the *Phenicians* look'd upon one another full of Amazement. One faid, this is *Orpheus*; for thus with his Harp he us'd to tame the favage Beafts, and draw after him both Woods and Rocks; 'tis thus he enchanted *Cerberus*, fufpended for a while

the

the Torments of *Ixion*, and of the *Danaids*, and prevail'd with the inexorable *Pluto*, to confent to the Releafement of the fair *Eurydice*. Another cry'd, No, 'tis *Linus*, the Son of *Apollo* ; another anfwer'd, You are miftaken ; this muft be *Apollo* himfelf. *Telemachus*'s Surprize was little lefs than that of the reft ; for he never knew before, that *Mentor* could play on the Harp with fo much Maftery, and fing fo divinely. *Achitoas*, who had, by this Time, thrown a Cloak over his Jealoufy, began to give *Mentor* thofe Commendations he deferv'd ; but he could not praife him without blufhing, neither was he able to finifh his Difcourfe. *Mentor*, who faw his Confufion, began to interrupt him, and endeavour'd to comfort him by giving him all the Praifes he deferved. But *Achitoas* received no Confolation ; becaufe he perceiv'd that *Mentor* furpafs'd him yet more by his Modefty, than by the Charms of his Voice.

In the mean time, *Telemachus* faid to *Adoam*, I remember you fpoke to me of a Voyage you made into *Bœtica*, after we left *Egypt* ; and becaufe *Bœtica* is a Country, of which common Fame relates fo many incredible Wonders, vouchfafe to tell me whether all that is faid of it be true. I will gladly, reply'd *Adoam*, give you a Defcription of that famous Country, which deferves your Curiofity, and which far furpaffes whatever Fame proclaims about it ; whereupon he thus began :

The River *Bœtis* runs through a fruitful Land, blefs'd with a temperate, and ever ferene Sky. The Country has its Name from the River, which difcharges its Waters into the great Ocean, near the Pillars of *Hercules*, and not far from that Place where the furious Sea, breaking through its Banks, di-

divided heretofore the Land of *Tarſis* from *Great Africa.* This Country ſeems to have preſerv'd the Delights of the Golden Age. Here the Winters are mild, and the fierce Northern Winds never blow; the ſcorching Heat of the Summer is ever allay'd by refreſhing *Zephyrs*, which riſe towards Noon to cool the ſultry Air; ſo that the whole Year is but a happy Marriage of the Spring and Autumn, which ſeem ever to go hand in hand together. The Land, both in the Valleys and the Plains, yields every Year a double Harveſt; the Roads are hedg'd with Bay-Trees, Pomegranate-Trees, Jeſſamines and other Trees, ever green and ever in Bloſſom. The Hills are overſpread with numerous Flocks of Sheep, whoſe fine Wool is a choice Commodity among all the Nations of the World. There are a great many Mines of Gold and Silver in this beautiful Country; but its rude Inhabitants, contented and happy with their Plainneſs, diſdain to count Gold or Silver among their Riches, and only value what is really neceſſary to anſwer the Exigencies of human Nature.

When we firſt began to trade with that Nation, we found Gold and Silver employ'd among them about the ſame Uſes as Iron; as for Example, for Ploughſhares. As they had no foreign Trade, ſo they wanted no Coin. Moſt of them are either Shepherds or Huſbandmen: Artificers and Tradeſmen there are but few in this Country; for they only tolerate thoſe Arts which ſupply the Neceſſaries of Life; and beſides, though moſt of the Inhabitants either follow Agriculture, or the tending of Herds and Flocks, yet they are ſkill'd in thoſe Arts which are requiſite to the Support of their plain and frugal way of Living. The Women ſpin that ſilky Wool
I told

I told you of, and make of it extraordinary fine Stuffs of a marvellous Whitenefs; they bake the Bread, drefs the Victuals; and all thofe Labours are eafy to them, for in this Country their ordinary Food is Fruit and Milk, and very rarely Flefh; out of the Leather of their Sheep-fkins, they make thin Shoes for themfelves, their Hufbands, and their Children, they make Tents, fome of wax'd Skins, and others of Barks of Trees; they make and wafh all the Garments of the Family, and keep the Houfes in wonderful Order and Neatnefs. Their Cloaths are eafily made; for in this mild and happy Climate, they only wear a thin and light Piece of Stuff, neither cut nor few'd, and which, for Modefty's Sake, every one laps about his Body in long Folds, and in what Form he pleafes.

The Men, befides Hufbandry, and the tending of their Herds and Flocks, have no other Art to exercife, but the working and fafhioning of Wood and Iron; and even in thefe they feldom make any ufe of Iron, unlefs it be for Tools neceffary for Agriculture. All thofe Arts which refpect Architecture, are altogether ufelefs to them; for they never build Houfes. It argues, fay they, too great a Fondnefs · for the Earth, to build a Dwelling upon it, much more lafting than one's felf; it is fufficient to have a Shelter againft the Injuries of the Weather. As for all other Arts, fo much efteem'd among the *Grecians*, the *Egyptians*, and other civiliz'd Nations, they abhor and deteft them, as the Inventions of Vanity and Luxury.

When they hear of Nations that have the Art of erecting ftately Buildings, of making Gold and Silver Houfhold Goods, Stuffs adorn'd with Embroidery and precious Stones, exquifite Perfumes,

delicious

delicious and dainty Diſhes of Meat, and Inſtruments of Muſic, whoſe Harmony inchants the Soul, they anſwer in theſe Words : Thoſe Nations are very ui - happy, thus to beſtow ſo much Time, Labour, and Induſtry, upon the corrupting of themſelves. Thoſe Superfluities ſoften, intoxicate, and torment the Poſ- ſeſſors of them, and tempt thoſe that are depriv'd of them, to acquire them by Injuſtice and Violence. Can that Superfluity be call'd a Good, which ſerves only to make Men wicked ? Are the Men of thoſe Coun- tries more ſound, ſtrong, and robuſt than we ? Do they live longer ? Are they better united among them- ſelves ? Is their Life more free from Cares, more calm, and more chearful ? Nay, on the contrary, they muſt needs be jealous of one another, devour'd by ſhameful and gloomy Envy, ever diſquieted by Ambi- tion, Fear and Avarice ; and incapable of enjoying plain, unmix'd, and ſolid Pleaſures, ſince they are Slaves to ſo many imaginary Neceſſities, in which alone they place all their Felicity. Thus it is, con- tinu'd *Adoam*, that theſe wiſe men ſpeak, who owe all their Wiſdom to their diligent Study of ſimple Nature ; they have an Abhorrence for our Politeneſs, and it muſt be confeſs'd, that there is ſomething great in their amiable Simplicity : They live all together, with- out dividing their Lands ; every Family is govern'd by its Chief, who is real King of it. The Father of the Family has the Power to puniſh any of his Children, or Grand-children, that is guilty of an evil Action ; but before he inflicts the Puniſhment, he adviſes with the reſt of the Family. 'Tis rare indeed, that there is any Occaſion for Puniſhment ; for Innocence of Manners, Integrity, Obedience, and Abhorrence of Vice, dwell in this happy Place ; and one would think, *Aſtræa*, who is ſaid to have fled to Heaven, lies yet

K 4   con-

conceal'd here among thése People. There is no need
of Judges amongſt them, for their own Conſciences
judge them. All their Goods are in common; the
Fruits of the Trees, the Grain and Pulſe of the
Earth, the Milk of the Herds are ſo abounding, that
a People ſo ſober and moderate have no Occaſion to
divide them. Each Family, wandering up and down
in this happy Country, carry their Tents from one
Place to another, when they have eaten up the Paſtu-
rage, and conſum'd the Fruits of that Part where they
were ſeated before; ſo that having no private Intereſts
to maintain one againſt t'other, they all love one another with brotherly Love, which nothing can impair
or break in upon; tis the Contempt of vain Riches
and of deceitful Pleaſures, which confirms them in this
Peace, Union, and Liberty. They are all free, and
all equal.

There is no other Diſtinction among them, except
what is allow'd to the Experience of the ſage old Men,
or to the extraordinary Wiſdom of ſome young Men,
who being accompliſh'd in all Virtue, are equal to the
Elders. The cruel Outcries of Fraud, Violence, Per-
jury, Law ſuits, and Wars, are never heard in this
Country, cheriſh'd by the Gods. No human Blood
ever ſtain'd this Land; nay, even the Blood of Lambs
is ſeldom ſpilt in it. When theſe People hear of bloody
Battles, rapid Conqueſts, ſtate Revolutions, which are
frequent in other Nations, they ſtand perfectly amaz'd.
What, ſay they, are not Men ſubject enough to Mor-
tality, without inflicting on one another a violent and
haſty Death? Does Life, which is ſo ſhort, ſeem to
them too long? Are they ſent here upon Earth to tear
one another to pieces, and to make themſelves mutually miſerable?

Yet

Yet farther, thefe People of *Bætica* cannot conceive, why thofe Conquerors, who fubdue great Empires, fhould be fo much admir'd. What Madnefs is it, fay they, for a Man to place his Happinefs in governing others, which is fo painful an Office, if it be executed with Reafon, and according to Juftice? But what Pleafure can be taken in governing them againft their Confent? All that a wife Man can do, is to take upon him the governing of a docile People, whom the Gods have committed to his Care, or a People who entreat him to be their Father and Shepherd; but to govern Men againft their Will, is to make one's felf moft miferable, only to gain the falfe Honour of keeping them in Slavery. A Conqueror is a Man whom the Gods, being provoked at the Wickednefs of Men, have fent in their Wrath upon the Earth, to lay Kingdoms wafte, fpread every-where Terror, Mifery, and Defpair, and to make as many Slaves as there are Freemen. Is it not Glory enough for a Man, that thirfts after Fame, to rule thofe with Prudence whom the Gods have put under him? Does he think he cannot merit Praife, unlefs he becomes violent, unjuft, infulting, ufurping, and tyrannical over all his Neighbours? War fhould never be thought on, but for the Defence of Liberty. Happy he, who being a Slave to no Man, has not the mad Ambition of making another Man his Slave. Thofe mighty Conquerors, whom they reprefent to us with fo much Glory, are only like overflowing Rivers, which appear majeftic, but deftroy all the fertile Fields which they fhould only refrefh.

After *Adoam* had given this Defcription of *Bætica*, *Telemachus*, charm'd with his Relation, afk'd him feveral curious Queftions. Do thefe People, faid he, drink Wine? They are fo far from drinking it, reply'd *Adoam*, that they never care to make any; not

that

that they want Grapes, since no Country whatsoever produces more delicious; but they content themselves with eating Grapes, as they do other Fruits; and dread Wine as the Corrupter of Mankind. 'Tis a kind of Poison, say they, which raises Madness. It does not directly kill a Man, indeed, but it makes him a Beast. Men may preserve their Health and Strength without Wine; and with it they run the risk of losing their Health, and destroying their Morals.

Then, said *Telemachus*, I would fain know what Laws are observ'd relating to Marriages in this Nation. No Man, reply'd *Adoam*, can have more than one Wife, whom he must keep as long as she lives. The Honour of the Men in this Country depends as much on their Fidelity to their Wives, as the Honour of the Women depends, in other Countries, on their Fidelity to their Husbands. Never were People so honest, nor so inviolably chaste. The Women here are beautiful and agreeable, but plain, modest, and laborious. Marriage here is peaceful, fruitful, and spotless. The Husband and Wife seem to be but one Soul in two Bodies; they bear an equal Part in all domestic Cares; the Husband manages all the Concerns abroad, the Wife keeps close to her Housewifry at home; she comforts her Husband, and seems to be made only to help and pleasure him; she gains his Confidence, and contributes less by her Beauty, than her Virtue, to heighten the Charms of their Society, which endure as long as they live. Sobriety, Temperance, and Purity of Manners, make the Lives of these People not only long, but free from Diseases. Here are Men of an hundred, and of an hundred and twenty Years old, who are yet hearty and chearful.

One Thing more that I want to know, added *Telemachus*, is, how they avoid going to War with their Neighbours,

Neighbours.   Nature, said *Adoam*, has separated them
from other People, on one Side by the Sea, and on
the other Side by high Mountains towards the North.
Besides this, the neighbouring Nations bear them
great Respect, on account of their Virtue ; and when
they fall out among themselves, they frequently make
choice of these People to determine their Differences ;
and have often entrusted to them the Lands and Towns
that were in dispute among them.   As this Nation
never committed any Violence, no body distrusts them.
They laugh, when they hear of Kings who cannot
settle and adjust among themselves the Frontiers of
their Territories.   Is it possible, say they, for Men to
fear they shall ever want Land ?   There will ever be
more than they can cultivate : And, as long as there
shall remain free and waste Lands, we would not
so much as defend our own against such of our
Neighbours, as should strive to take them from us.
Pride, Arrogance, Treachery, and the Lust of Dominion, were never heard of among the Inhabitants of
Bætica ;   so that their Neighbours never have Occasion
to fear such a People, nor can they ever hope to make
such a People fear them, which is the Reason that
they never molest them.   These People would sooner
forsake their Country, or meet their Death, than sub-
mit themselves to Slavery.   Thus they are as difficult
to be enslav'd, as they are incapable of desiring to
enslave others :   Which causes so profound a Peace betwixt them and their Neighbours.

    Adoam ended this Discourse, with an Account of
the Manner of Traffic between the *Phenicians* and
those of *Bætica*.   These People, said he, were amaz'd
when they saw strange Men come from so far on the
Waves of the Sea.   They suffer'd us to lay the Foundation of a City in the Isle of *Gades*.   They even received

ceived us amongſt themſelves with great Kindneſs, and
gave us part of all they had, without taking any
Payment for it.   Moreover, they offer'd us all that
was left of their Wool, after they had ſufficiently
provided for their own Uſe, and indeed ſent us a rich
Preſent of it.   'Tis a Pleaſure to them to give their
Overplus liberally to Strangers.

As for their Mines, they gave them up to us without any manner of Uneaſineſs, becauſe they made no
Uſe of them ; they fancy'd Men were not over wiſe to
ſearch with ſo much Pains in the Bowels of the Earth,
for what could not make them happy, nor ſatisfy any
real Neceſſity.   Do not dig, ſaid they to us, ſo deep
into the Earth ; content yourſelves with ploughing
and tilling it, and it will afford you real Goods that
will nouriſh you ; you will reap Fruits from it that are
more valuable than Gold and Silver, ſince Men deſire
neither Gold nor Silver, but only to purchaſe Suſte-
nance for human Life.

We would often have taught them Navigation, and
have carry'd the young Men of their Country into *Pheni-*
cia ; but they would never conſent that their Children
ſhould learn to live after our manner.   They would
learn, ſaid they to us, to ſtand in need of thoſe Things
that are become neceſſary to you ; they would have
them ; and would forego Virtue to gain them by unjuſt
Methods.   They would grow, like a Man who has good
Legs, but having diſuſed walking, brings himſelf at laſt
to the ſad Neceſſity of being always carry'd, like a ſick
Man.   As for Navigation, they admire it indeed, as
an induſtrious Art ; but they believe it to be a pernicious Art.   If thoſe People, ſay they, have enough
to ſupport Life in their own Country, what do they
ſeek in another ?   Are they not contented with that
which ſuffices the Wants of Nature ?   They deſerve

to

to be fhipwreck'd for feeking Death in the midft of
Tempefts, to fatiate the Avarice of Merchants, and
gratify the Paffions of other Men.

Telemachus was ravifh'd at *Adoam's* Difcourfe ; he
was highly delighted to find, that there was yet a
People in the World, who, following the true Dictates
of Nature, were, at once, fo wife and fo happy. Oh !
how vaftly the Manners of thefe People differ from
the vain and ambitious Maxims of thofe who are accounted wifer ! We are fo vitiated, that we can
hardly think that fo natural a Simplicity can be real.
We look upon the Morals of thefe People only as a
fine Fable, and they ought to look upon ours as a
monftrous Dream.

The END *of the* EIGHTH BOOK.

THE

THE

ADVENTURES

OF

TELEMACHUS.

BOOK IX.

The ARGUMENT.

Venus, *still enrag'd against* Telemachus, *sues to* Jupiter *for his Destruction ; but the Destinies not permitting him to perish, that Goddess goes to* Neptune, *to concert means to drive him away from* Ithaca, *whither* Adoam *was conducting him. They employ, for that Purpose, a deceitful Deity, who imposes upon the Pilot* Athamas, *and makes him steer full sail into the Port of the* Salentines, *thinking he was arrived at* Ithaca. Idomeneus, *their King, receives* Telemachus *into his new City, where he was actually preparing a solemn Sacrifice to* Jupiter, *to obtain Success in a War against*

the

Book. IX.

the Mandurians. *The Prieſt, conſulting the Entrails of the Victims, gives him hopes of Succeſs, and intimates that he ſhall owe his Happineſs to his two new Gueſts. This unhappy King implores their Aid againſt his Enemies, and promiſes them all manner of Aſſiſtance.*

 HILST *Telemachus* and *Adoam* were thus diſcourſing together, neglectful of Sleep, and not perceiving that the Night was already half ſpent, a deceitful unfriendly Deity led them far wide of *Ithaca*, which their Pilot *Athamas* ſought for in vain. *Neptune*, though a Friend to the *Phenicians*, could no longer endure to think that *Telemachus* had eſcap'd the Storm that had daſh'd him againſt the Rocks of *Calypſo*'s Iſland. *Venus* was yet more incens'd, to ſee that young Man triumphing, after his Conqueſt over *Cupid* and all his Charms. In the Height of her Paſſion, ſhe quitted *Cythera*, *Paphos*, *Idalia*, and all the Honours which are paid to her in the Iſle of *Cyprus*; ſhe could no longer ſtay in thoſe Places where *Telemachus* had deſpis'd her Power; and thereupon ſhe flies to bright *Olympus*, where the Gods were aſſembl'd round the Throne of *Jove*. From this Place, they behold the Stars rolling beneath their Feet: They ſee the terreſtrial Globe, like a ſmall Clod of Clay; the vaſt Seas appear to them only like Drops of Water, with which this Clod is a little moiſten'd; the largeſt Kingdoms are in their Eyes but a little Sand covering the Surface of this Clod. The numberleſs Multitudes of People, the mighty Armies ſeem to them but as Ants, contending for a Tuft of Graſs upon this Clod. The
                                                                Immortals

Immortals laugh at the moſt weighty Affairs that agi-tate feeble Mortals, and their moſt important Concerns appear to them like the Play-games of Children. That which Men call Glory, Grandeur, Power, profound Policy, ſeem to theſe ſupreme Deities to be nothing but Miſery and Folly.

'Tis in this Abode, ſo much elevated above the Earth, that *Jupiter* has fix'd his immovable Throne: His Eyes pierce into the deepeſt Abyſs, and viſit even the moſt ſecret Receſſes of the Heart. His ſweet and ſerene Aſpect diffuſes 'Tranquility and Joy throughout Univerſe. On the contrary, when he ſhakes thoſe majeſtic Curls that adorn his awful Head, he makes both Heaven and Earth to rock: The Gods them-ſelves, dazzled with the beamy Glory that ſurrounds him, approach with trembling.

All the celeſtial Deities were now about him. *Venus* preſented herſelf with all thoſe Charms that ſpring from her divine Perſon; her looſe flowing Gown was more ſplendid than all the Colours with which *Iris* decks herſelf amidſt the duſky Clouds, when ſhe comes to promiſe to diſmay'd Mortals the Ceſſation of a Tempeſt, and to declare to them the Return of fair Weather. Her Robe was faſten'd by that cele-brated Girdle on which are repreſented the Graces; the comely Treſſes of the Goddeſs were negligently ty'd behind by a Locket of Gold. All the Gods were ſurpriz'd at her Beauty, as if they had never ſeen her before, and their Eyes were dazzled, like the Eyes of Mortals, when *Phœbus*, after a tedious Night, comes to illuminate the Earth with his Rays. They look'd on each other with Aſtoniſhment, but ſtill their Eyes center'd on *Venus*; and they perceiv'd thoſe of the Goddeſs were bathed in Tears, and that a Cloud of Sorrow overcaſt her Face.

Mean

Mean while fhe advanc'd towards the Throne of *Ju-piter*, with a foft, light Step, like the rapid Flight of a Bird cleaving the vaft Space of the yielding Air. He look'd upon her with Complacency, fmil'd kindly on her, and then, rifing up, embrac'd her. My dear Daughter, faid he to her, what is it grieves you? I can't fee your Tears without Concern: Fear not to unbofom yourfelf freely to me; you know my Tender-nefs and Indulgence for you.

Venus anfwer'd him with a gentle Voice, but in-terrupted with deep Sighs: O Father of Gods and Men! Can you, who fee all Things, be ignorant of the Caufe of my Sorrow? *Minerva* is not fatisfy'd with overthrowing the very Foundations of *Troy's* ftately Town, which I protected; fhe is not contented to be thus dreadfully reveng'd on *Paris*, who had preferr'd my Beauty to hers; but fhe likewife conducts over Land and Sea the Son of *Ulyffes*, that cruel Deftroyer of *Troy*. *Telemachus* is accompany'd by *Minerva*; which occafions her Abfence from this divine Affembly. She ied this rafh Youth into the Ifle of *Cyprus* to affront me. He has defpis'd my Power; he would not condefcend fo far as to burn Incenfe upon my Altars; he has exprefs'd an Abhorrence of the Feftivals that are celebrated in my Honour; he has lock'd faft his Heart againft all my Pleafures. In vain has *Neptune* ftirr'd up againft him the Winds and Seas, at my Defire; *Telemachus*, caft by a dreadful Shipwreck on *Calypfo's* Ifland, has triumphed over *Cupid* him-felf, whom I fent thither to foften the Heart of this young *Greek*. Neither *Calypfo's* blooming Youth and Charms, nor any of her Nymphs, nor even the burning Shafts of Love, could get the Afcen-

dant

dant over *Minerva*'s Arts. She fnatch'd him from the Ifland———behold how I am defeated———a Stripling triumphs over me ———

Jupiter, to comfort *Venus*, faid to her : Is it true, my Daughter, *Minerva* guards the Heart of this young *Greek* againft all your Son's Arrows ; and prepares for him a Glory, which never yet was merited by a young Man. I am forry he has defpis'd your Altars, but cannot fubject him to your Power. I confent, to gratify you, that he ftill fhall wander both by Sea and Land ; that he fhall live far from his own Country, expos'd to all Sorts of Miferies and Dangers : But the Fates will neither fuffer him to perifh, nor his Virtue to be overcome by thofe Pleafures with which you decoy Mankind. Take Comfort, therefore, my Daughter : Content yourfelf with ruling over fo many other Heroes, and fo many of the immortal Powers. Here he fmil'd on *Venus*, with the utmoft Grace and Majefty. A radiant Flafh, like the moft piercing Lightning, darted from his Eyes. Then, tenderly kiffing *Venus*, he diffus'd an Odour of *Ambrofia*, which perfum'd *Olympus* all around. The Goddefs could not but be fenfible of this favourable Reception from the greateft of the Gods. In fpite of her Tears and Grief, a vifible Joy o'erfpread her Face. She let down her Veil to hide her blufhing Cheeks, and to cover the Confufion fhe was in. The whole Affembly of the Gods applauded *Jupiter*'s Anfwer ; and *Venus*, without lofing a Moment's Time, haftened to *Neptune*, to concert with him the Means of revenging himfelf on *Telemachus*. She repeated to *Neptune* what *Jupiter* faid to her. I knew before, reply'd *Neptune*, the unalterable Decree of Deftiny ; but

but if we can't fink *Telemachus* to the Bottom of the Sea, let us not at leaft omit any thing that may make him wretched, and retard his Return to *Ithaca*. I cannot confent to the deftroying of the *Phenician* Ship, in which he is embark'd; I love the *Phenicians*; they are my People; no other Nation in the Univerfe cultivates my Empire as they do; the Sea, through their Means, is become a Bond that ties together all the Nations of the Earth; they honour me with continual Sacrifices on my Altars; they are juft, prudent, and induftrious in their Commerce; they diftribute the Conveniencies of Life, and Plenty through all the World. No, Goddefs, I can't admit one of their Veflels fhould be wreck'd; but I will make the Pilot lofe his Courfe, and fail wide of *Ithaca*, whither he is bound. *Venus*, fatisfy'd with this Promife, forc'd a malicious Smile, and then return'd in her flying Chariot, and alighted on *Idalia*'s flowery Meads, where the Graces, the Smiles, and the Sports, exprefs'd their Joy to fee her again, dancing around her on the Flowers which perfume that charming Place.

Neptune immediately difpatch'd a deceitful Deity, like the God of Dreams, fave only that Dreams never deceive but during the Time of Sleep; whereas this Deity fafcinates Mens Senfes when they are awake. This malignant Deity, attended by a numberlefs Crowd of wing'd Delufions fluttering round him, came and pour'd out a fubtle and enchanted Liquor upon the Eyes of the Pilot *Athamas*, who was attentively confidering the Brightnefs of the Moon, the Courfe of the Stars, and the Port of *Ithaca*, whofe fteep Rocks he had already difcover'd pretty near. In this very Moment, the Pilot's Eyes could difcern no thing as it really was; a falfe

Sky

Sky and a mock Land prefented themfelves to him;
the Stars feem'd to have chang'd their Courfe, and
to have gone backwards in their fhining Orbits; all
Olympus feem'd to move by new Laws; the Earth
itfelf was alter'd; a falfe *Ithaca* ftill offer'd itfelf to
his View to amufe him, while at the fame time he
was going farther off from the true one. The more
he approach'd towards this deluding Reprefentation
of the Ifland, the farther this Image recoil'd from
him; it ftill fled from before him, and he knew
not what to make of its Retreat: Sometimes he
thought he already heard the Noife ufual in a
Port; and fo he was ftrait preparing, according to
the Orders he had receiv'd, to fteal afhore on a little
Ifland near the great one, to fecure the Return of
this young Prince againft the Violence of *Penelope's*
Lovers, who had confpired againft him. Sometimes
he dreaded the Shelves, which are fo numerous on
that Shore, and he fancied that he heard the hollow
roaring of the Waves dafhing againft thofe Shelves.
Then all on a fudden he perceiv'd that the Land appear'd at a much greater Diftance: The Mountains
feem'd to him like fo many little Clouds, which
fometimes darken the Horizon while the Sun is fet-
ting. Thus was *Athamas* perplex'd, and the Impreffion of the deceitful Deity, which had bewitch'd
his Eyes, fill'd him with a Sort of Apprehenfion,
which till then he was a Stranger to. He was even
inclin'd to believe that he was not awake, and that
he was under the Illufion of a Dream. Mean
while, *Neptune* commanded the Eaft Wind to blow,
in order to drive the Ship on the Coaft of *Hefperia:*
The Wind obey'd him with fo much Vehemence,
that the Ship foon arriv'd at the Place *Neptune* had
appointed.

Already

Already had *Aurora* proclaim'd the approaching Day ; already had the Stars, which dread the Rays of the Sun, and are fhy of him, begun to hide in the Ocean their dufky Fires, when the Pilot cry'd out : I can no longer doubt it; we are now touching the very Ifland of *Ithaca* ; rejoice, *Telemachus*, for in an Hour, you fhall fee *Penelope* again, and perhaps *Ulyffes* repoffefs'd of his Throne. At this Cry, *Telemachus*, who was lock'd faft in the Arms of Sleep, awakes, ftarts up, goes to the Steerage, embraces the Pilot, and with his Eyes fcarce open, furveys the neighbouring Shore, and figh'd when he could not perceive that it was the Coaft of his own Country. Alas ! where are we, faid he. This is not my dear *Ithaca*. *Athamas*, you are deceiv'd ; you are but little acquainted with that Coaft fo far diftant from your own Country. No, no, reply'd *Athamas* ; I can't be deceived in my Knowledge of the Bearings of this Ifland : I have been a great many times here ; I know the fmalleft Rock belonging to it ; the Coaft of *Tyre* is fcarce more recent in my Memory : See that Mountain there jutting out ; behold that Head-land rifing like a Tower : don't you hear thofe Billows that break themfelves againft thofe other Rocks, that with an angry Brow feem to threaten the Sea with their Fall ? But don't you fee that Temple of *Minerva*, which falutes the Clouds ? Yonder is the Houfe and Caftle of your Father *Ulyffes*. O *Athamas* ! reply'd *Telemachus*, you are deceiv'd ; I fee, on the contrary, a very high, but level Coaft ; and I perceive a Town, but it is none of *Ithaca*. O Gods, it is thus ye deride and mock poor Mortals !

Whilft he was faying thefe Words, all of a fudden the Eyes of *Athamas* were reftor'd to their
wonted

4

wonted Certainty, and the Charm diffolv'd :. He perfectly furvey'd the Shore as it really was, and acknowledg'd his Error. I own, O *Telemachus*, cry'd he, fome envious Deity has enchanted my Eyes. I thought I faw *Ithaca*, and a perfect Image of it prefented itfelf to my Fancy; but now it is vanifh'd like a Dream : I now behold another City, and it is doubtlefs *Salentum*, which *Idomeneus*, who fled from *Crete*, has lately founded in *Hefperia*; I perceive its rifing Walls, as yet' unfinifh'd; I fee a Port not yet entirely fortified.

Whilft *Athamas* was taking notice of the feveral Works newly erected in this growing City, and whilft *Telemachus* was bewailing his Misfortune; the Wind that *Neptune* caufed to blow, drove them full Sail into a Road where they found themfelves under Shelter, and juft by the Haven.

Mentor, who was no Stranger, either to *Neptune*'s Revenge, or the cruel Devices of *Venus*, only fmil'd at the Miftake of *Athamas*. When they were in this Road, *Mentor* fays to *Telemachus*, *Jupiter* is making Trial of you; but will not fuffer you to be deftroy'd : On the contrary, he only tries you to point out to you the Road of Glory. Think on the Labours of *Hercules*; let your Father's Atchievements be ever prefent to your Mind. He, who knows not how to fuffer, is not magnanimous. By Patience and Fortitude you muft tire out that mercilefs Fortune, which takes Delight in perfecuting you. I am lefs afraid, with regard to you, of the rigorous Treatment of *Neptune*, than I fear'd the infinuating Careffes of that Goddefs who detain'd you in her Ifland. What do we ftay for? Let us enter the Port; thefe People are our Friends; we are come among the *Greeks. Idomeneus*, who himfelf

has

has been ill ufed by Fortune, will have Pity on the
Diftrefs'd. They prefently enter'd the Port of
Salentum, where the *Phenician* Ship was receiv'd
without any Obftruction, becaufe the *Phenicians* are
in Peace and Commerce with all the People of the
World.

Telemachus beheld with Admiration, this growing
City. As a young Plant, which having been
nourifh'd by the Night's fweet Dew, at Break of
Day feels the Sun-beams coming to embellifh it ; it
grows; it opens its tender Buds ; it ftretches out its
green Leaves ; it blows its fragrant Flowers with a
thoufand new Colours ; every Moment you look
upon it, you perceive a new Luftre : So flourifh'd
Idomeneus's new City on the Sea-fide. Each Day,
each Hour it rofe in Magnificence, and prefented
afar off to Strangers at Sea, new Embellifhments of
Architecture, which tower'd to the very Skies. All
the Coaft refounded with the Cries of the Work-
men, and the Strokes of Mallets and Hammers ;
while, by the Help of Cranes and Ropes, Stones travell'd through the Air : All the leading Men of the
City fpirited up the Populace to their Work, as foon
as *Aurora* appear'd ; and King *Idomeneus* himfelf gave
Orders every where, and forwarded the Works with
an incredible Diligence.

Hardly was the *Phenician* Veffel got into Port,
ere the *Cretans* gave to *Telemachus* and *Mentor* all
the Tokens of a fincere Friendfhip : They haften'd
away to inform *Idomeneus*, that the Son of *Ulyffes*
was arriv'd. The Son of *Ulyffes !* cry'd he, of
Ulyffes ! He ! that dear Friend, that wife Hero, by
whom we at laft laid ftately *Troy* in Duft ! Bring
him to me, and let me fhew him how much I
lov'd his Father. Hereupon they prefent to him
Tele-

Telemachus, who telling him his Name, fues for Hofpitality. *Idomeneus* anfwer'd him with a courteous fmiling Countenance : Though no Body had told me who you are, I fhould certainly have known you. You are *Ulyffes* himfelf ; behold his very Eyes darting forth Fire, his fteady Look, his Mien at firft cold and referved, which cover'd fo much Sprightlinefs and fo many Graces ! I perceive even that fubtle Smile, his eafy negligent Demeanour, his gentle Speech, plain and infinuating, which perfuaded, without allowing Time for Sufpicion. Yes, you are the Son of *Ulyffes* ; but you fhall be mine too. O my Son, my dear Son, what Accident brings you to this Climate ? Is it to feek your Father ? Alas ! I can tell you nothing of him ; *Fortune* has perfecuted both him and me : It was his ill Fate not to be able to find his Country again : and 'twas mine to find my Country again, fill'd with the Hatred of the Gods againft me. Whilft *Idomeneus* was fpeaking thefe Words, he look'd wiftfully upon *Mentor*, as one whofe Face he was no Stranger to, but whofe Name he could not recal.

And now *Telemachus* anfwer'd him with Tears in his Eyes : O King, pardon the Grief, which in defpight of me, will break out at a Time when I ought to exprefs nothing but Joy and Gratitude for your Generofity to me. By your lamenting the Lofs of *Ulyffes*, you yourfelf teach me how much I ought to be affected with my Misfortune, in not finding my Father. 'Tis now a long, long while, I have been in fearch of him through all the known Seas. The incens'd Gods permit me not either to fee him again, or to know whether he be fhipwreck'd, or to return to *Ithaca*, where *Penelope* pines

pines away with a longing Defire to be freed from
her importunate Suitors. I thought I fhou'd have
found you in the Ifle of *Crete*; I was there inform'd
of your cruel Deftiny, but little thought of ever
coming near *Hefperia*, where you have founded a new
Kingdom; but Fortune, who makes us Mortals her
Play-game, and now obliges me to wander from Place
to Place, and keeps me ftill from *Ithaca*, has at length
caft me upon your Shore. Of all the Difafters fhe has
expofed me to, this is what I the leaft repine at; for
though fhe drives me from my native Country, ye fhe
brings me acquainted with the moft generous of all
Kings.

At thefe Words, *Idomeneus* gave *Telemachus* a kind
Embrace, and leading him into his Palace, faid to
him; Who is that wife old Man that accompanies
you; for methinks I have feen him fomewhere? 'Tis
Mentor, reply'd *Telemachus*; *Mentor*, the Friend of
Ulyſſes, to whom he committed the Government of
my Infancy: What Tongue can exprefs how much I
am oblig'd to him!

Thereupon, *Idomeneus* ftepping to *Mentor*, and
taking him by the Hand; You and I, faid he to
him, have feen one another before. You may remember the Voyage you made into *Crete*, and what
good Advice you gave me; but, at that Time, the
Heat of Youth, and the quick Relifh of fenfual
Pleafures hurry'd me away; fo that my Misfortunes
alone have been able to teach me what I would not
believe. Would to the Gods I had taken your Advice, O fage old Man! But I am amaz'd to fee that
you are not in the leaft alter'd in fo many Years; your
Face is as frefh and fanguine as ever, the fame ftrait
and vigorous Body, only your Hair is grown fomewhat hoary.

Great King, anſwer'd *Mentor*, were I a Flatterer,
I would tell you likewiſe, that you ſtill preſerve that
Bloom which ſhone in your Face before the Siege
of *Troy :* But I had rather diſpleaſe you, than offend
againſt Truth.   Beſides, I find by your wife Diſcourſe, that you do not love Flattery, and that a
Man runs no Hazard in being ſincere with you.
Therefore, I muſt needs tell you, you are very
much chang'd, and that 'twas ſcarce poſſible to have
known you again.   I am not a Stranger to the Cauſe
of it; 'tis occaſion'd by your many and great Sufferings; but you have been a great Gainer by your
Misfortunes, ſince you have acquir'd Wiſdom.   A
Man may very eaſily comfort himſelf for the Wrinkles
of his Face, ſo long as his Heart is exercis'd and
fortified in Virtue.   Moreover, know, *Idomeneus*,
that Kings always wear away faſter than other Men.
In Adverſity, the Fatigues of the Mind and Body
make them old before their Time :   In Proſperity,
the voluptuous Enjoyments of an eaſy Life, waſte
their Strength even, more than the Toils of War.
Nothing is more detrimental to Health than im-
moderate Pleaſure.   From hence it proceeds, that
Kings ,either in Peace or War, do continually labour
under ſuch Pains or Pleaſures, as bring upon them
old Age before its natural Seaſon.   Whereas a ſober,
temperate, and plain way of Living, free from In-
quietudes and Paſſions, regular and laborious, keeps
all the Limbs of a wiſe Man in a vigorous Youthful-
neſs, which, without theſe Precautions, flies faſt away
upon the Wings of Time.

Idomeneus, charm'd with *Mentor*'s Diſcourſe, would
for a long time have liſtened to him, had they not
come to put him in mind of a Sacrifice which he
was to make to *Jupiter*.   *Telemachus* and *Mentor*
follow'd

follow'd him, furrounded by a great Croud of People, who with much Eagernefs and Curiofity gaz'd
at the two Strangers. The *Salentines* faid one to
another, Thefe two Men are very different; the
young one has a certain amiable Livelinefs beyond
Expreffion; all the Graces of Youth and Beauty are
diffus'd over his whole Face and Perfon; but this
Beauty has nothing effeminate nor languid; though he
is in the tendereft Bloffom of Youth, yet he appears
vigorous, ftrong, and inured to Labour. But this
other, though far older, has loft nothing at all of his
Strength : His Mien indeed feems at firft not fo majeftic, nor his Countenance fo graceful; yet if you
look nearer, you will find in his Simplicity the Marks
of Wifdom and Virtue, with a furprizing Grandeur
of Deportment. When the Gods defcended to Earth
to reveal themfelves to Mortals, they undoubtedly
appeared in the like Figures of Strangers and Tra-
vellers.

By this time they were arriv'd at the Temple of
Jupiter, which *Idomeneus*, who was defcended from
that God, had adorn'd with much Magnificence.
It was envion'd with a double Row of Marble Pillars,
like *Jafper:* The Chapiters were of Silver: The
Temple was all incrufted with Marble, where *Baffo
Relievos* rofe, reprefenting the Transformation of *Jupiter* into a Bull, the Rape of *Europa*, and her Paffage through the Sea into *Crete*. The Waves feem'd
to reverence *Jupiter*, though he was in a ftrange
Form. Then there was reprefented the Birth and
Youth of *Minos*; afterwards, that wife King in a more
advanced Age difpenfing Laws to the whole Ifland, in
order to render it for ever flourifhing. There likewife
Telemachus took notice of the principal Occurrences at
the Siege of *Troy*, where *Idomeneus* had acquired the

L 2 Repu-

Reputation of a great General. Amidſt the Repre-
ſentation of theſe Actions, *Telemachus* look'd for his ·
Father, and found him taking the Horſes of *Rhcſus*,
whom *Diomedes* had juſt killed ; in another Place diſ-
puting with *Ajax* for the Arms of *Achilles*, amidſt an
Aſſembly of the *Grecian* Commanders : And, laſtly,
his coming out of the fatal Horſe to give Death to ſo
many *Trojans*.

Telemachus preſently knew him by all theſe famous
Actions, which he had ſo often heard of, and which
Mentor himſelf had frequently repeated to him. The
Tears preſently guſh'd from his Eyes ; he chang'd
Colour ; Grief was ſpread all over his Face : *Idomeneus*
perceiv'd it, though *Telemachus* turn'd aſide to conceal his Trouble. Don't be aſham'd, ſaid *Idomeneus*
to him, to let us ſee how much you are mov'd with
the Glory and Misfortunes of your Father.

Mean while the People aſſembled in great Crowds
under the vaſt Porticoes form'd by the double Row
of Columns which ſurrounded the Temple. There
were two Companies of young Boys and Girls, who
ſung Hymns in Praiſe of the Thunder-graſping God.
Theſe Children, who were ſelected for their Beauty,
had their long Hair ſpread abroad upon their Shoulders ;
their Heads were perfum'd and crown'd with Roſes,
and they were all cloath'd in white. *Idomeneus* offered
in Sacrifice to *Jupiter* a hundred Bulls, to render the
God propitious to him in a War which he had undertaken againſt his Neighbours. The Blood of the
Victims, ſmoaking on every Side, ſtreamed into the
capacious Goblets of Gold and Silver.

The aged *Theophanes*, beloved of the Gods, and
Prieſt of the Temple, kept, during the Time of the
Sacrifice, his Head cover'd with one End of his
purple Robe ; then he conſulted the Entrails of the
Victims

3

Victims ftill panting; after which, afcending the facred Tripod, O ye Gods, cried he, what are thefe two Strangers whom you have fent into thefe Parts? Had they not come among us, the War lately entered upon would have been fatal to us, and *Salentum* would have fallen to ruin ere it had been well raifed above-ground. I have in myEye a youngHero, whomWifdom leads by the Hand,——No Mortal dares fay more. ——In fpeaking thefe Words, his Looks were wild, and his Eyes fparkled with Fire; he feem'd to gaze on other Objects than thofe that were before him; his Face was inflamed, his whole Body was in Emotion; he rag'd and grew diftracted; his Hair briftled up; his Mouth foam'd; his up-lifted Arms ftood motionlefs in the Air; his loud Voice was ftronger than any human Voice; he was breathlefs, and could no longer contain within him the Deity he was poffefs'd with.

O happy *Idomeneus*, cry'd he again, what do I fee? What Misfortunes avoided! What amiable Peace at home! But abroad, what bloody Wars! What Victories! O *Telemachus!* thy Labours exceed thy Father's: The proud infulting Enemy groans in the Duft, whilft thy Sword flafhes over his Head: The brazen Gates, the inacceffible Ramparts fall at thy Feet——O mighty Goddefs! Let his Father——brave Youth! in time thou fhall re-vifit——At thefe Words his Speech fail'd him, and he continued, as it were, by irrefiftable Neceffity, in a Silence full of Aftonifhment.

The People were frozen with Fear: *Idomeneus* fhiver'd, not daring to bid him make an end. *Telemachus* himfelf, furpriz'd, hardly underftood what he had heard; fcarce could he believe that he had heard fuch high Predictions. *Mentor* alone was un-

aftonifhed

aftonifhed at the Divine Spirit. You hear, faid he to *Idomeneus*, the Purpofe of the Gods; that whatever Nation you have to fight againft, the Victory fhall be in your Hands, and you will owe to your Friend's youthful Son the Profperity of your Arms; therefore be not jealous of him, but make a right Ufe of what the Gods beftow on you by his Means.

Idomeneus, being not yet recovered out of his Amazement, ftudied in vain for Words; his Tongue continu'd motionlefs. *Telemachus*, more Mafter of himfelf, faid to *Mentor*; even fo much promis'd Glory does not move me; but what can be the Meaning of thofe laft Words, *Thou fhalt revifit?* Is it my Father, or only *Ithaca*, that I fhall fee again? Ah! why did he not make an end? He has left me more in doubt than I was before. O *Ulyffes!* O my Father! Is it poffible that I fhould ever fee you again? Can it be true? But I flatter my-felf——O cruel Oracle! thou delighteft in fporting with an unfortunate Wretch: One Word more, and I had been at the Height of Happinefs.

Accept with Reverence what the Gods reveal, faid *Mentor* to him, and attempt not to difcover what they are pleafed to keep fecret. Rafh Curio-fity deferves to be put to confufion. 'Tis out of a fupreme Goodnefs and Wifdom that the Gods conceal from feeble Mortals their Deftinies, involved in an impenetrable Darknefs. It is indeed of Advantage to forefee what depends on our Endeavours, in order to a due Performance; but 'tis no lefs advantageous to be ignorant of what the Gods defign to do with us, and of what it is not in our Power, by any means, to avert.

Telemachus,

Telemachus, touch'd with thefe Words, contain'd himfelf, though not without the greateft Reluctance. *Idomeneus*, who by this time had conquered his Surprize, began to thank great *Jove* for fending to him the young *Telemachus* and the wife *Mentor*, in order to make him victorious over his Enemies. And, after he had given them a noble Entertainment, fubfequent to the Sacrifice, he fpoke thus to the two Strangers.

I acknowledge, I was but a Novice in the Art of Governing, when I return'd into *Crete*, after the Siege of *Troy*. You know, dear Friends, what Misfortunes difabled me from reigning over that great Ifland, fince you tell me that you were there after I left it. Yet I am happy, exceeding happy, if the fevereft Strokes of Fortune can be of Ufe towards my Inftruction, and teach me to be Mafter of my Paffions. I croffed the Seas like a Fugitive, whom the Vengeance of Gods and Men purfues. All my paft Grandeur ferved only to render my Fall the more ignominious and infupportable. I fought a Shelter for my Houfhold-Gods upon this defert Coaft, where I found nothing but wild uncultivated Lands, overrun with Thorns and Bryers, covered with thickfet Trees as old as the Earth itfelf, and almoft inacceffible Rocks, which ferved for Harbour to the wild Beafts. Yet fuch was the Extremity to which I was reduced, that I was glad to poffefs this favage Land, and to make it my Country in company with a fmall Handfull of Soldiers and Friends, who were fo kind as to take Share in my Misfortunes, deftitute of all Hopes of ever feeing again that fortunate Ifland, where the Gods caufed me to be born, that there I might reign. Alas! faid I to myfelf, what an Alteration is this! what a dreadful Example am I to all Kings! what

whole-

wholefome Inftructions may they draw from my Mif-
carriages! They fancy they have nothing to fear,
becaufe of their Elevation above the reft of Mankind; whereas it is that very Elevation that ought
to make them fear every thing. I was dreaded by
my Enemies, beloved by my Subjects; I commanded
over a powerful and warlike Nation ; my Name was
fpread abroad upon *Fame's* fwift Wings into the moft
diftant Climates; I reign'd in a delicious, fruitful
Ifland ; each Year an hundred wealthy Cities paid
me Tribute ; my People acknowledged me to be the
Offspring of *Jupiter*, who was born in their Country ;
they lov'd me as the Grandfon of the fage *Minos*, by
whofe Laws they are become fo powerful and fo happy.
What was there wanting to my Felicity, except the
knowing how to enjoy it with Moderation? But my
own Pride, and the Flattery of others, which I liften'd
to, overturn'd my Throne. In like manner will all
Kings fall, that fhall give themfelves up to their own
Paffion, and the deceitful Counfels of Flatterers. In
the Day-time, I endeavoured to put on a chearful
Countenance, and fuch as feemed full of Hope, in
order to keep up the Spirits of thofe who had follow'd
me. Come on, faid I to them ; let us build a new
City, to make us amends for our Loffes : We are
furrounded by Nations who have fet us a noble Example for fuch an Enterprize : See there *Tarentum*
rearing up its Head juft by us ! *Phalantus*, with his
Lacedemonians, founded that new Kingdom. *Philoctetes*
has built upon the fame Coaft another great City,
which he calls *Petilia*. Such another Colony is *Meta-*
pontum. And fhall we be out-done by thofe Strangers
who are Wanderers like ourfelves ? *Fortune* has
dealt with us all alike, and has not ufed us worfe than
them.

Whilft

Whilst I endeavoured, by such Expressions as these' to mitigate the Distresses of my Companions, I smothered a deadly Grief at the Bottom of my Heart: It was to me a mighty Consolation whenever the Day withdrew its Light, and the Night came to wrap me up in Darkness; for then I was at liberty to moan my wretched Fate. Two bitter Floods of Tears rolled from my Eyes, and balmy Sleep was an utter Stranger to me. The next Day I resumed my Toils with indefatigable Fervor, and that's the Reason, *Mentor*, you find me so much alter'd for the worse.

After *Idomeneus* had made an end of relating his Sufferings, he begged *Telemachus* and *Mentor* to give him their Assistance in the War wherein he was engaged. I will, added he, most carefully send you back to *Ithaca*, as soon as the War is over; and in the mean while, I will send out Ships, far and wide, to learn News of *Ulysses*. Wherever he is thrown, either by stormy Winds or angry Gods, I will take care to bring him back. Heaven grant he still be living! As for you, the best Ships that ever were built in the Island of *Crete* shall be fitted out to carry you home: They are built of Timber felled on the true Mount *Ida*, where *Jupiter* was born: That sacred Wood can never perish in the Waves; the Winds and Rocks do awfully respect it; and *Neptune*'s self, even in his highest Rage, dares not to stir the Billows up against it. Rest therefore assured, that you will happily return to *Ithaca*, and that no adverse Deity shall be any longer able to make you wander upon so many Seas any more. The Passage is so short and easy; send away the *Phenician* Vessel that brought you hither, and think now of nothing but how to acquire the Glory of establishing the new Kingdom of *Idomeneus*, which is to be the Recompence of all his Sufferings. 'Tis at this Price,

L 5 O Son

O Son of *Ulysses*, that you must be esteemed worthy
of your Father: And though harsh Destiny should
have already sent him down to *Pluto*'s gloomy Realm,
yet *Greece*, overjoy'd, will find him again in you.

At these Words, *Telemachus* interrupting *Idomeneus*,
Let us, said he, send away the *Phenician* Vessel. What
do we stay for? Why don't we this Moment take up
Arms, and attack your Enemies, who are now become
ours? If we were victorious, when in *Sicily* we
fought for *Acestes*, who was a *Trojan*, and a professed
Enemy of *Greece*, shall we not be yet more ardent, and
more befriended by the Gods, when we fight for one
of those *Grecian* Heroes, who levelled to the Ground
that unjust City of *Priam?* The Oracle we have just
now heard will not suffer us to doubt it.

The END *of the* NINTH BOOK.

THE

Book X.

THE

ADVENTURES

OF

TELEMACHUS.

BOOK X.

The ARGUMENT.

Idomeneus *acquaints* Mentor *with the Reasons of his making War against the* Mandurians ; *and relates to him, that they had at first yielded to him the Coast of* Hesperia, *where he had founded his City ; that they retired to the neighbouring Mountains, where some of them having been abused by a Party of his Men, they had deputed to him two old Men, with whom he had. agreed upon Articles of Peace; and that, after an Infraction of that Treaty, by some of* Idomeneus's *Men, who knew nothing of the Peace, the* Mandurians *were*
preparing

preparing to make War against him. Whilst Ido-
meneus was telling this Story, the Mandurians, *who*
had taken up Arms with great Expedition, appeared
at the Gates of Salentum. Neftor, Philoctetes, *and*
Phalantus, *whom* Idomeneus *thought to be neuter,*
came against him in the Army of the Mandurians.
Mentor *goes forth from* Salentum *by himself, to pro-*
pofe Conditions of Peace to the Enemy.

ENTOR, with a ferene compofed
Countenance, looking upon *Telemachus,*
who now burnt with a noble Ardour
for the Fight, thus befpoke him : I am
much pleafed, O Son of *Ulyffes,* to fee
in you fo laudable a Paffion for Glory ; but remember, that the greateft Renown of your Father, was
his approving himfelf the wifeft and moft moderate
Commander among the *Greeks,* when that fam'd
Siege of *Troy* was carrying on. *Achilles,* though both
invincible and invulnerable, though he carry'd Terror
and Death wherever he fought, yet could not mafter *Troy*; he fell himfelf beneath the Walls of that
proud Town, which triumph'd over him who conquer'd *Hector :* But *Ulyffes,* whofe Valour was governed by Prudence, carried Fire and Sword amidft
the *Trojans*; and to his Hands is owing the Fall of
thofe high and ftately Towers, which, during ten
long Years, defied all confederate *Greece.* As
much as *Minerva* is fuperior to *Mars,* fo much
does a well-weigh'd provident Valour furpafs a boifterous and favage Boldnefs. Firft then, let us enquire into the Circumftances of this War that is to
be carried on ; I, for my part, decline no Danger ;
but 'tis my Opinion, *Idomeneus,* that you ought
firft

firft to let us know whether your War be a juft one; fecondly, againft whom you wage it; and, laftly, what number of Forces you have to juftify the Hope of a happy Iffue.

Idomeneus reply'd: At our firft Arrival here, we found a favage People, who lived in the Woods upon what they killed in hunting, and fuch Fruits as the Trees fpontaneoufly produce. Thefe People who are called *Mandurians*, were fo terrified at the Sight of our Ships and Arms, that they made all the hafte they could into their Mountains; but the Soldiers, whofe Curiofity led them to view the Country, and likewife being minded to hunt down fome of their Stags, met with fome of thofe favage Run-aways,, whofe Leaders thus accofted our Men: We have forfaken the agreeable Shore, and yield it to you; we have nothing left but wild Mountains, almoft inacceffible; and 'tis but juft that you leave us in Peace and Liberty there: We have met you wandering, difperfed, and weaker than we; fo that we have it in our Power, if we will, to take away your Lives; nor can your own Companions have the leaft Sufpicion of what's become of you; but we have no Inclination to imbrue our Hands in the Blood of thofe who are Men like ourfelves. Go your ways, and forget not that you owe your Lives to our Principles of Humanity. Remember it is from a People you call rude and uncivilized, that you receive this Leffon of Forbearance and Generofity.

Thofe of our Men, who were thus let go by the *Barbarians*, return'd to the Camp, and related what had happened to them. Our Soldiers were vex'd at it; they were afhamed that *Cretans* fhould owe their Lives to fuch a Gang of Fugitives, who

feemed

feemed to them more like Bears than Men. Thereupon they went out a hunting in greater Numbers than at firft, and furnifh'd with all manner of Arms: They did not go very far ere they met with the Savages, and attacked them; the Engagement was fharp; the Darts flew on both Sides like Hail in a Storm; the Savages were forced at laft to retire to their fteep Mountains, whither our Men durft not purfue them.

A while after, thofe People fent to me two of their wifeft old Men to fue for Peace: They brought Prefents along with them, confifting of the Skins of wild Beafts which they had killed, and various forts of Fruits, fuch as the Country affords. After they had given me the Prefents, they began thus:

O King, in one Hand thou feeft we bear the Sword, and in the other an Olive-branch (for they had actually each in their Hand) chufe therefore, which thou wilt, Peace or War. We, for our parts, would chufe Peace; and for the Sake thereof we have not been afhamed to yield thee the pleafant Sea-fhore, where the fertile Land, impregnated by the Sun, abounds with fo many and fuch delicious Fruits. Yet Peace is fweeter than all thofe Fruits; and for that Reafon we retired into thofe fteep Mountains cover'd with everlafting Ice and Snow, where we never behold either the Flowers of the Spring, or the rich Fruits of the Autumn. We have in Abhorrence that Brutality which, under the plaufible Names of Ambition and Glory, madly ravages whole Provinces, and fpills the Blood of Men, who are all Brethren. If that falfe Glory affects thee, we are not fuch Fools as to envy thee; we pity thee, and beg the Gods to preferve us from the like Madnefs. If the Sciences, which the *Greeks*

are

are so careful to learn, and if that Politeness they take so much Pride in, serves only to inspire them with such a detestable Injustice, we look upon it as our great Happiness to be without those Advantages; we will glory in being still ignorant, and being *Barbarians*, but withal, just, kind, faithful, disinterested, satisfy'd with little, and despising that idle Delicacy which brings along with it a Necessity of enjoying a great deal. What we hold in greatest Esteem is Health, Frugality, Liberty, Vigour of Body and Mind, the Love of Virtue, the Fear of the Gods, a kind Disposition towards our Neighbours, Constancy to our Friends, Honesty towards every body, Moderation in Prosperity, Fortitude in Afflictions, Courage to declare the Truth at all Times, Detestation of Flattery. Such are the People whom we now offer to thee for Neighbours and Allies. If the Gods, in Anger to thee, do so far infatuate thee, as to cause thee to refuse this Peace, thou shalt find, when it is too late, that those People who are Lovers of Peace out of a Principle of Moderation, are the most formidable in War.

While these old Men were thus speaking to me, I thought I should never satiate my Eyes with looking upon them: They had long uncombed Beards, short hoary Hair, thick Eye-brows, sparkling Eyes, a resolute Look, an Utterance grave and full of Authority, Manners plain and ingenuous. The Furs, which served them for Cloaths, were fastened negligently over their shoulders, and discovered their bare Arms, more nervous and brawny than even those of our Wrestlers. The Answer I gave those two Envoys was, that I desired Peace. We thereupon settled between us several Conditions, upon each other's Faith: We invok'd all the Gods to witness

the

the Treaty; which done, I sent them back again with
Presents: But the Gods, who drove me from the
Kingdom of my Ancestors, were not yet tired with
persecuting me. Our Huntsmen, who could not so
soon have Information of the Peace we had just made,
happened to meet the same Day a great Company of
those *Barbarians*, as they were attending their Ambas-
sadors in their Return from our Camp. They fell
upon them with Fury, killed many of them, and
pursued the rest into the Woods: And thus the War
is kindled anew. It is the Opinion of these *Barbarians*, that they can no longer safely trust either our
Promises or Oaths.

In order to distress us the more, they have called
to their Assistance the *Locrians*, *Apulians*, *Lucanians*,
the *Brutians*, the People of *Crotona*, *Neritum*, and
Brundusium. The *Lucanians* use Chariots armed
with keen Scythes. The *Apulians* are every one of
them covered with the Skin of some wild Beast which
they have killed; they carry in their Hands great
wooden Clubs, full of large Knobs, beset with Iron
Spikes; they are, for the generality, as tall as Giants,
and their Bodies are so robust, by hardening themselves in the most laborious Exercises, that their very
Looks strike Terror. The *Locrians*, who come
from *Greece*, do still retain something of their Original, and have more Humanity than the rest; but,
with the exact Discipline of the *Greek* Troops, they
have the additional Advantages of being as lusty as
those *Barbarians*, by habituating themselves to a
hardy Way of living, which makes them invincible:
They have a sort of light Bucklers, made of twisted
Withies, cover'd over with Skins! and they use long
Swords. The *Brutians* are nimble-footed like Bucks
or Does; and, when they run, one would think that
even

even the tendereſt Blade of Graſs is hardly depreſſed by their Feet; they ſcarcely leave any Prints of their Steps in the Sand itſelf; they ruſh ſuddenly on their Foes, and are gone again with the ſame Rapidity. The People of *Crotona* are very ready at ſhooting Arrows; few of the ordinary Sort among the *Greeks* can draw a Bow like the leaſt expert of theſe *Crotonians*; and if they ſhould ever apply themſelves to our Games, they would infallibly carry the Prize; Their Arrows are ſteep'd in the Juice of certain poiſonous Herbs, which are ſaid to come from the Banks of *Avernus*, and whoſe Wounds are incurable. As for thoſe of *Neritum*, *Meſſapia*, and *Brunduſium*, all they have to boaſt of is a great Strength of Body, and an untaught artleſs Valour. As ſoon as they ſee their Enemies, they rend the Skies with ſuch hideous Out-cries, as are really frightful: They are pretty dexterous at the Sling, and darken the Air with Showers of Stones; but they obſerve no Order in fighting. This, O *Mentor*, is what you deſired to know: You are now let into the Occaſion of this War, and are informed what ſort of Enemies we have to deal with.

As ſoon as *Idomeneus* had given them this Account, *Telemachus*, impatient to engage, thought there was no more to do than to take up Arms. *Mentor* ſtopped him a ſecond time, and thus addreſſed himſelf to *Idomeneus:* How comes it, that theſe ſame *Locrians*, who are of a *Grecian* Stock, do thus confederate with the *Barbarians* againſt *Grecians?* How comes it, that ſo many *Greek* Colonies are in a flouriſhing Condition upon this Sea-Coaſt, without being engaged in the ſame Wars with you? You ſay, O *Idomeneus*, that the Gods are not weary of perſecuting you; but I ſay, they have not yet done

instruct-

inftructing you: It is ftrange, that fo many Mif-
fortunes, as you have gone through, fhould not
have yet taught you what you ought to do, in order
to prevent a War! What you yourfelf juft now
related, concerning the Honelty of thofe *Barbarians*, fuffices to fhew, that you might have lived in
Peace with them; but Pride and Haughtinefs are
always attractive of the moft dangerous Wars. You
might have given them Hoftages, and taken fome of
theirs; and it would have been an eafy Matter for
you to have fent fome of your Captains along with
their Ambaffadors, to have reconducted them fafe
Home. Nay, fince the Renewal of the War, you
ought to have pacify'd them, by reprefenting to
them that they were attack'd purely through Ignorance of the Treaty that had been made with them:
You fhould have offered them all the Security they
could poffibly demand; and have denounced the fevereft Punifhments againft thofe of your Subjects
who fhould give the leaft Interruption or Difturbance
to this Alliance. But, pray, what has happen'd fince
this Rupture?

To this *Idomeneus* reply'd; I thought it would
have been a bafe and abject Submiffion in us to have
courted thofe *Barbarians*, who had now affembled
in hafte all their moft ferviceable Men, and fuch as
were fit to bear Arms, and implored the Affiftance
of all the neighbouring Nations, to whom they
made us odious and fufpected. Thereupon I thought
that the beft Courfe I could take, was immediately
to make ourfelves Mafters of certain narrow Paffes
in the Mountains, that were ill guarded. Thefe we
feized without much Difficulty; and by that means
put ourfelves into a Condition of annoying thofe
Barbarians. In thefe Defiles I have caufed ftrong

                                          Towers

Towers to be erected, from whence our Men may,
with their Darts, gaul and overwhelm fuch of our
Enemies as fhall come down from the Mountains
into our Country; and at the fame time, we may enter into theirs, and deftroy their chief Settlements
whenever we pleafe. Thus, with Forces much inferior, we are able to make head againft that innumerable Multitude of Enemies which furrounds us.
This being the prefent State of our Cafe, it would
be a difficult Matter to treat of Peace with them:
For we cannot give up to them thofe Towers, without expofing ourfelves to their Incurfions; and they
look upon them as Citadels intended by us to bring
them under Slavery.

Mentor made this Reply to *Idomeneus*: You are a
wife King, and are pleafed with hearing the Truth
delivered to you without any difguife: You are not
like thofe foolifh Men, who are afraid of feeing it,
and who, for want of Courage to correct their
Faults, employ their whole Authority to maintain
what they have once done amifs. Know then, that
this barbarous People gave you an admirable Leffon,
when they apply'd to you for Peace. Was it out of
Weaknefs they fu'd for it? Did they want Courage,
or foreign Affiftance, to make head againft you?
You manifeftly fee they did not, fince they are fo
inur'd to War, and fupported by fo many formidable
Neighbours. Why did not you imitate their Moderation? But a miftaken Shame, and a falfe Honour,
have caft you into this Misfortune: You were afraid
of making the Enemy too proud, but did not fear
the making them too powerful, by uniting fo many
Nations in a Confederacy againft you, through
your haughty and injurious Conduct. What are
thofe Towers, you fo much boaft of, good for?
unlefs

unlefs it be to bring all your Neighbours under a
Neceffity, either of deftroying you, or perifhing themfelves, in order to keep off an approaching Slavery.
You rear'd up thofe Towers for your Security only,
and it is by means of thofe very Towers, that you
are now threatned with fo imminent a Danger.
The beft Bulwark of a State is Juftice, Moderation, Integrity, and the Affurance your Neighbours have, that you will never encroach upon their
Lands. The ftrongeft Walls may fall, through a
thoufand unforefeen Accidents; Fortune is caprici-
ous and uncertain in War; but the Love and Confidence of your Neighbours, who have experienced
your Moderation, is what renders a State invincible,.
and what makes it fcarce ever fo much as attempted
againft. Nay, though an unjuft Neighbour fhould
attack it, all the reft who are concerned in its Prefervation, do prefently take up Arms in its Defence :
The Support of fo many Nations, who find their
true Intereft in maintaining yours, would have
ftrengthened you much more, than thefe Towers,
which render your Misfortunes irretrievable. Had
you at firft taken care to prevent the Jealoufy of all
your Neighbours, your infant City would have flou-
rifhed in a happy Tranquillity, and you would have
been the Arbiter of all the Nations of *Hefperia.*
But, waving all other Confiderations, let us now
confine ourfelves to examine which Way you can
repair what is paft, by taking proper Meafures for
the Time to come. You told me juft now, that
there are upon this Coaft feveral *Greek* Colonies :
Thefe People cannot but be inclin'd, from the Dictates of Nature, to affift you ; for fure they have not
forgot either the great Name of *Minos,* Son of *Jupiter,* or your Labours in the Siege of *Troy,* where you

fo

fo often fignalized yourfelf among the *Grecian* Princes, in the common Caufe of all *Greece.* Why don't you endeavour to bring thofe Colonies over to your Side.

They are all refolv'd, anfwer'd *Idomeneus,* to remain neuter: Not but that they had fome Inclination to affift me, but they were deterred from doing, it, by the mighty Noife this City has made, from its very Beginning. Thofe *Grecians,* as well as the reft, were afraid we had fome Defign upon their Liberty. They were apprehenfive, that after we had fubdued the *Barbarians* of the Mountains, we fhould pufh our Ambition yet farther. To conclude, they are all againft us: Thofe very People, who declare not openly againft us, would yet be glad to fee us reduced, and the univerfal Jealoufy deprives us of all Alliance.

O ftrange Extremity! reply'd *Mentor.* By endeavouring to appear too powerful, you ruin your Power, and whilft you are both feared and hated abroad by your Neighbours, you at home exhauft yourfelf, by the vaft Expences you muft needs be at to maintain fuch a War. O wretched, doubly wretched *Idomeneus,* whom even this Misfortune' has inftructed but by halves! muft you needs have a fecond Fall to teach you to forefee the Evils which threaten the greateft Kings? But leave it to my Management, and only give me a particular Account of thofe Cities that refufe to enter into an Alliance with you.

The principal of them, faid *Idomeneus,* is *Tarentum.* About three Years ago *Phalantus* laid the Foundation of it. He had got together in *Laconia* a vaft Number of young Men, who were born of Women that had forgot their abfent Hufbands during

the

the Siege of *Troy*. When thefe Hufbands came home, the Women did all they could to pacify them, by denying the Faults they had committed in their Abfence. Thefe numerous Youths born out of Wedlock, being difclaimed both by Father and Mother, gave themfelves up to an unbounded Licentioufnefs: But their Diforders being check'd by the Severity of the Laws, they united together under *Phalantus*, a bold, intrepid, ambitious Captain, who, by plaufible Infinuations, had got the Dominion of their Hearts. He came to this Shore with his young *Laconians*, who have made *Tarentum* a fecond *Lacedæmon*. On the other Side, *Philoctetes*, who fignalized himfelt at the Siege of *Troy* by carrying thither *Hercules's* Arrows, has rear'd in this Neighbourhood the Walls of *Petilia*, a City which is indeed lefs powerful than *Tarentum*, but far more wifely governed. Laftly, We have hard by us the City of *Metapontum*, founded by the wife *Neftor* and his *Pylian* Subjects.

How! reply'd *Mentor*; have you *Neftor* in *Hefperia*, and could you not make him your Friend? *Neftor*, who faw you fo often fight againft the *Trojans*, and who then was fo much your Friend? I loft his Friendfhip, anfwer'd *Idomeneus*, by the Artifice of thofe People, who have nothing barbarous but their Name; for they had the Dexterity to perfuade him, that my Defign was to make myfelf the Tyrant of all *Hefperia*. We will undeceive him, faid *Mentor*. *Telemachus* faw him at *Pylos*, before he came to fettle a Colony here, and before we undertook our long Voyages in queft of *Ulyffes*: He cannot yet have forgotton that Hero, nor thofe Expreffions of Tendernefs which he ufed to his Son *Telemachus*. But the chief Point will be to cure his Diftruft:

Diftruft: Thofe Sufpicions you raifed in the Minds of your Neighbours have kindled this War, and it muft be extinguifhed by removing thofe Sufpicions. Once more I fay, let me alone to manage it.

At thefe Words, *Idameneus*, embracing *Mentor*, melted into Tears, and for a while could not fpeak a Word. At laft, with fome Difficulty, he expreffed himfelf in this Manner: O wife old Man, fent by the Gods to rectify all my Errors! I confefs, I fhould have had no Patience, if any other man durft have talk'd fo freely to me as you have done. I own, that you, and none but you, can difpofe me to fue for Peace. I was refolv'd either to conquer all my Enemies, or perifh in the Attempt; but it is much fitter for me to be led by your wife Counfels, than by my own Paffion. O happy *Telemachus*, you never can go aftray like me, fince you have fuch a Guide! *Mentor*, you may act entirely as you pleafe; all the Wifdom of the Gods is in you: Not even *Minerva's* felf could have given more wholefome Counfel: Go, promife, conclude, make any Conceffion that is in my Power; *Idomeneus* will approve whatever you think fit to do.

Whilft they were thus difcourfing together, there was heard on a fudden a confus'd Noife of Chariots, Horfes neighing, Men rending the Skies with horrible Howlings, and Trumpets that fill'd the Air with martial Clangors. The general Cry is, The Enemies are come, they have gone round about to avoid the guarded Defiles: They are come; they are ready to befiege *Salentum*. The old Men and the Women are under the greateft Confternation. Alas! fay they, why were we fated to forfake our dear Country, the fertile Ifle of *Crete*, and follow an unhappy Prince through fo many Seas, to build a

4   City

City which will now be laid in Afhes like *Troy?* They faw from the Top of their new-rais'd Walls, the neighbouring Fields crowded with approaching Enemies, whofe Helmets, Cuiraffes, and Bucklers, glittering in the Sun, dazzled the Beholders Eyes : They faw likewife the briftling Pikes, which cover'd the Ground, in like manner as when it is cover'd by a plenteous Crop, which *Ceres* is preparing in the Fields of *Enna* in *Sicily* during the fcorching Heats of Summer, to recompenfe the Labours of the Husband-man. And now they perceived the Chariots arm'd with fharp Scythes, and could diftinguifh the feveral People that were come againft them.

Mentor, the better to difcover them, afcends a lofty Tower , *Idomeneus* and *Telemachus* follow near him : He was no fooner come there, but he percei-ved on one Side *Philoctetes*, and on the other *Neftor* with his Son *Pififtratus*. *Neftor* was eafily known by his venerable old Age. What, cry'd *Mentor*, you thought, O *Idomeneus*,· that *Philoctetes* and *Ne-ftor* would only remain neuter ! But fee, they have taken Arms againft you ; and, if I miftake not, thofe other Troops which march in fo good Order, and in fo leifurely a Manner, are a Body of *Lacede-monians*, commanded by *Phalantus*. All are againft you ; there is no neighbouring Nation upon this Coaft whom you have not made your Enemy, without de-figning it.

Having thus fpoke, *Mentor* haftens down from the Tower; makes towards one of the City Gates, on that Side where the Enemy were advancing, and caufes it to be opened. *Idomeneus*, furprized at his majeftic Deportment in doing thefe Things, durft not fo much as afk him what was his Defign. *Mentor* waves with his Hand, that no-body fhould follow him

him. He goes directly towards the Enemy, who were amazed to fee a fingle Man prefenting himfelf to them; he holds up to them at a Diftance an Olive-branch as a Token of Peace; and when he was come within hearing, he requir'd them to convene their Commanders, who inftantly affembling themfelves together, he thus fpoke to them:

O generous Men, affembled out of fo many Nations that flourifh in rich *Hefperia*; I know what brings you hither is only the common Intereft of Liberty. Your Zeal I commend; but fuffer me to point out to you an eafy Way to preferve the Liberty and Honour of all your People without the Effufion of human Blood.

O *Neftor*, O wife *Neftor*, whom I perceive in this Affembly, you know full well how dreadful War is, even to thofe who juftly undertake it, under the Protection of the Gods! War is the greateft Evil with which the Gods afflict Mankind. You can never forget what the *Greeks* fuffer'd for Ten long Years before the curfed Walls of *Troy*. What Divifions were there among the Leaders! What Caprices of *Fortune!* What Havock of the *Greeks* was made by *Hector*'s Sword! What Defolation in all the moft powerful Cities caus'd by the War during the tedious Abfence of their Kings! In their Return home, fome fuffer'd Shipwreck at the Promontory of *Caphareus*; and others met a fatal Death even in the Bofom of their Spoufes. O ye Gods, 'twas in your Wrath you arm'd the *Greeks* for that glorious Expedition! O ye Inhabitants of *Hefperia*, I wifh the Gods may never grant you fo ruinous a Victory! *Troy* it is true, is now in Afhes; but it had been better for the *Grecians*, were fhe ftill in all

her Glory, and that bafe *Paris* had ftill enjoy'd un-molefted, his infamous Pleafures with *Helena*. O !
Philoctetes, you who ha·e been fo long unhappy, and abandon'd in the Ifle of *Lemnos*, do you not fear to meet with the like Difafters in another War? I know that the People of *Laconia* have likewife expe-rienc'd-great Mifery, occafion'd by the long Abfence of their Princes, Captains, and Soldiers, who went againft the *Trojans*. O *Grecians*, you who are come into *Hefperia*, your coming hither was only occafion'd by a Train of Misfortunes, which were the fad Con-fequences of the *Trojan* War !

After *Mentor* had faid this, he goes forward to-wards the *Pylians*; and *Neftor*, knowing him again, advanced likewife to falute him. O *Mentor*, faid he to him, I am glad to fee you again : 'Tis now many Years fince I firft faw you in *Phocis :*· You were then but fifteen Years of Age : but yet I even then forefaw that you would prove as wife a Man as I now find you to be. Pray let me know by what Accident you was brought into thefe Parts, and what Expedient you defign to propofe in order to pre-vent this War, which *Idomeneus* has brought upon himfelf ? He has forced us to attack him : We defire nothing but Peace : It was the general Intereft of every one of us to defire it : But we could no longer live fecure with him : He has violated all his Engage-ments with his neareft Neighbours : Peace with him would not be Peace : but only an Opportunity for him to break our League, which is our only Refource. He had too plainly difcover'd to all the other People his ambitious Defign of enflaving them, and has left us no other Means to defend our Liberty, than the ufing our utmoft Endeavours to overthrow his new
                                                  King.

Kingdom. His Breach of Faith has reduc'd us to the Neceffity either of deftroying him, or becoming his Slaves. Now if you can find a Way to remove our juft Fears, and fettle a firm and lafting Peace, all thofe Nations whom you fee here, will willingly lay down their Arms, and with Joy confefs that you excell us in Wifdom.

Mentor anfwer'd: You know, wife *Neftor*, that *Ulyffes* committed his Son *Telemachus* to my Care. This young Man, impatient to know what was become of his Father, went firft to *Pylos*, where you gave him all the kind Reception he could expect from one of his Father's cordial Friends: You likewife appointed your own Son to conduct him on his Way: He after this undertook great Voyages at Sea; he has vifited *Sicily*, *Egypt*, the Ifle of *Cyprus*, and that of *Crete*; and at laft the Winds, or rather the Gods, have driven him on this Shore, as he endeavour'd to return to *Ithaca:* And we are come here very feafonably to prevent the Mifchiefs of a furious War. 'Tis not *Idomeneus*, but the Son of the wife *Ulyffes*, and myfelf, who will now anfwer for the Performance of every thing that fhall be ftipulated.

While *Mentor* was thus difcourfing with *Neftor* in the Middle of the Confederate Troops, *Idomeneus* and *Telemachus*, with all the *Cretans* in Arms, kept their Eyes fix'd on him from the Top of the Walls of *Salentum:* Their Thoughts were intent how *Mentor*'s Propofals would be receiv'd, and they would have been glad to have heard the wife Conferences of thofe two old Men. *Neftor* had been ever efteem'd the moft experienc'd and moft eloquent of all the *Grecian* Kings: It was he who during the Siege of

Troy,

Troy, curb'd and reftrain'd *Achilles*'s boiling Wrath, *Agamemnon*'s Pride, *Ajax*'s Fiercenefs, and the impetuous Courage of *Diomedes:* Soft Perfuafion fiow'd from his Lips like a Stream of Honey: His Voice alone was always liften'd to by all thofe Heroes who were filent whenever he began to fpeak: He alone knew how to appeafe wild Difcord in the Camp. The Infirmities of frofty Age began indeed to creep on him, but yet his Expreffions were full of Strength and Sweetnefs: He repeated Things paft in order to inftruct Youth by his confummate Experience; and though he was fomewhat flow of Speech, yet he delivered himfelf with admirable Grace.

This old Man, fo much admir'd throughout *Greece*, feem'd to have loft all his Majefty and Eloquence as foon as *Mentor* appear'd with him. He feem'd perfectly wither'd and deprefs'd with Years, as he ftood by *Mentor*; whereas old Age feem'd to refpect and reverence *Mentor*'s ftrong and vigorous Conftitution. *Mentor*'s Words, tho' grave and plain, carry'd along with them a Sprightlinefs and Authority which began to be wanting in *Neftor*'s: Whatever he fpoke was concife, exact, nervous; he never us'd vain Repetitions, never departed from the Point in hand. If he was oblig'd to fpeak often of the fame Thing, the better to inculcate it, or to perfuade others, he did it by a new Turn, and by fenfible Comparifons. He had a certain ineffable Complaifance and Gaiety, whenever he had a mind to infinuate fome Truth, or adapt himfelf to the Occafions of thofe he had to deal with. Thofe two venerable Men yielded a moving fort of Spectacle to fo many affembled Nations. While all the Allies that were come

againft

againſt *Salentum* crowded upon one another to hear their wife Diſcourſe, *Idomeneus*, with his People, endeavour'd, with greedy and attentive Looks to find out the meaning of their Geſtures and Countenances.

The E N D *of the* TENTH BOOK.

THE
ADVENTURES

OF

TELEMACHUS.

BOOK XI.

The ARGUMENT.

Telemachus, *seeing* Mentor *amidst the Confederates, has a mind to know what passes between them.* He causes *the Gates of* Salentum *to be opened to him, goes and joins* Mentor, *and his Presence contributes to make the Allies accept the Conditions of Peace which* Mentor *proposed to them on the Part of* Idomeneus. *Idomeneus, whom* Mentor *sends for out of the City into the Army, accepts of all the Articles that had been agreed on.* Hostages *are exchang'd, and a common Sacrifice is made between the City and the Camp, in Confirmation of this Alliance. The Kings enters* Salentum *as Friends.*

AND

Book XI.

N D now, *Telemachus*, being grown impatient, flips from the Multitude that were about him, runs to the Gate *Mentor* went out at, and imperiously orders it to be opened. Presently after, *Idomeneus*, who thought he was still by his Side, wonder'd to see him running crofs the Fields, and making towards *Neftor*. *Neftor* knew him again, and made all the Hafte, his Age allow'd, to go and meet him. *Telemachus* flew to embrace him, and grafp'd him in his Arms without being able to fpeak. At laft he cry'd out: O my Father, for I am not afraid to call you fo; the Misfortune of not finding my true Father, and the generous Favours I have received from you, give me a Right to ufe that endearing Name! My Father, my dear Father, how blefs'd am I to fee you, and oh that I could fee *Ulyffes* too; Yet if any thing could make me amends for being deprived of him, 'tis certainly the finding him again in you.

Neftor could not refrain from weeping at thefe Words, and he was touch'd with a fecret Joy in feeing thofe Tears which with wonderful Grace ran down *Telemachus*'s Cheeks. The Beauty, Gentlenefs, and noble Affurance of this unknown Youth, who without any manner of Apprehenfion, crofs'd through fo many Enemies, ftruck all the Confederates with Amazement. May not this, faid they, be the Son of that old Man, who came to fpeak with *Neftor?* It muft be fo; he can be no other, they have both the fame Wifdom, in the two oppofite Seafons of Life. In the one, fhe only begins to bloffom; in the other, fhe bears a plentiful Harveft of the ripeft Fruits.

Mentor,

Mentor, who was highly pleafed to fee how effec-
tionately *Neftor* received *Telemachus*, laid hold of
that happy Opportunity, and [faid to him: This is
the Son of *Ulyffes*, fo dear to all *Greece*, and to yourfelf, O wife *Neftor!* Here I deliver him up to you
as an Hoftage, and the moft precious Pledge that can
be given you for the faithful Performance of *Idomeneus's*
Promifes. You may eafily imagine, that I fhould be
forry if the Lofs of the Son fhould follow that of the
Father, and that the unhappy *Penelope* fhould up-
braid *Mentor* with facrificing her Son to the Ambition of the new King of *Salentum*. With this
Pledge, who voluntarily offers himfelf to you, and
whom the Gods, who are Lovers of Peace, have fent
to you, I will proceed to lay before thefe affembled
Nations, fuch Propofals, as may eftablifh a folid Peace
to all future Ages.

At the Mention of Peace, there was heard a confufed Noife among the Ranks. All thofe different
Nations murmur'd with Anger and Refentment,
thinking fo much Time loft as was fpent without
fighting: They fancied that the Intent of all thefe
Speeches was only to fufpend their Fury, and by
that means to rob them of their Prey. The *Mandurians* in particular were enraged, to think that *Idomeneus* fhould ever have it in his Power to deceive
them again: They often attempted to interrupt
Mentor, fearing left his wife Difcourfes fhould draw
off their Allies; nay, they began to diftruft all the
Greeks that were in the Affembly. *Mentor* perceiving
this, made it his Bufinefs to increafe their Jealoufy,
the better to difunite the Counfels of thofe different
Nations.

I confefs, faid he, that the *Mandurians* have juft
Reafon to complain, and to demand Satisfaction for
the

the Wrongs that have been done them; but then again, it is not reasonable that the *Greeks*, who plant Colonies in this Country, should be suspected, and odious to the ancient Natives of the Place. On the contrary, the *Greeks* ought to be united together, and make themselves respected by others: The only thing they must observe, is to be contented with what they enjoy, and never to invade the Territories of their Neighbours. I know that *Idomeneus* has been so unhappy as to occasion Jealousies among you; but it will be no difficult Matter to remove all your Suspicions: *Telemachus* and myself offer to become Hostages; we will be answerable for *Idomeneus*'s Integrity, and will remain in your Hands till every thing that shall be promised is faithfully performed. What you are incensed at, O *Mandurians*, is that the *Cretan* Troops have seiz'd by Surprize the Passages of your Mountains; and thereby can, in despite of you, enter, whenever they please, the Territories, whither you retired when you left them the flat Country near the Sea-shore. The Defiles which the *Cretans* have fortified with high Towers, full of armed Men, are therefore the real Cause of this War. Pray answer me, can you alledge any other?

Upon this, the Chief of the *Mandurians* came forwards, and spoke thus: Have we left any thing unattempted to avoid this War? The Gods are our Witnesses that we did not renounce Peace, till Peace had irrecoverably fled from us, through the restless Ambition of the *Cretans*, and the Impossibility of trusting to their Oaths again. Senseless Nation! who forced us against our Will, to the hard Necessity of acting a desperate Part against them, and seeking our Safety in their Ruin. As,

long

long as they keep thofe Paffes, we fhall ever believe
that they mean to encroach upon our Lands, and to
bring us under Subjection.   If they really intended
to live in Peace with their Neighbours, they would
be contented with what we fo voluntarily yielded up
to them, and would not labour to preferve an Entrance into a Country, upon whofe Liberty they
have no ambitious Defign.   But you know them
not, O wife old Man ; whereas, to our great Mif-
fortune, we know them but too well.   Ceafe then,
thou Favourite of the Gods, ceafe to obftruct a
War fo juft and neceffary ; without which *Hefperia*
can never hope to enjoy a lafting Peace.   O ungrateful, treacherous, and cruel Nation, whom the
angry Gods have fent amongft us to trouble our Repofe, and punifh us for our Faults !   Yet, after you
have punifhed us, O ye Gods, you will revenge us
too : Neither will you be lefs juft to our Enemies than
to us.

At thefe Words all the Affembly was in an Emotion ; it feem'd as if *Mars* and *Bellona* went from
Rank to Rank, rekindling in each Breaft the Rage
of War, which *Mentor* endeavoured to quench ; who
thus refum'd his Difcourfe :

Had I nothing but Promifes to make to you,
you might refufe to truft to them : But the Things
I offer to you are real, and before your Eyes.   If
you are not content to have *Telemachus* and myfelf
for Hoftages, I will caufe to be put into your Hands
twelve of the moft noble and valiant *Cretans :* But
it is juft that you likewife fhould give Hoftages ;
for though *Idomeneus* fincerely defires Peace, yet it is
not through Fear or Cowardice that he defires it :
He defires Peace juft as you yourfelves fay you defire
it, upon Principles of Wifdom and Moderation, and
not

not out of a bafe Love of an eafy effeminate Life, nor out of Fear of the impending Dangers of War. He is prepar'd either to die or to conquer; but he prefers Peace to the moft pompous Victory. He would be afhamed to fear being overcome; but he fears to be unjuft, and is not afhamed to redrefs what he has done amifs. Though he offers Peace with Sword in hand, he is not for prefcribing the Conditions of it with Imperioufnefs; for he fets no Value upon a forced Peace: He would have a Peace, which fhould be to the Satisfaction of all Parties; a Peace that may for ever put an end to all Jealoufies, allay all Refentments, and remove all Diftrufts. In a word, *Idomeneus* has all thofe Sentiments which I am fure you wifh he fhould have. All that now remains to be done is, to perfuade you into a Belief of it; which will be no difficult Tafk, provided you will hear me calmly, and without Prejudice.

Liften then, O ye warlike Nations; and you, O ye wife and united Captains; give ear to what I offer you from *Idomeneus.* It is not juft, that he fhould have it in his Power to enter the Countries of his Neighbours; nor is it juft, that his own Territories fhould be expofed to the Incurfions from them: He therefore confents, that thofe Paffes which he has fortified with high Towers, may be kept by neutral Troops. You *Neftor,* and you *Philoctetes,* are *Greeks* by Birth; yet, upon this Occafion, you have declared againft *Idomeneus;* and therefore you cannot be fufpected of being too partial to his Interefts. What animates you is the common Intereft of the Repofe and Liberty of *Hefperia;* be you then the Truftees and Keepers of thofe Defiles which occafion'd this War. You have no lefs Reafon, nor is it lefs your Intereft, to hinder the old Inhabitants of of *Hefperia* from deftroying *Salentum*, a new *Grecian* Colony, like that which you have founded, than to hinder *Idomeneus* from ufurping the Lands of his Neighbours. Do you keep an equal Balance between both of them; and, inftead of carrying Fire and Sword among a People whom you ought to love, referve to yourfelves the Honour of being Judges and Mediators. You will undoubtedly anfwer, that you would be extremely pleafed with thefe Propofals, could you be fure that *Idomeneus* would faithfully perform them : And, as to this point, I am going to give you Satisfaction.

For the Security of both Parties, there will be the Hoftages I mentioned before, to continue till all thofe Defiles be put into your Poffeffion. Now, when the Safety of all *Hefperia*, and even that of *Salentum* and *Idomeneus*, fhall be at your Mercy, will you not be contented ? What can you diftruft after this, unlefs you are afraid of yourfelves ? You dare not truft to *Idomeneus*; and yet *Idomeneus* is fo far from having any Defign of deceiving you, that he is willing to truft you. Yes, he will entruft you with the Repofe, Lives, and Liberties of all his People, together with himfelf. If you are really defirous of a good Peace, behold fhe offers herfelf to you, and leaves you no Pretence for rejecting her. Once again, think not that 'tis Fear obliges *Idomeneus* to make you thefe Offers; no, 'tis Wifdom and Juftice that engage him to take this Courfe; nor fhall it affect him in the leaft, fhould you impute to his Weaknefs what is the Effect of his Virtue. In his firft Attempts he committed fome Faults, and he glories in acknowledging them as fuch, by preventing your Demands in this Manner. 'Tis Weaknefs, 'tis ridiculous Vanity, 'tis ftupid Ignorance of a

2   Man's

Man's own Intereft, to think to hide his Faults by
endeavouring to maintain them with Pride and
Haughtinefs. He, who owns his Faults to his Enemy
and offers to repair them, fhews thereby, that he
can never more enter upon Thoughts of committing
them, and that at the fame time the Enemy has all
things to fear from fo wife and fo fteady a Conduct,
unlefs he makes Peace. Beware, left you give him,
in his turn, Occafion to lay the Blame at your
Door. If you flight Peace and Juftice which now
offer themfelves to you, Peace and Juftice will take
their Revenge. *Idomeneus*, who before ought to have
feared the Gods would have been incenfed againft
him, will now have them on his Side againft you.
Telemachus and myfelf will fight in this good Caufe ;
and I call all the Gods, both celeftial and infernal,
to be Witneffes of the juft Propofals that I now make
to you.

At thefe Words, *Mentor* lifted up his Arm on
high, to fhew to the People the Olive-Branch which
he had in his Hand, in token of Peace. The Commanders, who were nearer him, were aftonifhed
and dazzled with the Divine Light which darted
from his Eyes ; he look'd with a certain Majefty
and Authority, far beyond what is ever feen in the
moft eminent among Mortals. The Charms of his
fweet, yet commanding, Eloquence ftole away all
Hearts : It was like thofe enchanting Spells which,
in the deep Silence of the Night do, on a fudden,
ftop, in the midft of Heaven, the Motion of the
Moon and Stars, calm the raging Sea, fupprefs the
Winds, make the Billows fubfide, and fufpend the
Courfe of rapid Streams.

Mentor feem'd in the Middle of thefe furious People like *Bacchus* when he was furrounded by Tygers,
who,

who, forgoing their natural Fiercenefs, and attracted by the Efficacy of his foft, melodious Voice, came and lick'd his Feet, and fawningly paid Submiffion to him. At firft, a deep Silence was obferv'd throughout the whole Army; the Commanders gazed on one another, unable to refift this Man, or comprehend what he was. All the Troops were motionlefs, and kept their Eyes fixed upon him ; not daring to fpeak or make the leaft Noife, for fear he fhould have fomething farther to fay, and they fhould obftruct his being heard. Though they thought it impoffible that what he had faid could be capable of any Addition, yet they wifhed his Speech had been longer: Every thing he had faid remain'd, as it were, engraven in their Hearts. As he fpoke he commanded at once the Love and Belief of his Hearers; and every one was greedily attentive to catch the leaft Syllable that iffued out of his Mouth.

After a continued Silence for fome time, a kind of a foft Noife began to fpread itfelf by little and little. It was not now the confufed Noife of People murmuring with indignation; on the contrary, 'twas a gentle favourable Whifpering. Each Man's Face difcovered a certain Serenity, and an Afpect already mecken'd. The *Mandurians*, who were fo highly provok'd, let their Weapons drop to the Ground. The rough *Phalantus*, with his *Lacedemonians*, were furprized to feel their Hearts fo mollify'd. The others began to figh for that happy Peace which had been fet to their View. *Philoctetes*, who by experiencing the Hardfhips of Fortune, was more fenfible than any other, could not with-hold his Tears. *Neftor*, not being able to fpeak for the Tranfports in which this Difcourfe had put him, affectionately embrac'd *Mentor*, without being able to utter a Word;

Word; and all the People at once, as upon a Signal given, cry'd out, O wife old Man, you have difarm'd us ! Peace ! Peace !

Neftor, a Moment after this, was going to begin another Speech, but all the Troops being impatient, and fearing left he fhould ftart fome Difficulty, once again, cry'd out Peace ! Peace ! Nor would they give over, till they had made all their Leaders cry out with them, Peace! Peace!

Neftor, perceiving it was no time to make a fet Speech, contented himfelf with faying : You fee, O *Mentor*, what wonderful Efficacy the Words of a good Man have. When Wifdom and Virtue fpeak, they hufh all the boifterous Paffions ; our juft Refentments change into Priendfhip, and four Animofities into Wifhes for a durable Peace. We accept the Peace you offer us. At the fame time all the Commanders held up their Hands in token of Confent.

Mentor ran to the City Gate to caufe it to be opened, and to bid *Idomeneus* come forth now without any Fear. *Neftor*, in the mean time, embraced *Telemachus*, and faid to him : Thou amiable Son of the wifeft of all the *Greeks*, may'ft thou be no lefs wife, but far more happy than he ! Have you learnt nothing concerning him ? The Memory of your Father, whom you fo much refemble, has help'd to ftifle our Indignation. *Phalantus*, though rough and fierce, and though he had never feen *Ulyffes*, could not be unmov'd at his and his Son's Misfortunes. And now they were going to prefs *Telemachus* to relate what had befallen him, when *Mentor* return'd with *Idomeneus*, and all the *Cretan* Youth attending him.

At the fight of *Idomeneus*, the Allies felt their Refentments kindling a frefh ; but *Mentor*'s Words

2   quench'd

quench'd the growing Fire. Why do we delay, faid he, to conclude this holy Alliance, of which the Gods will be both Witnefſes and Defenders? May they revenge it, if any impious Wretch dare to violate it, and may all the Horrors of War, inftead of overwhelming the faithful and innocent People, fall on the perjur'd execrable Head of that ambitious Man, who fhall flight the facred Ties of this Alliance! May he be hated by Gods and Men! May he never enjoy the Fruit of his Perfidy! May the infernal Furies, under the moft hideous Forms, appear to him, and fill him with Rage and Defpair! May he be ftruck dead, without any hope of Burial! May his Body become a Prey to Dogs and Vultures! And may he for ever be more feverely tormented than *Tantalus*, *Ixion*, and the *Danaids*, in the deep Abyfs of *Tartarus*! But no,———rather may this Peace be as firm and immoveable as the Mountain of *Atlas*, that fupports the Heavens! May all 'thefe People religioufly obferve it, and tafte the Fruits of it from Generation to Generation! May the Names of thofe who fhall have fworn to it, be ever commemorated with Love and Reverence, by lateft Pofterity! May this Peace, founded on Juftice and Integrity, be a Model of every Peace, that fhall hereafter be made among all the Nations of the Earth! And may all People who are defirous to tafte the Happinefs of Peace and Union, imitate the Example of thofe of *Hefperia*!

At thefe Words, *Idomeneus*, with the other Kings, fwore to maintain the Peace, on the Conditions agreed to; and twelve Hoftages were exchang'd on both Sides. *Telemachus* would needs be one of the Hoftages for *Idomeneus*, but *Mentor* was not allow'd to be one of them, becaufe the Al

lies

lies defired that he might remain with *Idomeneus*, to have an Eye upon him and his Counfellors, till the entire Execution of the Articles fworn to. Between the Town and the Camp were facrificed an hundred Heifers, white as Snow, and as many Bulls of the fame Colour, whofe Horns were gilded and adorned with Garlands. The dreadful Bellowings of the Victims that fell beneath the holy Knife, made all the neighbouring Hills refound; the reeking Blood ftream'd on all Sides; exquifite Wines were in Abundance pour'd out for the Libations; the *Harufpices* confulted the panting Entrails: And the Priefts burnt upon the Altars vaft Quantities of Incenfe, which form'd a thick Cloud, and perfum'd all the Country round with the fweet Odour thereof.

Mean while, the Soldiers on both Sides, regarding each other no longer as Enemies, began to entertain one another with their Adventures; they already gave a Relaxation to their Labours, and did beforehand tafte the Sweets of Peace. Many of thofe, who had follow'd *Idomeneus* to the Siege of *Troy*, knew again the Soldiers of *Neftor*, who had fought in the fame War. They affectionately embraced each other, and mutually related what had befallen them, after they had ruined that towering City, the Ornament of all *Afia*. And now they lay down on the Grafs, crown'd themfelves with Flowers, and quaffed the Wine that was brought from the Town in large Veffels to celebrate fo happy a Day.

Of a fudden *Mentor* faid: O Kings! O ye affembled Captains! henceforth, under feveral Names, and feveral Leaders, you fhall be but one People; for thus the juft Gods, who are Lovers of Men whom they created, are pleafed to be the eternal Tie

of

of their perfect Concord. All Mankind is but one Family, spread over the Face of the whole Earth. All Men are Brethren, and, as such, ought to love each other. Curse on those impious Wretches, who seek a cruel Glory in the Blood of their Brethren, which is indeed their own Blood! War, it's true, is sometimes necessary; but it is a Shame to Humanity that it should be inevitable in more favourable Circumstances. O ye Kings! think not that War ought to be desired for the Acquisition of Glory. True Glory is not to be found separate from Humanity. Whoever prefers his Ambition before a Sense of Humanity, is a Monster of Pride, not a Man; and shall never attain any other than a false Glory; for true Glory consists solely in Moderation and Goodness. Men, indeed, may flatter him, to gratify his foolish Vanity; but when they are in secret, and may speak their Minds sincerely, they will say of him, that he has so much the less deserv'd Glory, as he has desired it with an unwarrantable Passion. Men ought not to have any Esteem for him at all, since he has so little valued Men, and has been so lavish of their Blood, through brutal Vanity. Happy is that King, who loves his People, and is beloved by them; who confides in his Neighbours, and in whom his Neighbours confide; who, instead of making War upon them, prevents any War they may have with one another; and who gives Occasion to all the foreign Nations to envy the Happiness of his Subjects, in having him for their King. Resolve then to meet from time to time, O you who govern the most powerful Cities of *Hesperia!* agree to meet once in three Years in a general Assembly, where all the Kings here present may attend to renew the Alliance by a fresh Oath, to

strengthen

ſtrengthen the promiſed Friendſhip, and to conſult about your common Intereſt. As long as you are united, you will enjoy in this fine Country, Tranquillity, Glory, Plenty ; and abroad you will always be invincible. It is only Diſcord, the Child of Hell, and ſent from thence to torment Mortals ; it is only ſhe, I ſay, that can diſturb the Felicity which the Gods are preparing for you.

Neſtor reply'd, You ſee by the Readineſs with which we came into the Peace, how far we are from deſiring War out of Vain-glory, or an unjuſt Eagerneſs to aggrandize ourſelves at the Expence of our Neighbours. But pray what's to be done when we find ourſelves near a violent Prince, who knows no Law but his Intereſt, and who neglects no Opportunity of invading the Territories of other States ? Think not that I glance at *Idomeneus* ; no, I have no longer ſuch a Thought of him ; 'tis *Adraſtus*, King of the *Daunians*, from whom we have every thing to fear. He contemns the Gods, and thinks that all Mankind are only born to be ſubſervient to his Glory, and to be his Slaves. He will not have Subjects of whom he may be both the King and Father ; he muſt have Slaves and Adorers, and have divine Honours paid him. Hitherto blind Fortune has favour'd his unrighteous Enterprizes. We haſten'd to attack *Salentum*, to get rid of the weakeſt of our Enemies, who had juſt begun to eſtabliſh himſelf upon this Coaſt, with a Reſolution to turn our Forces afterwards upon that other more powerful Enemy. He has already taken ſeveral Towns from our Allies ; the *Crotonians* have already loſt two Battles in fighting againſt him ; he ſticks at nothing to gratify his Ambition ; Force or Fraud is all alike to him, provided he can but cruſh his Enemies. He has amaſs'd together

gether vaft Treafures ; his Troops are difciplin'd and
harden'd to War ; his Generals are experienc'd; he
is well obey'd ; he himfelf inceffantly watching over
all thofe who act by his Order : He feverely punifhes
the leaft Faults; and largely rewards the Services
that are done him : His perfonal Valour fuftains and
animates that of his Troops : He would be an ac-
complifh'd King, if he fquar'd his Actions by the
Rules of Juftice and Integrity ; but he neither dreads
the Gods, nor the Upbraidings of his Confcience :
Reputation he reckons as nothing; he looks upon it
as a vain Phantom, which can affect none but poor,
low, groveling Spirits ; he efteems nothing as a real
and folid Good, but the Advantage of poffeffing great
Riches, the being dreaded, and trampling all Mankind under foot. His Army will foon appear upon
our Territories ; and if the Union of fo many People
prove ineffectual againft him, there is an End of our
Liberty. It is therefore the Intereft of *Idomenus,* as
well as ours, to oppofe this tyrannical Neighbour,
who can fuffer nothing free to be near him. If we
fhould be ever overcome, *Salentum* would be threat-
en'd with the fame Mifery : Therefore let us haften
jointly to prevent it. Whilft *Neftor* was thus fpeaking, they mov'd towards the City ; for *Idomeneus* had
invited all the Kings, and the principal Commanders,
to come and pafs the Night there.

The END *of the* FIRST VOLUME.

A N

AN
INDEX

OF THE

PRINCIPAL MATTERS

Contain'd in the

FIRST VOLUME.

. A.

ÆOLUS,

An INDEX.

B.

C.

CAPHAREUS

An INDEX.

An INDEX.

An INDEX.

An INDEX.

READ.

TELE-

An INDEX.

VOLUP-

An INDEX.

F I N I S.